The Princess School

Special Edition
Books 1–3

The
Princess School

Special Edition
Books 1–3

Jane B. Mason ॐ Sarah Hines Stephens

SCHOLASTIC INC.

New York   Toronto   London   Auckland   Sydney
Mexico City   New Delhi   Hong Kong   Buenos Aires

The Princess School #1: If the Shoe Fits, ISBN 0-439-54532-3, Copyright © 2004 by Jane B. Mason and Sarah Hines Stephens.

The Princess School #2: Who's the Fairest? ISBN 0-439-56553-7, Copyright © 2004 by Jane B. Mason and Sarah Hines Stephens.

The Princess School #3: Let Down Your Hair, ISBN 0-439-62939-X, Copyright © 2004 by Jane B. Mason and Sarah Hines Stephens.

12 11 10 9 8 7 6 5 4 3 2 1   6 7 8 9 10/0

Printed in the U.S.A.   23

ISBN 0-439-85198-X

First compilation printing, January 2006

Contents

The Princess School

If the Shoe Fits

For David and Anica, with thanks for the royal treatment.

—JBM & SHS

Chapter One
Ella

"Ouch!" Ten-year-old Ella Brown's bare foot came down on a sharp rock. Lifting the skirts of her hand-me-down gown, she hopped on her left foot to inspect her right. No damage, just dirt.

I should be used to dirt, she thought grimly.

With a sigh, she continued gingerly down the lane, picking the least muddy path. She wished yet again that she had a decent pair of shoes for her first day of Princess School.

Her old shoes were full of holes and blackened with soot — too shabby to wear, even with a secondhand dress. They were fine for chores, but not for Princess School. At Princess School the right pair of shoes could make all the difference. Ella ought to know.

Biting her lip, Ella remembered the mysterious shoes that had arrived the night before her Princess School entrance interview — the grueling interrogation every prospective princess faced in order to gain admittance. The shoes sparkled in their velvet-lined box. A small bow shimmered on each curved toe. They were perfect! Until she put them on. As soon as they were on her feet, Ella realized they were much too big.

Of course she had worn them to the interview anyway. Even though they were made of glass, too big, and *really* uncomfortable, they were better than the grubby slippers she had. Ella would rather go barefoot than be seen entering Princess School in *those*.

She stepped over a small puddle in her path and sighed again. It was, quite simply, a miracle that she had been accepted at Princess School at all. And Ella was pretty sure she knew who to thank for it. The telltale sparkle on those new shoes, and the fact that her fairy godmother had recently accepted a job in the Princess School administrative chambers, could only mean one thing. Somebody had been up to a little bobbity-boo.

Ella smiled. Her fairy godmother, Lurlina, looked out for Ella when no one else did. She didn't always get things exactly right . . . like the time she was trying to help clean and decided to banish all of the dust and pet hair from the house. The poor cat was bald for months. But Lurlina *almost* always made things better. And this morning Ella was counting on that.

She hoped Lurlina could make her some new shoes with a quick wave of her wand (and get the size right this time). All Ella had to do was get to Princess School early enough to find her fairy godmother without anyone noticing she was barefoot. That shouldn't be too hard, right?

Looking down, Ella saw her muddy toes peeking out from under her dress. If she bent her knees slightly and walked with her back straight, her hem brushed the ground (gathering *more* dirt), but it hid her feet completely.

"This just might work," Ella said to herself, half smiling.

Then she rounded the corner and the gleaming towers of Princess School came into view. They pierced the sky like jeweled points on a crown. Beneath the stone spires, the enormous arched entrance was swarming with gilded carriages, teams of horses, coachmen, servants, and dozens of novice princesses.

Ella's bent knees suddenly felt weak.

For the first time in her life, Ella wished she were sitting in the kitchen peeling potatoes or sweeping cinders back into the fireplace. At least there she knew what she was doing. It was awful to admit, but she felt more at home in front of the hearth than in a school full of girls in gowns.

How will I ever fit in here? Ella wondered. Doubt swept over her as she realized she wasn't at all sure she would. As she gazed at the fanciful scene before her, she felt the urge to turn and run.

Suddenly the pounding of hooves and rattling of wheels jolted her out of her thoughts. Just in time she dove out of the way of a speeding coach. By pressing against the bushes on the side of the road she only barely managed to keep from being run down.

The coach whizzed past in a blur of blue and gold. One of the large, spoked wheels bumped into a rut in the road and a shower of mud splashed onto Ella's skirts.

With her heart beating fast and her fists clenched in anger, Ella peered after the racing carriage. It was her father's coach! And the piercing cackles and disgusting, snorting laughs echoing out of the windows were all too familiar. Her lying stepsisters!

What were Hagatha and Prunilla doing in her father's coach? Ella fumed. That morning, after Ella served them breakfast, Hag and Prune told their mother they were getting a ride to Princess School with Prince Hargood.

"Such a waste to send the whole coach for just one girl," Ella's stepmother, Kastrid, had said. She flashed a crooked smile as Ella cleared the breakfast dishes and hurried downstairs to finish pressing Hagatha's gown and Prunilla's hair ribbons. "Ella, you can walk."

Ella knew Hag and Prune had lied on purpose. She swiped at her skirts angrily. They couldn't get over the fact that Ella was starting at *their* school — and heaven forbid they should all arrive together! The older girls didn't think Ella could make it at Princess School.

Ella had hoped that starting Princess School would change things at home. That her stepsisters would stop ordering her around and insulting her. That her stepmother would stop treating her like hired help. That her father would stand up to his new wife. But if today's start was any indication, nothing had changed, and nothing ever would.

"There's no way I'm going to spend the rest of my life in my stepmother's kitchen," Ella said out loud, giving her skirts a final swipe. She would show her awful stepsisters she was as good as they were, even with a muddy dress and bare feet.

Bent knees wobbling, Ella headed for the drawbridge that led up to the school's entrance. Several long-necked white swans glided in the moat beneath the bridge.

They look more regal than I do, Ella thought. She held her head a little higher. If she was going to get in unnoticed, she had to look like she belonged. Luckily most of the other students were too excited to pay attention to a shabbily dressed new girl. But Ella found it difficult not to stare at them. They were lovely, with fancily braided and coiled hair. They wore gowns of every color — in silk and velvet and brocade. The fine fabrics glimmered in the sun. Clustered in small groups, the girls chatted animatedly with one another, making polite princess gestures with delicate fingers.

Ella looked past them toward the school entrance and her heart jumped. The white marble steps up to the school were so polished, the sun glinted off them. The carved wooden doors were as ornate as any gilded picture frame, and when a princess or member of the faculty stepped up to them, the heavy doors opened with a quiet *whoosh*. It sounded as if the castle itself were drawing a breath.

On either side of the doors, trumpeters raised long golden instruments to their lips. Then, with a few short blasts, they announced that the first day of the new school year was about to begin.

As she gazed at the castle that was to be her new school, Ella was filled with awe . . . and dread. Her stepsisters were right: She would never make it at Princess School.

You can't think like that, she scolded herself. *Be confident. You can do this.*

Ella squinched up her toes and walked more quickly

toward the steps. She needed to find Lurlina before class started. But with each step, she passed another perfect princess-in-training and her courage began to melt away. It seemed every novice she walked by was more beautiful than the last. They were all so well pressed and dressed!

Here I am in dirty rags, and I don't even have shoes on! Ella thought. *Lurlina* has *to come through.*

At the base of the stairs, Ella stopped in her tracks when she saw the prettiest girl yet. Her hair was the color of wheat in the sun. Her cheeks were like rose blossoms. Her eyes were bluer than the clearest lake.

"Do be careful, dear," the girl's mother cooed while her father wrung his hands nearby.

"Won't you please wear these gloves?" her father begged, holding out a pair of metal gauntlets suitable for a knight.

The beautiful girl smiled kindly at her parents, refusing the hand armor. Tiny fairies buzzed all around her, adjusting her collar, twisting an already-perfect curl, smoothing her delicate eyebrows, draping her skirts more elegantly down the stairs, twittering their advice in her ears.

Ella almost laughed out loud at the bustling fairies. What could they possibly do to make this girl more lovely?

Forgetting all about her own predicament, Ella

lifted her skirts to climb the stairs, the final ascent into Princess School. With a gasp, she saw her own pale naked foot shining like the moon on the stone stair. She quickly dropped her skirts back over it and looked around to see if anyone else had noticed. No one turned in her direction, except the beautiful girl with the fairies.

Ella stared into the other girl's deep blue eyes and waited. She waited for her to say something mean. To laugh and point. She waited to be ridiculed. Exposed as a fake. Thrown out of school! But all she saw in the other girl's eyes was curiosity.

"What is it, Rose?" the girl's mother asked anxiously.

"Are you afraid? Do you want me to come with you?" Rose's father asked, looking around to see what had caught his daughter's eye. "I can call the guards."

"Please, Father, it's nothing." Rose brushed her parents off with a smile. "I'm fine. And I'm going to school now. *Alone.*"

Ella watched, shocked and grateful, as the girl strode confidently up the stairs without so much as another glance in her direction. All eyes, it seemed, were on Rose. Ella took a cautious look around to see if anyone else had seen her. She could still make it inside unnoticed. Except . . .

Leaning against a banner pole, another girl peered

at her with an odd smile. The girl had an unbelievably huge coil of auburn hair piled haphazardly on her head, and her navy dress was strange — shorter than Ella's and looser. But before Ella could decipher the look on her face, the girl turned away and waved, not very royally, to a prince on the other side of the rose garden.

The prince returned the wave with a grin and then ducked inside an enormous manor house. Ella squinted into the distance. The sign over the door read The Charm School for Boys.

Ella's stomach gave a lurch. The Charm School! Every prince in the kingdom went there! And princes made her almost as nervous as princesses. Ella sighed. Why did *everything* make her so nervous?

With her feet hidden, knees bent, and stomach fluttering, Ella walked up the last few stairs and stepped through the already-open doors of her new school.

She felt her breath catch in her throat. The inside of Princess School was as overwhelming as the outside. The polished stone floor was an ornate pattern of square pink and white stones. The tall, narrow, diamond-paned windows reached from the floor to the ceiling, ending in delicately pointed tops. The ceiling itself was silver leaf, while the alabaster pillars between the endless arches were covered with carved roses and ivy.

Excited voices echoed loudly off the tall arches. Teachers stood in the glittering foyer, directing new students to class. For a moment Ella couldn't even move. Prospective princesses swarmed past her. Which way was her fairy godmother's chamber?

A woman in a red velvet gown approached Ella. "Your name?" she asked, eyeing Ella's mud-strewn gown warily.

"Cinderella Brown," Ella replied, her heart sinking. Out of the corner of her eye she could see the girl who'd been waving excitedly to the Charm School boy outside. She seemed to be watching Ella with renewed interest. A trumpet blast echoed down the hall, interrupting Ella's thoughts and distracting the other girl. There would not be enough time to find Lurlina before class. Ella would have to start Princess School barefoot and filthy.

Chapter Two
Rapunzel

Rapunzel followed the barefoot girl with the filthy gown into the large hearthroom and sat down in a velvet-cushioned, high-backed chair. The hearthroom was big and echoey, like most of the rooms in a castle. A fire burned in the grate of a large fireplace to take away the morning chill. Tapestries depicting kings and queens doing things kings and queens do lined the walls. But Rapunzel wasn't really looking at the furnishings. She was looking at the other girls. And she was scowling.

Okay, maybe she had been locked in a tower for years and years (and years), but she had never seen such a bunch of prissy girls in her life! With the single exception of the girl in the muddy gown, the room was filled with nothing but fancy-pants princesses.

Like Rapunzel, all of the girls in this class were at Princess School for the first time. They were first-years,

Bloomers. Girls returning for their second year were known as Sashes. Third-years were Robes, and the fourth and final-year students were called Crowns.

Rapunzel slouched. This bunch of Bloomers looked a little fidgety. Most of them had not taken their seats. They were introducing themselves with small nods and curtsies, exchanging compliments and pleasantries while Rapunzel sat back and chewed the end of her braid. If this was how Princess School was going to be, Rapunzel wasn't sure she could take it.

Rapunzel turned her narrowed eyes toward one of the prettiest Bloomers in the class, Briar Rose. Dressed in a stunning gown that matched her blue eyes, Rose had shining golden hair and a warm smile. She was completely surrounded by other novice princesses. Already they had a nickname for her: "Beauty." Ugh!

"I'll bet she is just full of herself," Rapunzel muttered to a sour-looking king on the tapestry closest to her. "And I bet she couldn't eat her way out of a gingerbread house."

Rapunzel had no respect for people who couldn't take care of themselves. After all, she had been taking care of herself since she was tiny — since Madame Gothel took her from her parents and put her in a thirty-foot tower.

"Nobody keeps me locked up," Rapunzel mumbled, though she had to admit she'd had some help escaping — at least the first time. She was only seven when Val, short for Prince Valerian, appeared at the base of the tower and called up to her.

Rapunzel's scowl disappeared when she thought about her friend. He might be a prince, but he would always be plain old Val to her. Val was eight when he first stumbled across Rapunzel's tower in the woods. He wasn't trying to save her or anything. He just wanted somebody to play with.

"Come down!" he'd called.

"How?" Rapunzel asked.

"Just climb!" he'd answered.

At first Rapunzel thought he was kidding. The tower was almost ten times her height!

"I bet you can't," Val teased.

So then, of course, she did. He coached her, pointing out places to put her hands and feet.

"I would have climbed up," Val said when Rapunzel finally made it to the bottom, "but heights make me vomit."

Rapunzel smiled as she remembered the incredible sense of freedom she'd felt that first time she'd escaped from the tower. Being cooped up was horrible! As the memory faded, Rapunzel saw a girl with silky brown hair and a pink gown curtsy in her direction. In an instant the scowl was back.

Rapunzel wished she were with Val right now. He wasn't very far away — just across the rose garden. Rapunzel was sure second-year Charm School could beat the pantaloons off of first-year Princess School. But she knew she had a better chance of turning into a frog than of getting into the all-boys' school.

Maybe I should have tried the Grimm School, Rapunzel thought as the first-year girls settled into their chairs with a swish of skirts. Glaring at the back of the perfectly postured princess in front of her, Rapunzel knew that would never have worked out, either. The Grimm School was actually closer to her tower than Princess School, but the students who went there were *spooky*. They were real witches! Not only did they learn to fly on broomsticks, which actually sounded kind of fun, they also practiced magic. They concocted potions and cast spells on anything and everything, from trees to animals to people. It was rumored that a few years ago a Grimm girl had even turned a princess into a lizard! And if you thought the students were bad, the teachers were positively evil. Rapunzel shivered. She'd had her fill of nasty sorceresses living with Madame Gothel.

Just then Madame Garabaldi, the Bloomers' hearthroom instructor, strode importantly into the room and held her arms wide for the pages to take her robe. Her silver-streaked hair was pulled into a tight bun, and her hazel eyes gazed sharply over her half-spectacles at the students. Madame Garabaldi cleared her throat as a scribe hurriedly passed scrolls to all the girls. Then, with a final horn blast, class began.

Rapunzel scanned the list of classes written on the silver-leaf-trimmed scroll she'd just received.

Fine Art of Self-defense

That sounded okay.

Frog Identification

Not too terrible.

History: Princesses Past and Present

Well, all right.

Stitchery: Needlework, Spinning, and Embroidery Basics

Were they serious?

Rapunzel gazed down at the scroll to read the final class:

Looking Glass Class — Hairdo How-to and Essential Self-reflection

With a moan, Rapunzel dropped the scroll on her desk and glanced around to see her classmates' reactions. The other Bloomers were gazing politely at Madame Garabaldi, who strode around the chamber, reading from an enormous scroll all of the rules the girls were expected to follow.

"Proper attire is to be worn at all times," Madame

Garabaldi enunciated. Her gaze left the list and settled on the barefoot girl who Rapunzel had noticed on the bridge. The girl's face reddened. It didn't look like much got past Madame G.

"Politeness must be observed," Madame Garabaldi rapped out. "Continuously maintain a regal countenance. Homework will be carefully completed. And you must *always* be prompt." Madame Garabaldi laid down the scroll.

"You will find," she continued, "that the punishments we serve here at Princess School are not nearly as harsh as those realities you will encounter once you graduate." Pausing for effect, Madame Garabaldi breathed a puff of air out her nose. She almost looked like a dragon. "Or perhaps you'd have a vine time living the rest of your days as a ridiculously colored squash?" She finished by gazing around the room, smiling at her own joke. But the smile was not exactly warm or welcoming.

Rapunzel stuffed her braid back in her mouth and chewed. Was this what it felt like to be nervous?

Suddenly the heavy classroom doors swung open with a *whoosh*, and the palest princess Rapunzel had ever seen stumbled in.

"Pardon the interruption, Madame Garabaldi," a page said, skirting the girl and bowing low several times before the stern teacher. His hands were shaking slightly. "May I present Snow White?" He gestured toward the pale girl with black hair before backing quickly out of the room, flourishing his pointy hat.

Snow White stood alone at the front of the room. All eyes were on her, and her too-short, high-collared, old-fashioned dress.

Madame Garabaldi was too angry to speak. Her lips quivered and she looked like she wanted to turn Snow White into a pumpkin. Everyone waited for her to say something.

But it was Snow White who spoke first.

Her berry-red lips turned up into a silly grin, and she gave a little wave to all the girls staring at her.

"Hi-ho, everyone!" she chirped.

Rapunzel let her braid drop from her mouth. *Things could be worse*, she thought. *I could be* her.

Chapter Three
Snow White

Snow White smiled at her new classmates. In spite of the scowling woman next to her, her heart was full of joy. She was at Princess School! And she was sure that each and every one of the girls looking at her would become a good friend.

"As it is your first day of Princess School, your tardiness will be excused," Madame Garabaldi said in a carefully controlled voice. It sounded as if her teeth were clenched. "But should it happen again, you will receive double tower detention. Be warned: Tardiness has been the demise of many a princess." The instructor looked pointedly at each girl in the class before turning back to Snow. "Please take your seat," she said in a low tone. "Now."

Snow shivered. The look on Madame Garabaldi's face reminded her of the way her stepmother, easily the most horrible person Snow had ever met, used to look at her over the dinner table. Snow's smile returned. *I don't miss that!* she thought. Surely her new teacher couldn't be as bad as her stepmother.

Snow hummed a little on the way to her seat — a new tune the birds had taught her just that morning. As she turned to sit she caught Madame Garabaldi's eye and the song quickly died in her throat.

Snow did not miss withering looks. Ever since she'd gone to live with her seven surrogates, the dwarves, she hadn't seen anything close to a glare. Until now.

Tomorrow, she told herself, *I'll just have to get up earlier.*

Snow hadn't meant to be late. But she'd needed to help pack seven lunches and see the dwarves off to work. Then she had stopped for a quick visit with Mother Sparrow, whose injured wing Snow was tending. It was almost healed. Snow swung her feet under her desk, thinking of her happy home in the forest.

Behind her, other Bloomers were starting to whisper.

"She doesn't look a thing like a princess! How did she get in?"

"And where did she get that outfit? Look at that collar!"

"I heard she was raised by gnomes."

Snow's feet swung more slowly under her desk. She would not let her good mood be ruined by gossip. She had come too far. She'd even walked past the

Grimm School *by herself* on the way here. She had been looking forward to this for months.

Life with the dwarves was good. Wonderful, even. They worked together to keep their small house tidy. Snow did most of the cooking (though the dwarves often offered to prepare the food, they *all* preferred her delicious soups and pies to their gray gruels and goulashes), but as she worked, the dwarves entertained her with music. And they were constantly doing nice things for Snow, like picking her flowers or bringing her an empty bird's nest. The only bad thing about her cottage life was that the dwarves worked a lot, and Snow got lonely while they were gone . . . even with the company of the woodland animals.

Snow smiled at a few of the girls seated close to her. *They'll like me once they get to know me*, she thought.

A couple of the girls turned away from Snow, but one or two returned her smile, including the friendly-looking, dirty-gowned girl just behind her.

Snow felt better already. Nothing kept her down for long. And look, at the front of the room Madame Garabaldi was reading the school announcements and looking a lot less stern.

"By decree, the Royal Coronation Ball will be held at the end of your second week at Princess School!" she announced. "At the ball, one student — the most elegant and graceful of all — will be crowned Princess of the Ball!" Madame Garabaldi practically beamed. She gazed into the distance and swayed back and forth to imaginary music.

The mood in the room changed at once as everyone pictured herself at the Coronation Ball. The girls began to murmur with excitement. Many of the Bloomers, like Snow White, were born princesses, but lots of them were merely princess hopefuls waiting for an opportunity to wear a crown. This could be their chance.

"The honor of being the Princess of the Ball is great," Madame Garabaldi went on, still smiling and swaying. "It cannot be won by birth or marriage. Indeed not. It is an honor bestowed by one's peers. Every girl in the school will get to cast a vote, and she who is most admired will be crowned."

A few of the princesses glanced expectantly at the beautiful princess with shining, wheat-colored hair and striking blue eyes.

"Of course," Madame Garabaldi continued with a mild look of disdain, "a Bloomer has not received such an honor in more than four dozen years. I certainly would not recommend getting your hopes up."

The excitement in the room faded as quickly as it had grown. Only Snow did not notice the change in the atmosphere. The room was silent when she clapped her hands together, unable to contain her enthusiasm.

"Oh my great golly goodness," she exclaimed. "My very first ball!"

Chapter Four

A Single Slipper

Ella slipped out of hearthroom the moment class ended. It was easy to go unnoticed now. The whole school was abuzz with talk of the ball. Ella made her way through the pink-and-white mazelike hallways, past the gilded, velvet-lined trunks where girls kept their books and supplies, and toward the flower-carved winding staircases leading to other wings of the castle. Around her she heard girls planning what they should wear.

"Do you think rubies go with silk?" a second-year Sash asked her friend as they strolled by, arm in arm.

"Oh, Arabelle! You *have* to wear your tiara," another girl said loudly to a group of her friends. "Have any of you seen it? It is royally gorgeous!"

Talk of ribbons, gowns, and jewels spilled off everyone's tongues. Ella wished she could stop and talk to the other girls. But what would she say? She didn't have a fancy hair ribbon to her name, let alone a gown suitable for a ball.

"At least I can finally get some shoes," Ella consoled herself. Maybe Lurlina could help her out with something to wear to the ball, too. Ella stopped in front of a heavy wooden door and slowly pushed it open. An ornately carved sign over her hand read PRINCESS SCHOOL ROYAL ADMINISTRATIVE CHAMBER.

"I'm looking for Lurlina Busybustle, if you please," Ella said with a curtsy to the woman behind the gilded desk.

"Oh, you must be Ella. Lurly left something for you," the woman said kindly. Then she began pawing through an enormous velvet bag filled with scrolls.

"You mean she's not here?" Ella asked. She felt a lump growing in her throat.

"Oh, no, dear," came the muffled reply from inside the bag. "Aha!" she said, emerging with a small scroll in her hand and a very disheveled hairdo. "Here we are. This should explain everything."

Ella was reaching for the scroll when a rather short page she hadn't even noticed leaped up and grabbed it. He gave the trumpeter by the door a sharp jab with his elbow, and after a few sour notes were played, the page cleared his throat to read.

After a moment of panic Ella calmed herself. "If

you don't mind," she said, putting out her hand, "I'd rather read it myself."

The page handed Ella the note sheepishly. "Of course, your nearly royalness, of course. My mistake," he said with a bow. "It's been such a long summer. I guess I'm anxious to read some decrees."

The page sat back down in the far corner and tilted his hat so it covered his eyes, and Ella began to read.

Halloo Dearie,

I forgot to tell you I am going to a fairy convention in Afaraway Land. I'll be back in three weeks. Sorry I'll miss the Coronation Ball. Have fun in Princess School. I knew you'd get in!

Love,
LB

P.S. Hope you are enjoying the shoes.

Ella's heart sank as she read. Three weeks! She couldn't possibly go barefoot for that long! What was she going to do? Bending her knees so her skirt touched the floor, Ella turned slowly toward the door.

"I have something else for you, too, dear. I think you left this at your interview." The woman behind the desk handed Ella a box. Inside it was one lovely, but oversized, glass shoe.

"Thank you." Ella smiled weakly, remembering the awful interview. She'd had to sit in a much-too-tall chair across from the Dean of Admissions, Miss Prim. And she'd had a terrible time answering the questions because all she could think about the whole time was how to keep her shoes from slipping off and breaking on the stone floor.

When Miss Prim had finally told her she could go, Ella was so anxious to get out of there she accidentally stepped out of one of her shoes. At first she was too embarrassed to go back for it. When she had summoned up her courage to reenter the dean's office, Miss Prim was holding the shoe in her hand, turning it this way and that and gazing at it with what looked like . . . admiration.

Ella couldn't ask for it back after that. Instead, with burning cheeks, she'd pulled off the other shoe, run all the way home, and received a serious lecture from her stepmother for being late. And of course, merciless teasing from Hagatha and Prunilla. Only her father had told her everything would be okay — but he'd told her in a whisper so his wife wouldn't hear. It wasn't particularly reassuring.

Ella gazed at the shoe in her hand. After her interview she'd been certain that the fancy footwear would keep her out of Princess School. Now she wondered if it had gotten her in.

Ella sighed. Little good the shoe would do her now without Lurlina to resize the pair. Ella tried not to think about how she was going to survive for three weeks without her fairy godmother — or what she would wear to the ball.

"Head down, feet covered," she mumbled to herself as she hurried toward her next class. Except for a large group of girls farther down the corridor, the halls were empty and the trunks were closed.

Ella did not want to be late and call attention to herself. But as she approached the group of girls, something made her slow. *Hungch-henh-henh-henh-hungch.* That laugh! Only Prunilla snorted like that when she laughed. And Hagatha's nasal cackle was echoing in the corridor as well.

Hagatha and Prunilla were standing in the center of a bunch of Bloomers Ella recognized from Madame Garabaldi's hearthroom. Ella backed into a doorway. She wasn't ready to deal with her stepsisters at school. Not with Lurlina gone. And not when they were laughing. Only one thing amused Hag and Prune: cruelty.

Ella carefully peeked around the corner to see what they were up to.

"It happens every year," Hagatha hissed at the big-eyed Bloomers. Prunilla nodded beside her sister. "Sometimes the wolf eats the princesses alive and they have to be chopped out. Sometimes he doesn't eat them at all, just chews up their limbs and spits out their bones!"

"Oh, no!" one of the first-years cried.

"How awful!" another shrieked.

The Bloomers pressed closer together. Some of them glanced over their shoulders. Only the girl with the massive, sloppily braided bun — Rapunzel — stood by herself. Her arms were folded across her chest. She didn't look scared but she was definitely listening.

"They come out of the woods and swim the moat." Prunilla made swimming motions with her arms. "They can smell Bloomer blood for miles, you know."

"I've never heard of a wolf that eats young girls!" a cheery voice from the Bloomer crowd protested. It was Snow White.

"These wolves do," Hagatha snapped back. "They're enchanted. The Grimm School sends them." Snow did not protest again.

"But you don't have to take our word for it," Prunilla said in singsong. "You'll see for yourselves soon enough!"

Hagatha and Prunilla pushed their way out of the crowd and sauntered down the hall. Then Hagatha turned quickly and snarled with her teeth bared, looking every bit as awful as a rabid wolf.

The shaken Bloomers screamed in terror and jumped back. All except Rapunzel, who followed the older girls down the hall, watching them with narrowed eyes.

Ella was dumbstruck. She didn't believe Hagatha and Prunilla's stories — not for a second. It was just like them to try to make the new girls scared. What shocked Ella the most was that Hag and Prune were being so terrible to, well, everyone! She always thought they saved their awfulness for her.

The thought of her stepsisters terrorizing her whole class made Ella furious. She wished like never before that she could stand up to them.

Then Ella had a terrible thought. What if everyone at Princess School found out Hagatha and Prunilla were her stepsisters? They might assume she was awful, just like them!

She would have to show the other Bloomers she was on their side. To do that she was going to have to stop going unnoticed. Ignoring her bare feet, Ella strode quickly down the hall. She beckoned to the still-cowering girls.

"Come on!" she called encouragingly. "We don't want to be late for class!"

One of the Bloomers, Snow White, smiled warmly at Ella. The rest of the girls were somber as they pressed together and shakily made their way down the hall.

Chapter Five
Rose

Madame Taffeta's skirts rustled as she gently took Rose's square of muslin and held it up for the rest of the princesses to see. "Note how the stitches are perfectly spaced and sized," she said, her gray eyes wide with admiration. Her round face was rosy from excitement. "Even the choice of thread color is perfect. The mossy green looks positively elegant against the cream muslin! And it's only our second day of classes!"

The girls were in Stitchery class, practicing basic threadwork. They sat in a large circle, each on a comfortable chair with a velvet cushion. Squares of plain muslin, spools of thread, needles, and shiny silver scissors sat on an ornately carved table in the center of the circle. A fire crackled cheerily at one end of the chamber.

Some of the Bloomers looked admiringly at Rose as the teacher held her muslin aloft. But others, including

Rapunzel, openly glared at her. Rose sighed and let her threaded needle fall to her lap, being careful not to let the sharp end touch her finger. Her stitches were straight, even, and perfectly sized, it was true.

Rose had been sewing for as long as she could remember, and with a disadvantage. Whenever Rose went near a needle, her parents forced her to wear a thimble on every finger, for fear she would prick herself. Rose didn't know why. It wasn't easy learning to sew with metal fingertips, but over time Rose had gotten good at it. So now, without those annoying thimbles, her stitching was even better — and she was faster at it. But she wished Madame Taffeta would stop making a fuss.

There was another girl who was fast — the friendly girl who'd been barefoot yesterday — Ella. She moved the needle and thread through the fabric so quickly, it was as if she desperately wanted the task to be done. She had already gone to the table to get a second and a third piece of muslin. Her stitches were almost as even as Rose's, and she had chosen a color that was almost identical to the mossy green. Why didn't Madame Taffeta compliment her?

As if deciding to squash any hope Rose had of ever being normal, Madame Taffeta began to speak again. "Briar Rose, would you like to demonstrate your perfect stitching technique? I'm sure the other girls would benefit greatly from an illustration of your talent."

Rose had no desire to demonstrate anything. For a moment she thought of pointing out Ella's fine stitches. But something stopped her. That first morning on the stairs, Ella had seemed terrified of being noticed. Standing up in front of the whole class might be even worse for her.

Rose stood and quickly ran her needle and thread through the muslin, making a straight line of even stitches.

"Perfect!" Madame Taffeta exclaimed. She snatched up the fabric and held it next to the window so the light shone behind it, making the stitches more visible.

Rose barely glanced at the muslin as she took her seat, but something outside the window caught her eye.

Oh my gosh! she thought, feeling her face flush with embarrassment. Was that Dahlia, one of her guardian fairies, hovering in midair?

The winged pest was spying on her! Rose quickly looked away, hoping Dahlia would disappear before anyone else saw her. That's when she noticed that Rapunzel was glaring at her for the second time in ten minutes. This time, Rose was ready. She glared right back. It wasn't as if she *asked* for this attention. Rapunzel's eyes widened in surprise before she lowered them back to her stitching.

Rose blew out her breath. Being so blessed and so protected was driving her crazy!

I wouldn't even mind being teased by the older girls! Rose thought desperately. Most of the Bloomers were miserable and terrified, and for good reason. The first day and a half of school had been grueling, and not just because of the rules and coursework. Terrible things had been happening to them!

First there was that horrible story about a cursed Grimm wolf eating the first-years. Rose wasn't sure she believed it, but the idea was enough to make anyone shiver. Then there were the trippings. An innocent Bloomer would be hurrying off to class when — *WHAM!* — she would suddenly find herself and whatever she was carrying sprawled across the cold stone floor. A few of the third-year Robes forced the new girls to guess their names, not letting them pass in the hall until they did so successfully. This usually made the Bloomers late for class, which got them in big trouble. But even tower detention (the punishment for being tardy) was not as humiliating as the drenchings. Some nasty Crowns rigged buckets of icy water over the trunks of unsuspecting Bloomers, soaking the girls as soon as the lids were lifted. Wet and shivering, the Bloomers would have to maintain their composure and dignity while they dried off as best they could and rushed off to wherever they had to go next.

Rose shuddered as she remembered that morning's drenching. It was early, and the sun had not yet peeked out from behind the clouds to warm the castle. The girl was small and had shivered uncontrollably as she made her way to class. Rose had wanted to go over and help the girl, but just then a group of Bloomers had come over to ask Rose what she was going to wear to the ball. Before she could break away, the cold and dripping girl was gone.

I'd like to do something about those cruel tricks, Rose thought. *Why can't the older girls just leave us alone?*

Except, of course, they *were* leaving Rose alone. She was getting the usual special treatment. And that was part of the problem!

The Self-defense class chamber was a giant room nearly as big as the school's stables. Thick, woven wool rugs covered the floor. There was no furniture, but to-day the room was decorated with large wooden props painted to look like trees and shrubs. The chamber looked like a forest.

The Bloomers stood in small groups waiting for Madame Lightfoot to give them instructions. Madame

Lightfoot was famous, the first princess in the land trained in the art of royal self-defense. Though she was the oldest teacher at Princess School, her braided gray hair was the only sign of her age. She was tall and stood so straight that her presence alone was intimidating. She was strict and did not tolerate students who did not work hard on their defense skills but her smile was never far below the surface.

Rose was eyeing the clusters of girls sprinkled throughout the room when Snow White skipped over. "I just loved your stitches!" Snow exclaimed. "If I could sew like that, the dwarves' clothes would almost never need mending. I swear I spend half my days restitching the same tears!" She let out a small giggle.

Rose had to smile. At least the pale girl's compliments were unique! "Do you really live with dwarves?" she asked, intrigued.

"Oh, yes!" Snow answered. "Seven of them! They are the funniest little men — a little strange at first, but really lovable once you get to know them. They bring me flowers and sing merry songs. Oh, and they protect me from —"

Just then Madame Lightfoot clapped her hands to get the girls' attention.

"Today we will be practicing the woodland-path-skip-trip," she announced. She moved swiftly around the room, pairing up the princesses. Rose was hoping she would be paired with Snow so she could learn more about the dwarves (like, how small were they? And would they be interested in meeting a bunch of fairies with too much free time?) but was not so lucky. Snow was paired with Ella. And Rose was paired with Rapunzel — the girl with the ridiculously long auburn hair and the mean stare.

Rapunzel gave a little snort when Madame Lightfoot pulled her and Rose together. The gleam in her eye was mischievous.

She looks like she wants to make a noose out of that hair and string me up, Rose thought. But she didn't care, and she wasn't afraid. It actually felt kind of nice to be scoffed at!

Madame Lightfoot went on, "This tactic is especially good when you find a devilish witch, wolf, or other beast of no-good nature sneaking up to devour you."

There was a chorus of shrieks, doubtless because of the rumored Grimm School wolf. Did Madame Lightfoot know about it? Rose wondered. Was that why she was teaching this skill during the first week of class?

"Ladies," the instructor said sternly, "we are here to learn to defend ourselves. Not to squeal and shriek like helpless children!"

The Bloomers quieted, and Madame Lightfoot continued. "Now, to begin the skip-trip, you must get into a good skipping rhythm. Whenever you are skipping through the forest, of course, you must continuously look from side to side for potential attackers. Keep your basket pushed back to your elbow so your hands are free. Then, when you see someone or something suspicious approaching you, throw out your forward skipping foot to knock the perpetrator off balance. That accomplished, grab your attacker around the neck and toss the scoundrel to the ground. It's really quite simple."

"It sounds mean!" Rose overheard Snow whispering to Ella. She watched as the shabbily dressed girl patted Snow's arm reassuringly. They had to be the nicest pair in the class!

Madame Lightfoot gazed around the chamber at the faces of the confused princesses. "Perhaps a demonstration," she said. "May I have a volunteer to be the scoundrel I am to trip?"

Rose was about to volunteer — maybe it would show the other girls that she didn't think she was too good to land flat on her face — when Rapunzel stepped forward. Madame Lightfoot immediately began to skip in slow motion. Rapunzel assumed a skulking pose and half-hid behind one of the wooden trees. She looked like she was just about to lunge at Madame Lightfoot when the teacher kicked her right foot to the side, knocking Rapunzel's left foot and throwing her off balance. An instant later, Madame Lightfoot tossed

Rapunzel over her shoulder and onto the soft green carpet like a small bale of hay. *Thud!* Rapunzel landed flat on her back.

Rapunzel beamed and leaped to her feet. "Incredible!" she said, not sounding very princesslike. Rose had to admire the girl's attitude. Would she have been as relaxed?

It didn't take long to find out. Madame Lightfoot instructed them to begin working in their pairs at once, and Rapunzel began skipping away. Rose lunged gracefully, but Rapunzel tripped her and tossed her to the ground like a sack of wet wool.

"Are you all right, Princess?" Rapunzel asked. Her voice was not entirely sincere, but Rose pretended not to notice.

"I'm fine," she replied pleasantly, getting to her feet.

Beside them, Snow and Ella were negotiating their own skip-trip. Ella was skipping and Snow was tripping — or, at least, she was trying to. As Ella approached, she slowed down, afraid to trod on Snow's foot. Snow kicked out her leg, but then threw out her hand to keep Ella from falling. Ella grabbed Snow's hand and sat down with a bump.

"Oops!" Ella giggled. "Maybe we should try that again. You don't have to be so nice, you know."

"Sorry," Snow apologized.

Those two are well matched, Rose thought. Then she

looked back at her own partner. She was well matched, too, she decided. Without even dusting herself off, Rose began her own skip, casting her eyes in all directions. Rapunzel came at her from behind a bush, but Rose was ready. She kicked out a leg with lightning speed and hurled Rapunzel to the ground so fast the girl got the wind knocked out of her.

Rose felt a little guilty. She hadn't meant to trip Rapunzel that hard. She was about to apologize when Rapunzel looked up, a wide grin on her face.

"Nice one!" she complimented Rose as she got to her feet and regained her breath. "Can you show me how to do it that fast?"

Rose grinned back. She had a sneaking suspicion she'd just made a friend. And not because she was pretty!

"Of course!" she replied.

Chapter Six
Step-by-step

Ella filled a platter with roasted meat and vegetables and hurried out to the dining room. She didn't want to listen to her stepmother or stepsisters complain about how slow she was. Or how lazy. Or how stupid. She was feeling deflated as it was.

It seemed that in the two days since she'd started Princess School, her stepsisters were more determined than ever to keep her swamped with chores at home. Suddenly the meals she had to prepare had seven courses instead of five. The mending basket was always overflowing. Hagatha and Prunilla had dirtied an extra gown a day, nearly doubling her laundry chores. Just yesterday they put in their winter furs to be aired, and it wasn't even October!

As Ella served the meat and vegetables, she tried not to look too tired. The more tired she appeared, the more her sisters ridiculed her.

"Everyone's talking about the Royal Coronation Ball at school, Mother," Prunilla said as she pecked at a scrap of meat. She looked scornfully at Ella holding the platter of food. "The meat is underseasoned again," she snapped. "Bring me the salt."

"You would think she would learn from her mistakes," Kastrid said coolly. "And yet we have to tell her again and again."

Ella knew the meat was seasoned perfectly. Besides, if she'd added any more salt, her stepsisters would complain that it was oversalted. She just couldn't win. Not since her father had married Kastrid.

"I think the meat is just right," Ella thought she heard her father murmur. She was standing right next to him with the platter. But if anyone else heard, they did not respond. With an aching heart, Ella wished her mother were still alive. How different things would be!

Ella sighed silently and handed Prunilla the glass bowl of salt that sat on the table, well within her reach. Her stepsisters never did anything for themselves if they could make Ella do it for them.

"Anyway," Prunilla said, casting a sideways glance at Ella, "they say the ball is going to be grander than ever this year. The ballroom floor is going to be repolished and the orchestra will have a dozen extra musicians! The fourth-year Crowns are in charge of decorating the ballroom, of course, but Headmistress

Bathilde has asked me to help decorate the ballot box!"

"You!" Hagatha cried, her eyes flashing with envy. "What about me?"

"Well, she asked *me*. But I suppose if you let me borrow your brocade cape I might let you help," Prunilla said coyly.

Hagatha scowled. "I was going to wear that cape, and you know it!" she howled.

"Girls, girls," Ella's stepmother said. "Let's not argue. Of course your sister will let you help with the ballot box," she told Hagatha. "And both of you will be beautifully dressed for the occasion."

"I'm sure all three of you girls will have a wonderful time at the ball," Ella's father added quietly.

The room fell silent, and for a moment Ella was grateful that her father had spoken up for her. But one glance at her stepmother's narrowing eyes told her she shouldn't be. The look on Kastrid's face was so cruel that Ella almost dropped the basket of bread she was holding.

"Ella is lucky to be attending Princess School at all," Kastrid snapped. "It has yet to be seen whether she deserves to go to the ball as well."

Ella looked over at her father, hoping he would say something else. His eyes flitted between his plate of food and his wife's angry face.

"But the ball is for all Princess School students, is it not, my sweet?" he said, almost in a whisper.

Kastrid slammed her wine goblet down on the table so hard that the red liquid spilled onto the white lace tablecloth — another stain for Ella to remove.

"We shall discuss this later, *darling*," Ella's stepmother declared, giving Ella's father a withering look. As Ella returned to the kitchen to finish preparing the dessert, her heart went out to her father. Being married to Kastrid could not be any easier than having her for a stepmother. And she knew he had married her because he thought she, his only child, needed a mother.

There was no mention of the ball during the rest of the meal. But as soon as Ella had cleared the dishes and filled the sink with hot water, her stepsisters flounced into the kitchen, talking loudly about the ball.

"I want all of my gowns cleaned and pressed so I can try them on and choose the one that makes me look prettiest," Prunilla announced.

"And I want each and every piece of my gold and silver jewelry polished to a perfect shine so I can choose the ones that bring out my eyes," Hagatha added.

Ella wanted to tell Hagatha that her beady eyes

were not her best asset. Why bring them out? And nothing could make Prunilla pretty, since her heart was as black as coal. But Ella said nothing, only continued washing the giant pile of dishes next to the stone sink.

"We're so sorry you won't be coming to the ball with us," Hagatha said in a sugary-sweet voice.

"Yes," Prunilla agreed. Her face contorted into a sneer. "Who will fetch our refreshments and adjust the skirts of our gowns?"

Ella gritted her teeth. *Politeness must be observed*, she told herself, repeating Madame Garabaldi's words. Somehow they fell flat. Still, Ella said nothing.

Then Hagatha's eyes glimmered, and she leaned back. Before Ella knew what was happening the soup tureen fell to the floor, smashing and splattering soup everywhere, especially all over Ella. Her stepsisters, of course, leaped out of the way just in time.

"What a mess!" Prunilla said. "You are as clumsy as you are slow!"

"You'd better clean it up before Mother finds out you broke her best tureen," Hagatha added.

Cackling like a pair of court jesters, the two left Ella alone in the kitchen with porcelain shards and spattered vegetable soup.

Ella held back tears as she got down on her hands

and knees to begin cleaning up the mess. As she sopped up the soup with a rag, she accidentally cut her hand on a broken tureen shard. In an instant her sadness disappeared, and she was filled with anger.

"I *will* go to the ball," she said aloud between gritted teeth. "And *not* to fetch cakes or adjust skirts!"

Chapter Seven
Mirror, Mirror

Rapunzel sighed. Looking Glass class was turning out to be as awful as she'd feared. Perching on a small velvet stool in front of a dressing table with a huge mirror was bad enough. Rapunzel didn't think she was much to look at, and staring at herself in the mirror only seemed to prove that she was right. Her freckled nose was straight. Her eyes weren't crossed or anything. And Rapunzel had always loved her hair — it was original and incredibly handy.

But in Looking Glass class, in addition to having to look at herself for more than an hour (boring), she was expected to weave fancy braids and twist curls and place hair clips just so. Rapunzel eyed the brush, comb, ribbons, hair clips, and curling iron in front of her. She was sure they would be of no help in tackling her untamable tresses.

Rapunzel held up a thick reddish-brown lock, eyeing it doubtfully. At the dressing table next to her,

Rose smiled encouragingly. "Just divide it into sections and weave them together," she said.

"Easy for you to say," Rapunzel replied, smirking. "Your hair doesn't resemble a ship's riggings!"

Rose giggled and continued to weave her golden tresses into a French braid. She didn't even have to pay attention to what she was doing. Instead, she was listening to the girl on the other side of her prattle on about the ball.

"I hear the crown is made of glittering diamonds!" the girl said, her blue eyes reflecting wide in the looking glass.

"I thought it was made of rubies," Rose replied.

"Someone told me it's made of both!" a third student said. "And sapphires, too!" A chorus of oohs echoed in the chamber.

"I hope a prince asks me to dance!" one of the Bloomers blurted out.

Suddenly the room filled with chatter about the Charm School for Boys. Everyone was giggling, and several girls blushed as well. Besides Rapunzel, only Ella was quiet. She seemed almost sullen as she combed and recombed the same lock of hair.

"I can't wait," said Snow White. "I've been practicing my dancing with the woodland animals."

"I hear the princes at Charm School are majestically cute!" another princess chimed in.

Rapunzel snorted. What was the big deal about boys? They were like girls, really — only different. She and Val had been friends for years, and he didn't make her blush or giggle –– more like belly laugh — and he was a boy.

For the millionth time, Rapunzel wished she were with Val instead of stuck at Princess School. Charm School was probably a blast!

While I'm here primping Val gets to fence and gallop on horseback! she thought miserably. *He's right on the other side of the gardens, and I never even see him!*

"Ah, girls," Madame Spiegel said, pulling Rapunzel out of her thoughts. The teacher was standing next to her dressing table at the front of the room, gazing at her own reflection, which was lovely. The young teacher had long, wavy blond hair, strikingly high cheekbones, and wide-set brown eyes.

"You can never be sure what will be reflected back at you when you look in a mirror," she said mysteriously. She caught Rapunzel's eyes in the looking glass. "Can you see your true self?"

Rapunzel made a face at herself and her hopelessly messy hair in the mirror. Of course she saw herself. Who else would she see?

Suddenly one of the girls — the tiny one who had gotten soaked by a bucket of freezing water the day before — leaped up off her stool with a shriek.

"Madame Spiegel," she cried. "I think there's something under my seat!" The poor girl had been moaning and twisting uncomfortably on her stool all morning. Rapunzel thought it was because she had caught a chill from the drenching. Now, she realized, it could be much worse.

The room went silent. The princesses' eyes widened. It couldn't be . . .

Without a word, Madame Spiegel went over to the princess's stool. Slowly and carefully she helped the girl remove cushion after cushion from her seat. Since the girl was so small, she had at least half a dozen piled on her chair.

The rest of the Bloomers exchanged silent glances while they held their breath, waiting to see what the lump was. Rapunzel hoped it was just a piece of batting that had gathered together inside one of the cushions. The other possibility was too horrible. Too cruel.

Finally Madame Spiegel lifted the last cushion from the girl's stool. There, slightly squashed but still intact, was a single pea.

At once the chamber was filled with cries of disbelief.

"A pea! A pea!" someone screamed.

"I don't believe it," another girl cried.

The princess who had been sitting on the pea fell to the floor in a faint.

Rapunzel felt sorry for the girl. Personally, she was not afraid of peas — she was pretty confident she could sit on one for hours and barely notice. But peas had sent several princesses into tailspins — robbing them of sleep, making it impossible for them to sit or lie down for days — some pea victims had even needed medical attention. Needless to say, most princesses were terrified of them. Rapunzel would never use the small round vegetable against another princess, not even a princess she didn't like. It was an unspoken rule — a princess pact.

"Who would do such an awful thing?" Rose said aloud as several girls gathered around the fallen princess.

"I have an idea," Rapunzel heard Ella say under her breath so quietly that Rapunzel was quite sure nobody else heard.

"Girls, we must remain calm." Madame Spiegel's voice was steady but strained. "Panic helps no princess." She crouched down over the princess who had fainted and held a small jar of smelling salts under her nose. The girl opened her eyes.

The tiny worry lines that had creased the teacher's flawless skin disappeared. "We must have courage and faith in ourselves," she said. "Without those things we will be defeated by unkind tricks such as these."

Madame Spiegel helped the victimized princess to

her feet, removed the pea from the stool, and set the cushions back on top.

Holding the offending pea at arm's length like a soiled diaper, Madame Spiegel ceremoniously carried the pea to the hearth and threw it directly onto the embers. The flames shot up and the pea exploded into several pieces before sizzling and disappearing into ashes. "Back to our looking glasses, ladies," she called.

Satisfied the offending vegetable had been properly disposed of, the girls sat back down on their stools, many of them checking for peas first.

Rapunzel watched Madame Spiegel stare at herself in a mirror. Then she turned back to her own reflection and wrestled once more with her unwieldy locks. A plain braid would be easy. But a French braid required small sections of hair — at least at first. And none of the clips on the dressing table looked remotely big enough for even a few strands of her thick hair.

Frustrated, Rapunzel grabbed the hot iron and began to wrap a piece of hair around it. But the iron was heavier than she expected, and she nearly burned her neck.

Just then another face appeared in Rapunzel's looking glass. It was Rose. Her hair had been neatly woven into three French braids, the ends of which were twisted into a neat bun at the nape of her slender neck.

"I hate those things," Rose whispered, pointing to the hot iron. "But I can show you a couple of braiding tricks."

"Great," Rapunzel said, smiling. She sat back, letting Rose take over. Obviously the girl knew what she was doing when it came to hair — just like she did in Self-defense. A few minutes later, Rose had half of the hair in a braid that ran partway down Rapunzel's back.

Grateful, Rapunzel turned her head to look at the sides. A beam of sunlight flashed on the mirror's surface. A second later it happened again. And again.

That's weird, Rapunzel thought. She had already put down her hand mirror. She glanced around the chamber and noticed that nobody else was using a small looking glass, either.

Flash. There it was again. She and Rose exchanged a glance in the mirror above her dressing table, and Rapunzel leaned over to look out the window. Halfway across the garden, she saw a boy standing outside the Princess School stables. Val! He was holding a piece of shiny metal, moving it back and forth so it reflected a beam of light into the Looking Glass chamber window!

"Who is that?" Rose whispered, leaning forward to get a better look.

"My friend Val," Rapunzel replied, waving at him. "He goes to the Charm School."

Rose nodded, looking impressed.

Val flashed his metal again and pointed toward the stables. Rapunzel grinned. Val had thought of the perfect meeting spot and signal!

Chapter Eight
Warts and All

Ella walked down the hall lost in thought. She was tired and shaken. The pea incident played again and again in her head. She was certain Hagatha and Prunilla were behind it — even if they didn't carry out the horrible deed alone. And for some reason their cruelties seemed especially harsh to Ella lately. Maybe it was because she had never seen her stepsisters terrorize other girls. Or maybe it was because she had seen true kindness in some of her teachers and classmates.

Ella's thoughts were interrupted as Snow skipped up beside her, humming a little tune. Looping her arm through Ella's, Snow pulled her toward their next class: Frog Identification.

"Aren't you excited?" Snow asked. "This is my favorite class. And today we get to work with real frogs!"

Snow's enthusiasm was infectious. Ella allowed Snow

to pull her along and felt her spirits being slowly lifted by the cheerful chatter.

"Of course I love Princess School," Snow babbled, "but I do miss the forest animals. They visit me every day when I'm home at the cottage. They don't talk much, but they're wonderful company! Have you ever spent time with a toad? I have. Frogs and toads aren't nearly as cuddly as deer and rabbits and squirrels. But I think they're just as cute — in a slippery sort of way! Don't you agree?"

Ella smiled and nodded. She didn't really find frogs appealing, but she did feel better.

They were almost at the Frog ID chamber door when a group of older princesses began to crowd around them and the rest of the Bloomers, shouting taunts. Ella saw her stepsisters in the middle of the hecklers and ducked her head.

"Watch out for warts!" Prunilla called.

"Careful, girls, don't get slime all over your gowns!" a Sash yelled.

"The poor Bloomers," teased Hagatha. "Where else but in frog class would they get dates for the ball?"

The hall was filled with taunting laughter, but Ella ignored it as Snow led her and the Bloomers into the frog chamber. It was the plainest room in the castle. A fireplace stood at each end to warm the rug-free space. A single row of simple wooden tables ran along one wall. Small cages were lined up on the tables, each one containing a captured frog.

"Step inside, girls," Madame Bultad called. "Contrary to Princess School rumor, there's nothing to be afraid of here."

The girls entered the chamber but stood in a group near the door — all except Snow, who immediately went over to the frog cages to say hello.

Madame Bultad, a squat woman with a broad face and almost-black eyes, cleared her throat. Ella thought the sound was remarkably similar to a croak!

"I know Frog ID is the subject of much ridicule," the teacher said. "But as I've told you before, the skills you are acquiring in this room are essential for every princess." She paused for effect. "Unless you would like to find yourself plagued by a frog that you are unable to identify as either a prince under a spell or a green-skinned trickster."

The girls peered nervously at the caged frogs, whispering to one another. Nobody liked to talk about frogs — they generally made princesses nervous. Ella didn't really mind them. She was used to seeing them at the pond near her home and occasionally in the kitchen garden where she grew vegetables.

Madame Bultad continued, "As we discussed, ordinary frogs have become very skilled at disguising themselves as the real thing in the hopes of being kissed by a princess . . . or a princess-in-training." She sprung open the latch of one of the cages and a large, shiny green frog hopped out. Madame Bultad picked it up with a graceful swoop of her arm.

"Notice the golden-hued warts that cover this frog's body."

"He's beautiful!" Snow cried, rushing forward to get a better look.

Ella couldn't help but smile. But Madame Bultad's face grew serious. "Perhaps, but looks can be deceiving. A decade ago these golden warts would have been a sure sign that this creature is actually a prince under an evil spell. But today's amphibians have cleverly adopted these false clues to fool the inexperienced princess. One out of every five ordinary frogs and toads will have golden warts, spots in a crown configuration on its head, or a similar feature. My advice is this: Do not act in haste. Look carefully. Study your subjects. Only then will you find a prince among frogs."

Madame Bultad smiled, and the frogs began to croak loudly.

"And now, ladies, it is time to release the frogs. Each of you shall step forward and open a cage."

While most of the girls looked at one another in disgust, Snow bounded forward and opened a cage, freeing a frog. Ella stepped up behind her and cautiously lifted a latch. She had never touched a frog before, but they couldn't be *that* bad.

"They're not wolves," Rapunzel called, echoing Ella's thoughts and stepping forward herself. "They're frogs!" She sprung a latch and a skinny frog leaped straight to the floor.

Soon the entire chamber was filled with hopping, croaking frogs. Ella had never seen so many amphibians in so many shapes and sizes. And many of them were quite clever. One actually winked at her!

Most of the princesses, though, were not amused — or even interested. Most of them screamed and tried to get away when a slimy green hopper drew near.

Ella studied a frog with a silver circle on top of its head. It was sort of sweet, but . . . slimy.

On the other side of the room, Rose moved graciously away from a dozen frogs that were all trying madly to get close to her.

Rapunzel, for her part, sat on the floor nearby talking very calmly to a particularly large, lumpy frog. "It's nice to see you again, Warty," she said. "And I'm sorry you've been captured. But I don't care how many hopping contests you've won for me — I'm not going to kiss you again!"

Just then, Rose calmly strode over, still being followed by at least twelve frogs. "Yech," she said in a very unprincesslike manner. "I don't care if you *are* under a curse. I'm not going to kiss any of you!" The frogs stopped hopping and croaking and just looked up at Rose, pouting.

Rose looked to Rapunzel for help, but Snow was first to speak. "Don't listen to them," she said, making a hammock in the skirt of her gown to gather up the frogs. "I'll kiss all of you, even if you aren't princes." The frogs hopped excitedly toward her.

"Or will that get me in trouble?" Snow turned to Ella.

Ella abandoned the frog with the silver circle and cautiously reached a finger out to pet one of the frogs in Snow's skirt. "Here, froggy, froggy," she said in a croaky voice. She softly stroked a lumpy frog's back. He actually wasn't as slippery as he looked!

Standing next to them, Rose giggled. The frog Ella was petting croaked loudly, and Ella laughed, too. Warty croaked next and hopped over to Snow. But he was so fat he couldn't jump high enough to get into her skirt-hammock.

"Here you go, Warty," Rapunzel said, giving him a little lift. "You've been putting away the mayflies, haven't you?" The frog flipped right over, letting out a long croak as he landed on the soft fabric of Snow's gown.

"You're welcome," Rapunzel said, laughing.

The next thing they knew, all four girls were giggling hysterically. Across the room, Madame Bultad opened her mouth to tell the girls to be quiet, but began to cough instead.

"Frog in her throat," Rose whispered. Ella and the other girls nearly fell to the floor laughing. They couldn't stop. Ella felt all of her fear and worry slipping away. Frog ID was turning out to be the best class so far!

Then, all of a sudden, the laughter was cut short. Screams from the hall filled the room. "A wolf! A wolf!"

Chapter Nine
Who's Afraid?

A dark-haired Bloomer who had just been to the little princesses' room burst back into Frog ID screaming, "There's a wolf in the hall!"

Leaving the classroom door standing wide open, the girl dashed for the high windows at the back of the room. In a split second her panic spread. Pandemonium broke out.

The loud ribbiting of frightened frogs was overwhelmed by the shrieks of even more frightened princesses. Frogs tripped over one another, trying to get back to the safety of their cages. Bloomers scrambled onto tables, trying to avoid the frogs and reach the high diamond-paned windows. Everyone's worst nightmare had come true. There was a wolf loose in the school.

Strangely, Briar Rose felt calm. She was rarely afraid, but maybe that was because everyone was usually so scared for her she didn't have to be. She moved toward the door, intending to close it and protect the others.

Out in the hall Rose heard another cry. "Help!" A Bloomer in a red cloak dashed past Rose. Chasing after the girl — and moving fast — was a flash of black fur. Rose heard a growl, or maybe a snort, before the chorus of screams behind her drowned out all other noise.

"Is that the wolf?" Snow pushed past Rose into the hallway. The wolf stopped running and stood its ground at the end of the hall. "Oh, isn't he sweet?" Snow crooned, taking a few steps toward the animal with her hand outstretched.

"Shouldn't we grab her?" Rapunzel was suddenly standing behind Rose. Ella was there, too. Madame Bultad, for her part, had hopped up on the tables with the rest of the Bloomers. Her bog-green skirts were hoisted to her knees, showing plenty of yellow stocking.

Before her new friends could pull Snow back inside the room, the wolf turned and ran awkwardly away. It looked as if its two front legs were stunted, and its fur was awfully loose.

A minute later Snow came back into the room. "It's gone!" she called to everyone on the tables, including the teacher. "Poor thing. He looked just awful!"

Rose smiled. Leave it to Snow to be worried about the invader!

Madame Bultad climbed off the table, crossed the room, and cautiously poked her head out the door. Then she cleared her throat. "All clear, girls," she said in her rumbling voice. "Now, stay together and get to your hearthroom while I report this to the administrative chambers!"

The Bloomers held hands and hurried past Rose, looking both ways. Some of them skipped, ready to try their skip-trip if necessary. All of them appeared frazzled. Even Snow.

"I think there was something wrong with that wolf," Snow said, turning back toward her friends, who were still standing by the door. Her voice was full of concern and her eyes were starting to well up with tears.

"I *know* there was," Ella replied over Rose's shoulder. Snow looked like she thought the wolf was hurt, but there was something in Ella's voice that let Rose know Ella was thinking along the same lines she was.

"To start with, that was no wolf," Rose said. She held out her hand to comfort Snow.

Ella nodded. "No. I've seen that fur before, and it doesn't belong to a wolf. It belongs to something worse — my stepmother."

"What do you mean?" Snow's dark eyes sparkled.

Rapunzel pushed a lock of black hair off Snow's porcelain face. Rose had felt like doing the same thing. There was something about Snow. She was so trusting, it made you want to take care of her.

"That was no wolf," Rose announced. "That was a person in a wolf costume."

"Hagatha . . . or Prunilla, one of my stepsisters," Ella added. She wrapped her arm around Snow and glared at the spot where the "wolf" had been. "Those girls live to torture others. I just wish we could prove it was —"

Suddenly Ella stopped talking.

All of the Bloomers had gone, but now a Robe stood in the hallway. She was dressed in a gorgeous sunset-orange dress and her jewels were lovely, but they looked out of place beside the sneer on her face.

"Hey, Cinder Blockhead," Prunilla spat at Ella. "I see you made a new friend." She gestured toward Snow, looking her up and down, obviously disapproving of her old-fashioned dress. "She's perfect for you."

"Leave us alone, Prunilla," Ella said softly.

Prunilla acted like she didn't hear Ella. She slowly walked closer to Snow, staring into her wide eyes. "Do you always look so stupid?" she said with disdain, screwing up her face even more.

"Oh, no," Snow answered sweetly. "I was just so worried about that poor wolf —"

"Never mind," Prunilla cut Snow off and her dark eyes settled on Rose.

Rose watched as Prunilla's whole face changed. She still wasn't what Rose would call beautiful, but the snarl was gone. Now her tiny lips turned up in a smile.

"Briar Rose!" she said in a sickeningly sweet voice. "I'm sure you must have better things to do than to waste your time with this pair of dirty Bloomers! We are reflected in the company we keep, you know. Why don't you come with me, Beauty? I can introduce you to some of the Robes. We usually don't associate with the younger girls, but for you we might make an exception." Prunilla extended her hand limply.

"Thank you. No," Rose replied coolly, stepping closer to Ella, Snow, and Rapunzel and giving Prunilla a steely look. "I don't think I could bear to see myself reflected in *your* shallow eyes."

Prunilla's mouth dropped open into a perfect "O." For a moment she did nothing, then her eyes narrowed into tiny slits. Her mouth closed and opened again. But she was silent as she turned on her heel and stomped away in a huff.

Suddenly Ella bent over, clutching her stomach. Her head bobbed and she gasped for breath. Rose put her hand to her mouth. She hoped she hadn't gotten Ella into trouble! Maybe she shouldn't have said anything to the nasty older girl.

"I'm sorry. Was I out of line?" Rose began.

Ella stood up. Her face was red and tears were running down her cheeks. But she was grinning from ear to ear.

"You might live to regret that," Ella gasped, still trying to control her laughter. "But if you ask me, it was worth it!"

Chapter Ten

Rapunzel's Surprise

Rapunzel ran down the hall as fast as she could. It felt good — no, great — not to worry about regal countenance and posture and poise and . . . UGH!

Because of the wolf scare, all of the princesses had been escorted from their hearthrooms to the far courtyard — away from the Grimm School woods — while the royal guards checked the halls. Rapunzel headed to the other side of the castle, toward the stables and Val. It was the perfect opportunity for her to slip away.

Racing out the front of the school, Rapunzel dashed down the steps and hopped the low wall separating the entrance from the rose garden. She ducked through the prickly bushes and sprinted the last few yards. She hoped Val would still be there. They had arranged to meet in the stables during lunch. The only problem was, Val's lunch ended just as Rapunzel's began.

"Don't worry. Nobody can keep me in," she'd told him. "Just be there." She had sounded confident, but if it hadn't been for this wolf scare, she didn't know how she would have made it in time.

"Val!" Rapunzel called as she flew into the enormous stables. Doves scattered, flying up to the rafters. The horses snorted and pawed the straw at the disturbance. Luckily, none of the stable hands were there. Rapunzel suddenly realized that she could get herself in trouble for being out of school if she was caught.

"Come out, come out, wherever you are," Rapunzel called more quietly. Val *had* to be there. She had stayed up late every night for three nights making him a surprise. She had wanted to give it to him that morning, but he'd left for school early — without her. She simply could not wait another second.

All Rapunzel heard were stomping feet.

Sinking down onto a bale of hay, Rapunzel pulled the surprise out of the pocket she'd stitched into her dress. It was a belt buckle. The buckle had been her father's. Or at least she assumed it had been. It was on the belt Madame Gothel had used to tie up all of her baby things when she whisked Rapunzel away from her parents. Only the buckle had never shone like it did now.

Rapunzel had spent hours polishing and polishing it for Val. She hoped he would wear it every day. That way he would always be ready to flash her messages from the Charm School. Now the buckle was as shiny as her looking glass. Almost. Rapunzel's reflection distorted in the metal and she stuck out her tongue. Wow. And she thought she looked funny in a regular mirror!

"I thought you said you weren't going to turn all prissy and vain on me." Val's laughing voice was muffled in the dim stable. But his smiling green eyes were unmistakable in the shafted light. "And here I find you gazing at yourself in anything that will cast a reflection! Maybe I should start calling *you* 'Beauty.'"

"Oh, stop!" Rapunzel threw the buckle at Val, who stopped teasing long enough to catch it. She felt a pang of guilt for telling Val about Rose's silly nickname, especially now that she really kind of liked the pretty princess. Rose was more than a lovely face. Much more. In fact, she might even be a great friend. But Rapunzel wasn't ready to tell Val about that now. She had other things to tell him about, like the buckle and her plan.

"What's this?" Val asked, turning over the shiny metal object and polishing it a little on his shirt.

"A suit of armor," Rapunzel said dryly. "What do you think?"

Val gave her a look and Rapunzel pulled the rest of her surprise out of her pocket. "*That* is so you can send me light signals when I'm in class on the north side of the building." She pointed at the buckle. "*This*," she said, handing him a small scroll, "is the start of our code."

Rapunzel had come up with several flash sequences that would allow her to communicate with Val. There wasn't too much you could say with light and mirrors. "Hello." "See you later." "Madame Spiegel has a nose like a toadstool." And the most important: "Meet me at the stables — quick!" Rapunzel and Val couldn't exactly have conversations, but it was enough to keep them connected and keep Rapunzel from feeling trapped at Princess School. Besides, once they got good at using it, the code could be expanded.

Val smiled. "What a waste. There you are learning how to do cross-stitch when you would do the most good in King Westerly's Secret Service."

"Hey, I've learned some defensive skills, too." Rapunzel feigned a skip-trip and Val backed away with his hands up.

"Mercy, Your Highness," he said with a bow. "I've heard all about how you can take down pretty girls." Val flopped back in the hay, stretching his long skinny legs. "How *is* Beauty, anyway?" he asked. His eyes twinkled.

"Don't tell me you're stuck on her, too." Rapunzel

knocked the prince's thin crown so it sat askew in his dark curly hair.

"Not stuck, just curious." Val shrugged. "What's she like? Is she just like the stories say?"

It was Rapunzel's turn to shrug. "She's okay." Funny. Last week Rapunzel had been enjoying telling Val all about the fancy frou-frou girls at Princess School and having a good laugh. But now she felt different. Some of the girls weren't so silly. Like when Snow had walked up to that wolf, or whatever it was. That was brave.

Things were changing. Rapunzel didn't feel good about poking fun at the princesses and she didn't know how to explain it to Val. Maybe she was making new friends. Maybe she was fitting in.

Suddenly Rapunzel wanted to get back to school, to see if she was missing anything. The "wolf" could come back at any time!

"So, send me a signal when you're in Chivalry," she said, standing up quickly and backing out of the stables.

"Hey, where are you going? I don't have to be back until the second trumpet blast." Val looked surprised.

"I have to get back before I'm missed. They might be taking scroll call after the wolf alert." Rapunzel ran out of the barn with a quick wave and a smile.

"What alert? What wolf?" Val called after her.

Rapunzel didn't stay to explain. She'd tell him later. Maybe she'd tell him about her new friends later, too.

Thinking about the girls she'd find at the far courtyard, Rapunzel smiled. And as she jumped the wall of the rose garden and hurried up the stone steps to Princess School, Rapunzel felt completely free.

Chapter Eleven
Best-laid Plans

The mood at Princess School was charged. Although the royal guards had declared the school grounds safe and Ella had tried to tell some of the Bloomers that the wolf wasn't really a wolf, everyone was on edge.

The girl who had been chased by the "wolf" had gone home to her grandmother's house. The rest of the Bloomers were so scared that they walked the hallways in groups or pairs, always looking over their shoulders. Ella walked alone, deep in thought.

Aside from the fact that she was used to being harassed, Ella was simply too exhausted to be afraid. She had been staying up later and later every night. After all of the extra chores were done she had important work of her own to attend to.

Ella had been cleaning the parlor when she came up with the idea. *If only my fairy godmother wasn't so far away,* Ella had thought lamentingly. *Her magic could take care of everything!* Running the feather duster over the scrolled backs of the velvet chairs, she remembered how much fabric had been left over after her stepmother had ordered the seats reupholstered. Kastrid had redecorated everything in the house the moment she moved in. Ella knew the changes had cost her father a small fortune. Kastrid adored spending her new husband's money. But Ella was sure her stepmother had done the redecorating for another reason: to destroy every whisper of her mother's memory. Although her stepmother might be able to make her family's riches disappear, she could not take away Ella's memories. They were safely locked in her head and heart forever.

Ella remembered her mother every day. Her mother had taught her so much before she died, like how to cook and sing, how to dance and garden, how to take care of herself and hold onto hope. Her mother was also the reason Ella could sew better than almost anyone in Stitchery. And there were yards and yards of unused velvet just sitting in the attic.

From the first night Ella had started on her gown she'd stayed up late, working by candlelight to keep her project a secret and to get it finished in time. She'd used one of her mother's too-tattered-to-wear gowns as a basis for the pattern. The gown was simple but elegant. The square neckline was high. The long sleeves were snug but not too tight. And the skirt was full, with tiny pleats going all the way around the bodice. After five nights of hard work, the gown was nearly done.

Maybe it was because she was so tired, but as she moved down the hall Ella felt as if she were in a dream. She could barely believe she would actually be going to the Royal Coronation Ball. She knew her father must have said something because just last night Kastrid had informed her through pursed lips that she could go. Ella supposed Kastrid had gone along with it because she knew her stepdaughter had nothing to wear.

"As long as you are keeping up in school," her stepmother had said tightly, "I can't stop you."

Now all Ella needed was to make it through her classes. But that was a little harder than it sounded. Being tired from her housework and her late-night sewing made it difficult to concentrate. During History: Princesses Past and Present, the letters on her scroll swam in front of her eyes. And when Madame Istoria asked her even a simple question, she sat there, speechless, until Rose whispered the answer in her ear. In Stitchery she kept losing her thread. In Looking Glass she barely had the strength to raise her arms over her head and form a braid! But she would do it. Nothing would keep her from going to the ball now.

Lost in a daze of exhaustion and dreaming of the ball, Ella stumbled in her paper-stuffed glass shoes toward Self-defense. She never even saw Prunilla coming.

"Cin-der-el-la," Prunilla said, drawing out Ella's full name. "Just the Bloomer I've been looking for!"

"Leave me alone, Prunilla. I don't want to be late for class." Ella moved to walk around her stepsister, but Prune quickly stepped back into her path.

"I wouldn't want that, sister dear," Prunilla said with mock sympathy. "It's just that you are so good at cleaning up messes — and I'm afraid there's a rather large one waiting for you in my trunk. I'm sure it won't take you too long to clean out — you already have the rags for the job. Or is that your dress?"

Ella sighed and looked Prunilla in the eye. The "rag" she was talking about used to be Prunilla's. "You might be able to force me to do things in front of your mother, but at school things are different," Ella said.

"Are they really?" Prune asked. The false sweetness was gone, and Prunilla's narrowed eyes looked smaller than ever.

Ella took a small step back. She knew she had just made a big mistake. "Yes," Ella said, her voice cracking.

"*Hungh,*" Prunilla snorted, amused by her own deviousness as she plotted her next cruel act. "We'll just see about that," she growled. "Because if my trunk isn't organized and scrubbed spotless by the time I am out of Fancy Dress class, I am going to tell Mother that it was *you* who ripped her black fur cape."

Ella's mouth dropped open. She wasn't sure what would be worse — getting in trouble at school or at home. And now it was sure to be both.

Prunilla wasn't even finished. "And if you want to be sure Mother's cape is the only thing that gets ripped, you'll scrub out Hagatha's trunk, too!" With one last nasty glare, Prunilla stomped down the corridor.

When the trumpets blew and classes started, Ella was walking away from the Self-defense classroom door. Almost every shred of hope drained out of her poor tired body as she hurried down the hall toward the older girls' trunks.

She knew she had to take Prunilla's threats seriously. She only hoped that if she did what she was told, her stepsister wouldn't carry out her threats anyway, for spite. All Ella could do was scrub out the trunks as quickly as possible and hope that Madame Lightfoot was more merciful than her stepmother. Ella crossed her fingers. If she wasn't, the little bit of hope she was clinging to would be dashed as well. Trouble in school would be the only excuse Kastrid needed to keep Ella from the Coronation Ball.

Ella lifted the curved lid of Prunilla's trunk and

winced. It was crammed with so much stuff she couldn't even see the velvet lining on the bottom.

It's worse than her closet, Ella thought as a waft of stale air drifted past her nose. With a heavy sigh, Ella began to pull things out — books, scrolls, capes, scarves, scraps of food. . . .

"Need some help?" a voice called out behind her.

Startled, Ella turned around to see Rapunzel, Snow, and Rose.

Ella's eyes widened. "What are you doing here? You're late for class. You'll get in trouble!"

"Correction," Rapunzel said. "We've already been to class. We noticed you weren't there and thought maybe something was wrong. So Rose here faked an injury in Self-defense. We're supposed to be on our way to the nurse's chamber."

"It's strange, but my leg is feeling much better," Rose said with a little smile.

"We still have to go to the nurse, but we have a few minutes to help," Rapunzel said. She surveyed the mess on the corridor floor. "What are you doing, anyway? And what's that smell?"

"That smell is odeur de Prunilla," Ella said. "She's making me clean out her trunk. And Hagatha's, too." Ella felt her throat tighten. "If I don't do it, she's going to get me in trouble with my stepmother!"

"I can't believe those awful girls are part of your family," Rapunzel said. "Maybe living alone in a tower isn't so bad after all," she added thoughtfully.

Snow White was carefully studying Prunilla's trunk. "This isn't as bad as the dwarves' cottage the first time I saw it," she said cheerfully. "If we work together, we can get it cleaned up in no time!"

"Which trunk is Hagatha's?" Rose asked. "Snow and I can clean that one while you and Rapunzel take care of this mess. If we hurry we can get it done and still get to the nurse's chamber before the end of class."

"Thank you!" Ella said, her heart lightening. She pointed to Hagatha's trunk, and the girls got to work organizing books and scrolls into neat piles, folding capes, and throwing out aging food.

"What a waste!" Snow exclaimed, holding up a rotten apple she'd unearthed. "Who lets a perfectly good apple go bad?" Her dark eyes were wide.

"A bad apple like Hagatha," Rapunzel replied grimly as she set a *Riddles and Names* textbook on top of the pile she was making.

They were almost done when Rose pulled a burlap sack out of the bottom of Hagatha's trunk. The sack had a small hole in the bottom, and black fur was sticking out.

"Hey, look at this!" Rose said excitedly. She reached

inside and pulled out a black fur cape with pointed fur triangles, like ears, attached near the collar.

"Wait a second," Rapunzel said. "That looks like a wolf costume!"

"The wolf costume one of my stepsisters was wearing when we were in Frog ID," Ella added.

"It's evidence!" Rapunzel said excitedly. "Now we can figure out a way to get even!"

Just then the five-minute horn blasted — class was almost over!

"We'll have to figure out what to do later," Rose said, quickly shoving the cape back into the bag and the bag back into the compartment. "Let's think about it tonight. Tomorrow we'll come up with a plan."

"You should get to the nurse's chamber," Ella said. "I can finish up here."

"Are you sure?" Snow asked.

"Positive," said Ella. "But you have to hurry or you'll be late!"

Chapter Twelve
Castle Skip-trip

The next morning in hearthroom, Rose watched the door like a hawk. She had a great vantage point from her seat, which was on the opposite side of the chamber from the door. She couldn't wait to see her friends and decide what to do about the fur cape they'd found in Hagatha's trunk. She was sure that Hagatha and Prunilla were responsible for a lot of the tormenting — and now the wolf! Seeking revenge on those nasty girls was going to be sweet!

"How are you going to do your hair for the ball, Beauty?" the girl sitting behind her asked.

Rose was so busy staring at the door she didn't answer. "Rose?" the girl tried again.

"I beg your pardon?" Rose tried not to look annoyed as she turned back to the girl. She didn't care about her hair or the ball! At least not at the moment.

Finally Rapunzel came through the door. But instead of coming right over to Rose, she sat down in her chair and began writing furiously on a scroll. *She must be working on something good,* thought Rose.

Snow came in next. She smiled and waved at Rose — and everyone else in the chamber — before she took her seat near the door. Rose was getting to her feet to go talk to her when Ella shuffled into the room like a scolded puppy. She didn't look at anyone as she took her seat in the back of the chamber.

I guess our plan can wait, Rose thought, sitting back in her chair. Suddenly she was much more worried about something else: Ella. Even though Ella's head was bent low, Rose could see the dark circles under her eyes.

Rose felt a pang of guilt. Here she was always complaining about her overprotective parents and the fawning teachers and princesses. She bet that nobody ever fawned over poor Ella. Those nasty stepsisters of hers made her life miserable — and not only at school, but at home, too! She was sure Ella's stepmother didn't adore Ella the way Rose's parents adored her.

I should count my blessings, Rose thought, *and quit feeling sorry for myself.*

Rose wanted to leap out of her chair and go over to Ella right that minute. But before she could move, Madame Garabaldi strode into the room and began to take scroll call. And then the door opened again, and a page scampered nervously up to Madame G. and handed her a roll of paper.

Rose watched Ella sink lower into her chair. A scroll delivered in hearthroom usually meant that someone was in trouble. And since Ella had missed all of Self-defense yesterday . . . well, it didn't look good.

Ella sat as still as a stone while Madame Garabaldi read the notice. When the teacher looked up, her dark eyes were narrowed over her spectacles at Ella. It took her exactly three seconds to cross to the back of the chamber.

"Cinderella Brown," she said, towering over Ella's small, slouched frame. "I have just been informed that you did not see fit to attend Self-defense class yesterday. Would you like to tell me what pressing engagement you chose to grace with your presence instead?"

Ella looked up at Madame Garabaldi, her face full of desperation. But she said nothing.

"Excuse me?" Madame Garabaldi's eyes dared the cowering girl to speak. "I can't hear you."

Across the chamber, Rapunzel opened her mouth to say something. But after a moment she closed it again. Rose couldn't blame her. Aggravating Madame Garabaldi further wouldn't do anyone any good.

"I see," said Madame Garabaldi, rising to her full height. "Perhaps a punishment of double tower detention would demonstrate to you and the rest of the students that attendance in class is *mandatory* at Princess School." She folded her arms across her chest and glared down at Ella, who was by now halfway under her writing desk.

"Sit up straight!" Madame Garabaldi barked. "Cowering is not acceptable for any princess — even one who has been caught blatantly disregarding the rules."

Rose wanted to leap to her feet and tell Madame Garabaldi to stop being cruel. Detention was punishment enough — especially for Ella, who would also get a second punishment at home. It was excessive to ridicule her in front of the class, too.

Madame Garabaldi turned on her heel, strode back to the front of the chamber, and continued taking scroll call. All eyes were on Ella. Rose tried to get her friend's attention but guessed that a sympathetic smile would not be enough to cheer Ella up. Ella appeared to be using all her strength to hold back tears. She sat staring straight ahead for the rest of class.

Finally, when the end-of-class trumpets sounded, Ella broke down sobbing and raced out of the chamber.

Rose was on her feet in an instant, but still wasn't fast enough. By the time she got out the classroom door Ella was a blur streaking down the corridor. Snow was right behind her. Rose lifted her skirts and hurried ahead, hoping she could catch them.

Just then Hagatha appeared out of nowhere, skipping down the hallway after Snow.

"I'm Snow White," Hagatha called. "I spend all day with dwarves and woodland animals, skipping through the forest!"

Rose saw Ella turn, her eyes full of tears and fury. Ella had clearly reached her breaking point.

Don't do anything, Ella! Rose thought desperately. *You'll just get yourself into more trouble!*

Rose rushed forward to stop her friend. But suddenly there was a swarm of princesses between her and Ella.

"I heard you got hurt in Self-defense," one of them said to Rose. "Are you all right?"

"I'm fine," Rose said brusquely, trying to get through. "I'm trying to get to my friends —"

Out of the corner of her eye, Rose saw Rapunzel break through the throng of princesses. With her left arm, she gently took Snow by the elbow, then did a graceful skip-trip with her right foot, sending Hagatha sprawling to the floor.

"Hey!" Hagatha screeched as Rapunzel linked her free arm through Ella's.

"Come on, girls," Rapunzel said loudly. "Let's go find some decent company."

Rose pushed her way past a final pair of princesses in time to see Ella, Rapunzel, and Snow disappear through the Princess School doors, their arms linked together.

"Help me up!" Hagatha screeched from the floor.

Rose barely heard her. She was too busy watching her new friends go off without her, leaving her alone in a crowd. Again.

Chapter Thirteen
Needle and Hay

"Do you think she is all right?" Snow asked, turning to look back at the fallen Hagatha. "That stone floor is pretty hard."

"Who cares?" Rapunzel replied with a snort. "She was making fun of you, Snow. She was being mean."

Rapunzel pulled Snow and Ella ahead, steering them out the Princess School doors, down the steps, and through the rose garden.

"Don't you know when someone isn't being nice?" Ella asked more gently.

"Not being nice?" Snow repeated aloud. "Why wouldn't a princess be nice? Everyone should be nice, right?" Since she had escaped living with her step-mother, Snow had not encountered anyone who wasn't nice. Not until she came to Princess School, at least.

"Besides, Hagatha's too mean to get hurt," Ella added, striding over the grass.

Snow nodded but now felt even more confused.

Since when did being mean keep someone from getting hurt? If that was true, her stepmother must never feel *any* pain!

"Really? Does being mean keep you from getting hurt?" Snow asked.

"Well, not exactly," Ella admitted.

Snow pushed all thoughts about meanness from her mind. She wanted to savor this moment. She hadn't even been at Princess School for two weeks, and she was out in the gardens with two new friends!

"Come on," Rapunzel said, steering them toward a cozy-looking building with a grass roof. "I want to show you someplace special before class starts."

Snow gasped again. It looked like Rapunzel was leading them toward the stables! She'd been dying to see inside the stables since she'd started at Princess School, to see where the animals lived. And now she was going to!

Rapunzel pushed open one of the heavy stable doors and pulled the girls inside. Holding a finger to her lips, she stood quietly for a minute to make sure the coast was clear. The only audible sounds were of horses munching hay.

"It's safe," Rapunzel reported. "There's nobody else here."

Snow took a deep breath, taking in the smell of clean hay and horses. "Ooooh," she said, excited. The stables were enormous, with row upon row of wooden stalls painted various pastel hues. A well-organized, cream-colored tack room stood just inside the door, housing gleaming saddles and bridles and halters. A giant hayloft extended over half of the ground floor.

"Look at the beautiful horses!" Snow rushed into a lavender stall that was home to a tall chestnut mare. "Hello, sweetie," she greeted, stroking the bridge of the mare's velvety nose. She gazed into the mare's liquid-brown eyes. No matter how much time she spent with them, Snow was always amazed at the gentleness she saw in animals' eyes.

"If I'd known I was coming today, I would have brought you a carrot," she said softly.

The mare let out a soft whinny, nuzzling Snow's arm.

"Next time." Snow giggled. "I promise." She turned in the direction of her friends. "I could stay here all day!" she called.

"Me too," Rapunzel agreed. "But we don't have all day. Come on!"

"Coming!" Snow called back. She wanted to greet each and every horse but knew she couldn't. So she said a quick hello to a few more, promising she'd bring them treats the next time she came, as she made her way back to her friends.

"I'm so sorry about your detention," Rapunzel was

saying. "And Madame Garabaldi. She was being really severe, even for her."

"Maybe she never gets hurt," Snow suggested, plopping down beside Ella.

Ella's eyes glistened with approaching tears. "I think she has it in for me, just like my rotten steps," she said mournfully.

Snow gave Ella's arm a comforting squeeze. "I know what that's like," she said. "My stepmother was so jealous of me, I had to leave my father's castle!"

Ella sighed. "Sometimes I wish I could leave," she said. "But then of course I'd never see my father."

Suddenly Snow felt a little bit sad inside. She knew *exactly* how Ella felt.

"That Hagatha deserves more than to fall flat on her face," Rapunzel announced, changing the subject. She was lying down on the clean straw, gazing up at the stable rafters.

"Tell me about it," Ella agreed, breaking a piece of straw between her fingers. "And what you just saw was her *good* side. She's even more horrible at home."

Snow felt awful for Ella. After all, Ella was just about the nicest person she'd met at Princess School. She reached out a hand to her friend. "Maybe you could come live with the dwarves and me in the forest cottage," she offered.

Ella's eyes welled up with fresh tears at Snow's kindness.

"We've got to do something about Hag," Rapunzel declared, jumping up and pacing the narrow stall. "And her awful sister, too." There was a moment of silence. "Not you, Ella," she added quickly. "Prunilla."

Ella wiped her tears and smiled. "I know," she said. "And *I know*. We *do* have to do something about them. But what?"

The girls were silent for a minute, thinking. And then, in the distance, they heard the muted trumpets signaling the next class.

"Oh my gosh!" Snow said, leaping to her feet.

Ella was up, too. "I can't be late again!" she exclaimed. "They'll lock me up!"

Falling over the skirts of one another's gowns, the girls burst out of the stall. They raced through the stable doors, across the rose garden, and up the Princess School steps.

Throwing open the front door, the girls burst into the school and ran — *smack!* — into Briar Rose.

Rose stood alone in the main entrance, sucking her finger. Her eyes looked a little droopy.

"Oh, no, are you hurt?" Snow asked, pulling Rose's finger from her mouth to take a look.

"It's nothing," Rose yawned. "Just a tiny pinprick. I'll be fine. Please don't fuss."

"What happened?" Ella asked. "You look kind of strange."

"I don't know, really. I just reached into my Stitchery basket and something jabbed my finger." Rose paused to yawn again and rub one of her eyes. "It was a needle, I think. But the funny thing is, I never leave my needles out. I always put them into my metal box."

Ella, Snow, and Rapunzel all looked at one another.

"Are you thinking what I'm thinking?" Ella asked.

"Prunilla was awfully angry when Rose didn't want to go off with her the other day," Snow said, remembering the scowl on the older girl's face.

"Exactly. And Hag and Prune never miss a chance to get even," Ella confirmed.

"Let's go back to the stables and figure out what to do." Rapunzel already had one foot out the door.

"We can't," Ella said. "If we miss class, we'll all get in trouble — Madame Garabaldi might even expel me. And believe me, there's nothing Hagatha and Prunilla would like better."

Chapter Fourteen
Sleeping Beauty

As her friends hurried her down the corridor to Stitchery, Rose's limbs felt weighted down. Her whole body was exhausted.

This is so weird, she thought. *I feel so sleepy.*

She longed to lie right down on the marble floor and take a nap but forced herself to stay awake. *I have to act perfectly normal*, she told herself firmly. *Or my parents are going to go crazy. And the fairies! They'll swarm the castle if they think there's something wrong with me. They might even pull me out of Princess School . . . just when it's getting interesting!*

"Rose, are you okay?" Ella's voice sounded kind of far away, even though Rose was standing right next to her. Rose felt a hand reach out to steady her.

"I'm fine," she said. "I'm just trying to think of what I'm going to tell Madame Taffeta when we get to class." Rose stifled a yawn. "She'll believe anything I say, so I think I should do the talking."

"Fine with me," Rapunzel said as they reached the door to the Stitchery classroom. She looked intently at Rose. "But are you sure you're okay?"

"Perfect," Rose said, trying to sound convincing. Gathering all her strength, she stood up straight and put her hand on the door. She took a deep breath and pushed the door open, leading her friends inside.

Even in her sleepy state, Rose could tell that Madame Taffeta was furious. Or was that panic? Her usually pleasant, round face was tight and her gray eyes looked as sharp as daggers.

"Where have you been?" the teacher asked in a raised voice. "I was so worried I was about to send a message to Madame Garabaldi."

Rose heard Ella gasp and immediately rushed forward, trying not to stumble. She curtsied. "My sincere apologies, Madame Taffeta," she said in her proper princess voice. "I truly regret that I've made all these girls late. You see, I've pricked my finger." She raised her wounded appendage to show the teacher and hide a yawn.

Madame Taffeta gasped in horror as several girls looked over at Rose in concern. "Why, Rose, whatever happened?"

"I came to class early to begin my work," Rose said, feeling almost lucid for the first time since the pinprick. "But while I was threading my needle I accidentally pricked my finger. I hurried to the little princesses' room to rinse it in clean water, and Rapunzel, Ella, and Snow were kind enough to help me and make sure I got safely back to class."

Madame Taffeta inspected the pinprick carefully, making sure it was not too deep. She looked really worried, and Rose felt a little sorry for her. It couldn't be easy to have Madame Garabaldi looking over your shoulder all the time. She probably waited for the teachers to make mistakes just like she did the students!

"Well, it does appear to be just a pinprick," Madame Taffeta said more calmly. "And you girls did a fine job cleaning the wound." She looked at each of the four of them in turn.

"Under the circumstances, I will dismiss your tardiness. I see no reason to report this little incident to Madame Garabaldi."

Rose saw Ella's shoulders relax in relief. She flashed a drowsy smile at her friends. Being the favorite pupil was finally doing some good! But as relief washed over her, so did another wave of sleepiness. All of a sudden she didn't have the strength to fight it anymore. Every pink stone on the cold hard floor looked as inviting as a feather-stuffed pillow. Her eyelids felt incredibly heavy. She needed a nap.

"I think I'll just lie down for a minute," Rose mumbled. Her limbs felt wobbly, like custard. She was grateful for the supportive arms of Rapunzel, Snow, and Ella as they led her over to a pile of large velvet cushions. She had a sleepy memory of having been worried that these girls weren't really her friends. Now she felt sure that they were.

"Is she all right?" Madame Taffeta's voice sounded as if it came from the other end of a long hallway.

"Of course," Rose heard Rapunzel say smoothly. Rose was grateful for her friend's resolve. Rapunzel always managed to stay calm, no matter what the circumstances. "She's just worn out from all the excitement," Rapunzel explained. Rose smiled sleepily. She wasn't sure about any excitement, but she was definitely worn out.

"Beauty is clearly distraught from her episode," Madame Taffeta said, clapping her hands briskly. It sounded to Rose as if Madame Taffeta were now a hundred miles away, but she didn't care. All she cared about was finally being able to sleep. . . .

A dozen pages responded to Madame Taffeta's clap. Scampering into the chamber, they quickly pulled a tapestry from the wall. Six of them held the sides, creating a curving bed, while the others filled it with cushions and helped Rose lie down upon it.

Rose was drifting off contentedly as Madame Taffeta sent another page scurrying to get some blankets. "Hurry now!" she called. "This princess needs a rest!"

Chapter Fifteen
The Perfect Dress

The candelabra beside Ella flickered and she inched closer to it. She could see fairly well in the dim light — she was used to the dark room. But she hoped that the little flames would help warm her cold fingers as she quickly stitched the hem of her ball gown.

Despite the cold and dark, Ella felt unusually happy. There had been no scroll sent home alerting her stepmother of her double tower detention — which hadn't been so terrible after all. She'd used the time to do her homework, and was almost caught up! And since Kastrid had been napping in the afternoons lately, she didn't even realize Ella had gotten home late. Rose had skillfully gotten them off the hook in Stitchery, and — most unbelievable of all — Hagatha and Prunilla hadn't breathed a word of her school trouble for two nights in a row. All her stepsisters talked about was the ball and their beautifully decorated ballot box.

Maybe they don't know about the detention, Ella thought, though it seemed unlikely. It was more probable that they knew that *she* knew about their wolf caper. Knowing Hag and Prune, they were keeping Ella's little secret for now, planning to blackmail her later if she opened her mouth.

It didn't matter. Ella felt too cheerful to let even Hagatha and Prunilla's schemes ruin her mood. With a smile on her face, Ella finished the last stitch on her hem, tied off the thread, and cut it with her teeth. She hung the deep-blue gown before the window and shook out the luxurious fabric of the skirt. With the stars twinkling behind it, the midnight-blue gown looked absolutely magical. It was perfect.

Gazing at the finished dress, Ella felt a little bit like she thought Snow must feel all the time. Without even thinking, she clapped her hands together and began to hum a little tune. It felt good, and before she knew it she was dancing around her tiny room, imagining the fun she was going to have at the ball. She had a dress, she had shoes (so what if they were stuffed with paper and made her a tad clumsy? They were still magic. . . .), and she had new friends. It was too good to be true.

WHAM! Ella's door suddenly burst open, slamming against the stone wall. Hagatha stood in the doorway, panting from the climb up the stairs and holding a torn petticoat — for Ella to mend, no doubt. Her beady eyes grew round when she saw Ella dancing.

Ella quickly tried to appear unhappy. Wiping the smile off her face, she slumped down beside the mending pile with a heavy sigh. Hagatha would take extra delight in tormenting her if she realized she was in a great mood.

"What's going on in here?" Hagatha puffed into the room holding the torn petticoat. "I was just bringing up this mending and I thought I heard singing." Hagatha looked around like she expected to find a chamber choir in the corner.

"Must have been the wind," Ella said, staring down at her lap and trying to look miserable. "My window doesn't shut all the way" — she gestured toward the window — "and sometimes . . ."

Ella trailed off. She followed Hagatha's gaze to the dress that hung from the windowsill and gasped.

She had made a terrible mistake. All she could do was hold her breath and wait to see what Hag would do next.

"It's perfect," Hagatha breathed. She rubbed her hands together as if to warm them before reaching out to touch the beautiful velvet fabric.

Ella cringed. "I, uh, made it myself," she explained. It sounded as if Hagatha's compliment had been almost genuine.

"It'll look *gorgeous* at the ball." Hagatha pulled the skirts across her chest. "On me. Doesn't it go well with my eyes? In this dress I will be crowned for sure!"

If she weren't completely horrified, Ella would have laughed out loud. The beautiful blue of the gown *might* match Hagatha's eyes, but they were so small and beady, no one would ever be able to tell. And the thought of anyone voting for Hagatha . . . it was too much.

"You won't be wearing that dress," Ella said, standing and mustering up as much courage as she could. "I will. I made it for myself." Ella swept the dress off the hanger and clutched it to her chest.

"You?" Hagatha scoffed. "You aren't even going to the ball!"

"I am so," Ella argued. "Father said so. Your mother agreed!"

Hagatha smiled slowly. She seemed more and more like Kastrid all the time. "That was before I told her about your trouble in school, Cinder dear."

"You didn't." Ella dropped onto her hard wood-frame bed.

"Of course I did." Hagatha held a hand out for the dress. "I didn't want you there embarrassing us. And don't worry, Mother will think of a suitable punishment so you don't miss class again." Hagatha jiggled her hand impatiently, waiting for Ella to give her the dress.

"Maybe I can't wear this dress, but neither will you," Ella said, standing up and moving to the far side of her small room. "I could tell your mother a few things, you know — like the things we found in your trunk!"

"I'll say you're lying," Hagatha shouted.

"My friends were with me," Ella yelled back.

"I'll tell her you planted it, then!" Hagatha was seething. She stomped her feet. Her face was red and blotchy and she was stepping closer and closer to Ella with each second.

"Girls!"

Without warning, a tall figure appeared in the door and Hagatha and Ella both fell silent. Kastrid appeared so suddenly, Ella was not sure how much she had heard. Or what she was going to say. With one step, Kastrid seemed to fill Ella's small room entirely. Behind her, Prunilla poked her head in, obviously not wanting to miss the fun.

"You *know* I cannot abide bickering," Kastrid said softly with her eyes closed. Then, without warning, she erupted like a volcano. "SO TELL ME WHAT IS GOING ON!"

"Mummy, she won't let me wear that dress," Hagatha whined and pointed at the dress Ella was still holding before wiping her nose on her sleeve.

"Of course she will," Kastrid said, her voice returning to a syrupy smoothness. She held out a long slender hand to Ella, who had no choice but to lay the gown across it. Though Ella had threatened to tell on Hagatha for all of the mean tricks, deep down she knew it was useless. Kastrid would believe whatever she wanted to, and that would be her daughters' lies. Even Ella's father was helpless when it came to dealing with Kastrid. When Kastrid was around, everything always went the way Hagatha and Prunilla wanted.

Kastrid held the dress up, inspecting it. She ran the material between her fingers and a small smile played on her lips.

"It's m-mine," Ella stammered foolishly. "I made it."

Kastrid turned. "With whose material?" she asked slowly, looking Ella right in the eye.

Ella was caught. In a moment her stepmother would be accusing her of stealing. Not that Kastrid would ever have used the remnants — until now they had been mere scraps to her. But the fabric wasn't really Ella's. Ella hung her head and braced herself for the lecture.

She did not expect the one she got.

"It doesn't matter." Kastrid held the gown up to Hagatha, and Prunilla rushed into the room for a closer look. "It doesn't matter because, Cinderella, you will not be going to the ball."

"But you said —" Ella protested, though she knew it was hopeless.

"I said you might go if you were doing well in school. Which your sisters tell me you are not." Kastrid looked at Ella disapprovingly. "I wish I could say I am surprised. I only hope your father can bear the shame should you be expelled."

Ella's face was hot. How dare Kastrid mention her father? He would never be ashamed of her! She would never be expelled from Princess School. Why, with the trouble Hagatha and Prunilla caused, *they* should be the ones to get expelled.

Ella longed to scream back at her stepmother. She wanted to yell at her: *You should be ashamed. Look at your daughters. They are such awful witches, they belong in the Grimm School!*

"The dress won't fit Hagatha," was all Ella could mumble. Her stepsister was much taller and heavier than Ella.

"Well, then, you will have to *make* it fit." Kastrid threw the dress on the bed beside Ella. "In time for the Coronation Ball, of course."

With that, Ella's stepmother turned and swept out of the room and down the long flight of stairs.

Prunilla looked as if she was about to roll on the floor laughing. Hagatha was grinning, too. "And I'll need this petticoat," she said, tossing down the torn garment in her best imitation of her mother. "By tomorrow." Then she turned and followed her sister out of the room.

Ella collapsed across her bed. And though Hagatha had slammed the door behind her, Ella could still hear her stepsisters' wicked cackling over her own quiet sobs.

Chapter Sixteen

Wake-up Call

"Maybe I should transfer to *your* school," Val said. He sounded serious. "Nothing that exciting is going on over at Charm — it's all codes and chivalry."

"That's not even half of it," Rapunzel said, picking up a flat rock as they passed the mill pond. "We think maybe Ella's horrid stepsisters are behind the drenchings and the pea incident in addition to the wolf stunt. You would not *believe* these girls. They're like miniature Madame Gothels!"

Rapunzel sent the rock sailing over the still water. It skipped once, twice, three times before sinking to the bottom of the pond. She was enjoying bragging to Val. Princess School really was exciting. "I think they might have been the ones to stash that needle in Rose's bag, too. Luckily she wasn't hurt too badly."

Val flung the rock he was holding and didn't even watch to see how many times it skipped. "Beauty's been hurt?" he asked. His voice was full of concern, and he grabbed Rapunzel's arm. "What happened? Is she okay?"

"She's fine." Rapunzel shook Val off her arm. "Just tired is all." She looked at Val with narrowed eyes. "Is this part of the whole chivalry thing? What's the big deal? She just pricked her finger!"

Rapunzel picked up her books and walked away from Val, down the road toward their schools. She was annoyed. Sometimes Val was a little *too* interested in Rose. Her every move seemed to fascinate him. But maybe there was reason to be concerned. Rose had been awfully hard to wake up after Stitchery. And yesterday she had almost fallen asleep again in every class. For two days her head had been bobbing around on her neck like a sprung jack-in-the-box — hardly a pretty sight.

"Wait up." Val jogged beside her. "Don't be jealous."

"Ha!" Rapunzel laughed. Jealous of what? Rose was even more of a prisoner than she was. It was astounding the way her family doted on her. They were always waiting for her the moment school ended and accompanying her in the morning, trying to get her to wear ridiculous protective clothing. Rose even told her that she thought the fairies spied on her during the day. If you asked Rapunzel, that much attention would be worse than being locked in a tower alone. Everyone was always so worried about Rose.

Rapunzel started walking again, fast. Then she broke into a run.

"Hey," Val called after her. "Hey!"

Rapunzel waved but did not slow her pace. She wanted to get to school early. She had some things to discuss with Ella, Snow, and Rose.

Rapunzel scanned the crowd on the bridge as she rushed across the moat. There was Snow. Snow spotted Rapunzel, too, and skipped over with a wave and a warm smile. Rapunzel raised her head and gave a nod, but she didn't smile. She was too worried. What if Rose had gotten worse after school yesterday?

With a crushing wave of relief, Rapunzel spotted Rose on the other side of the bridge. She was holding a large mug of tea and brushing off her fairies and parents. She still looked tired but very much alive. Rose saw Snow and Rapunzel, too, and started to make her way over.

As Rapunzel watched Rose try to shake her fairies and join them on the steps, she couldn't really blame Val for liking the girl. In addition to being beautiful, she was great. And so were her other new friends, Snow and Ella.

Speaking of which, where *was* Ella? Beyond the bridge on the muddy lane, Rapunzel saw a forlorn figure walking slowly toward the school. The girl's skirts dragged in the mud and her head hung so low it was surprising it wasn't getting wet and muddy, too. Ella.

Without a word, Rapunzel headed for her crestfallen friend. Snow followed. But Rose, who had waved her parents off at last, slumped against the chain of the drawbridge. She yawned as Snow and Rapunzel whisked past. "I just have to rest a moment," she said sleepily. "I'll catch up."

Ella looked worse close up than she did from a distance. Her eyes were red from crying. Her hair was a mess, even by Rapunzel's standards. And her shoulders were so slumped she looked like she was carrying the whole world upon them.

Poor thing, Rapunzel thought as she hurried to Ella's side. *She has to go home to Hag and Prune every night. And her stepmother!*

Ella stumbled in her paper-stuffed shoes and almost fell into the carriage ruts. Rapunzel and Snow got there just in time, and Ella leaned heavily on her friends' shoulders.

"I can't go to the ball," she sobbed. "Hagatha . . . told. . . . She . . ." Ella was crying too hard to even speak. It took several minutes for her to tell the whole story. By the time she finished, Rapunzel was fuming. Even Snow looked angry.

"How could they?" Snow asked, dumbfounded. "Why would they? It's just . . . it's just so *mean!*"

"That's right," Rapunzel said, herding her friends back toward the bridge where Rose was dozing on her feet. "I think somebody needs to teach them to be nicer. Lots nicer."

"That's a great idea!" Snow chirped.

Rapunzel chewed her braid. Ella nodded at her and, in spite of her sad face, Rapunzel could tell by the look in her eyes she was ready to strike back no matter what it cost.

The trumpets blasted a two-minute warning and most of the princesses picked up their skirts and headed inside.

Rapunzel's head was spinning. The ball was only two days away. There was no way she was going to let Ella miss it or her awful stepsisters enjoy it. But they would have to act fast.

"Wake up, Brainy Rose." Rapunzel gently flicked Rose with the end of her braid, startling her awake.

"I'm fine. I'm fine." Rose stood up straight, sloshing the giant mug of tea.

"I'm glad to hear it," Rapunzel said honestly. "Because we need your help." She pulled her friends into a tight circle. "We've got to come up with a plan. And we don't have much time."

Chapter Seventeen
Daring Rescue

Ella peered out of the small open window on the top floor of her father's manor. For once she was glad that Kastrid had moved her room to the distant turret over the kitchen, far from the other bedrooms in the house. There was less of a chance anyone would notice the slim figure climbing her way, stone by stone, up the outside wall. It was so dark, Ella could hardly see Rapunzel herself.

"Are you still there?" Ella whispered into the night.

"Of course," Rapunzel said. Her head appeared just below the window opening and she hitched a leg up over the windowsill. "Could you give me a hand, damsel in distress?"

Ella laughed. "My hero," she said, dragging Rapunzel through the small opening. Rapunzel fell the rest of the way through and onto the knotted rag rug Ella had painstakingly woven from small scraps of cloth.

"Ooph." The heavy sack tied across Rapunzel's

back flattened her to the floor. Ella stared. Even in this inelegant pose, Rapunzel looked regal in a lovely dark green velvet gown with golden ribbons woven through the sleeves.

"No time for swooning, Princess," Rapunzel said as she got to her feet. "We've got work to do if we're going to get you to the ball in time." Rapunzel handed Ella the sack and went back to the window. "Get going. I'll watch for our prince."

Ella could feel her heart pounding in her chest. She had never done anything this risky before. Or this fun.

With the bag slung over her shoulder like laundry, she tiptoed downstairs to her stepsisters' dressing rooms.

In Hagatha's room, Ella's blue ball gown hung at the ready. She had spent hours ripping out stitches and redoing them. And since Hagatha was going to the ball in a newly made gown, Prunilla had announced that Ella would have to refit *her* dress as well, embellishing it with additional ribbons and lace. Ella had taken careful measurements of both her stepsisters. "Mother always said the proper fit is important," she had told them.

"That's right!" Prunilla had snapped back at her. "So don't mess up, dunderhead."

Ella was sure she hadn't messed up. Both dresses would fit like the girls had been sewn into them. They would be . . . breathtaking. Literally. The gowns would be so tight, her stepsisters wouldn't be able to take a deep breath. But Ella knew Hag and Prune would be too vain to admit that their dresses were too small. Instead they would suffer through the evening, puffing and wheezing around the dance floor. Ella almost giggled at her own deviousness. And the gowns were only part of the plan.

Beneath each altered gown, Ella had already laid out each sister's pair of shoes. Now she replaced them with almost identical footwear . . . two sizes smaller.

The shoes had been Rapunzel's idea. But it was Snow who had made it happen. Snow's dwarves were friends with some talented elfin shoemakers who had crafted the replicas in exchange for a few of Snow's delicious pies. Ella ran a finger along the soft leather and giggled. The elves had done a wonderful job.

Ella stooped to retrieve Hag's and Prune's regular shoes but stopped when she felt Rapunzel's sack bump against her leg. There was something else inside. Digging down to the bottom, Ella pulled out a beautiful pair of golden suede shoes with tiny rosettes stitched to the sides. They were just her size. Ella's breath caught. Could they really be for her?

Slipping off one of her oversized glass shoes, Ella slid her small foot into the soft suede. It fit like a glove. She tried on the other and glanced at her reflection in the full-length dressing room mirror. The shoes were truly lovely, and as comfortable as a pair of well-worn slippers.

Ella picked up her stepsisters' properly sized shoes and stuffed them into Rapunzel's bag along with her glass slippers. Then she took one last look in the mirror at the golden beauties on her feet . . . and noticed that the door behind her was opening!

Ella slipped noiselessly out the chambermaid's exit and silently thanked Snow for the shoes. If she'd been wearing her awkward glass slippers she would have been caught for sure.

Upstairs, Rapunzel was walking slowly around Ella's bedroom. "Your room isn't much better than mine," she said when Ella came back in. She smiled down at the sight of the slippers on Ella's feet. "Pretty, aren't they?"

Ella nodded, a smile spreading across her face. "Beautiful," she said.

"Are your sisters getting ready?"

"They were just coming into the dressing room when I left. I almost got caught!" Ella said. She felt nervous and excited at the same time. She and Rapunzel giggled nervously. They could not keep still. Ella was eager to see the results of her handiwork, but she would have to wait.

At last Ella saw a tiny light flare outside. A moment later something shiny caught the light and reflected it into Ella's window. That was the signal.

Hagatha and Prunilla had been sent off in the carriage — the road would be clear.

Rapunzel took a hand mirror out of her pocket and flashed back. Then she unwound her l-o-n-g braid, tying one end around Ella's waist in case she fell. After helping Ella out the window, Rapunzel climbed out slowly behind her.

Ella's stomach flipped when she got all the way outside.

"Just take it easy. Feel the rocks with your toes and fingers and don't move until you've got a good hold." Rapunzel's voice above her was reassuring. "And don't worry — my hair has got you, too!"

"To your left," Val coached from the ground, shining his light up to help the girls.

"Don't listen to him. He can't climb a tree," Rapunzel joked.

"I heard that!" Val protested.

It was easier to climb down the wall than Ella thought. With a final leap she landed on the ground. She felt exhilarated.

"Ella, Val. Val, Ella." Rapunzel gestured between the two while she quickly recoiled her hair.

"Charmed," Val took Ella's hand and bowed deeply. His velvet breeches were caramel colored, and the tunic and cape he wore were deep burgundy.

"Likewise," Ella said with a giggle as Val helped her up onto the horse standing nearby. When Ella was seated sidesaddle, the young prince took his seat behind her and held another hand out to Rapunzel.

Rapunzel refused the hand, swinging up behind Val by holding onto the saddle and boosting herself up on a nearby rock. For the first time Ella noticed that Rapunzel's skirts were split like pants, but the slit was cleverly hidden in pleats. Smart.

"Let's ride," Rapunzel said when the three were all safely on the horse. Val flicked the reins. Ella grabbed the horse's mane and without another word they galloped down the dark road toward Princess School and the Royal Coronation Ball.

The towers of Princess School were bathed in flickering torchlight. Gilded flags flew from the castle turrets. And every guard, page, and trumpeter was dressed in purple and gold and standing in a long line that marked the entry to the school. Tonight was going to be a magical night.

As they raced by on horseback, Ella saw princes and princesses arriving in fine coaches. Even the teams of horses were dressed up with plumes on their heads and silver bells on their halters.

Skirting the edges of the school, Val turned his horse and nudged him with his heels. The horse went from a gallop to a run. Before Ella could cry out in alarm, she and the horse and Val and Rapunzel were sailing over the Princess School moat and trotting toward the stables. When they entered the warm stables Ella slid to the hay-strewn floor with a wide smile on her face. Already this had been one of the best nights of her life.

"You made it!" Snow called. She elbowed Rose awake and pulled her out of the stall they had been hiding in. Snow and Rose both looked lovely. Snow's deep-red gown was the color of her ruby lips and looked so elegant against her alabaster skin that it didn't matter that the hem was too short or that the collar was old-fashioned. And Rose! Her gown was lavender satin with tiny opalescent pearls stitched over the bodice and skirt. Ella noticed that Val seemed to think Rose looked beautiful as well — he was staring at her with his mouth slightly open.

"I guess you'd better see to King," Rapunzel said, kicking Val lightly in the shin. "You know, your *horse*?"

Val quickly pulled his eyes away from Rose and closed his mouth. "Of course," he said. "I'll see you ladies at the ball."

"Did you get the shoes?" Snow asked.

"Oh, yes!" Ella replied. She lifted her tattered gown to show her friends. "They're beautiful. Thank you so much!"

"Ella, look!" Snow exclaimed. "Rose and I brought you something to wear, too!" Next to the horse bridles hung two ball gowns. Ella knew at once which one was Snow's — the hard white collar was a dead giveaway. Maybe Snow could pull off that look with her pale skin, dark eyes, and red lips, but Ella's delicate features would be lost in the stiff whiteness.

The other dress was from Rose's collection. It was pale, pale blue like the summer sky through a thin layer of cloud, but it shone golden on the edges like sun peeking through.

"You have to wear this one," Rose yawned, sitting down on a bale of hay. "It'll look royal on you."

Rapunzel agreed, and Ella slipped the dress on.

"Oh!" Snow cried as soon as the tiny buttons on the back of Ella's dress had been hooked and she spun around to show the girls. Snow couldn't say anything more. The fit was perfect.

"What about the hair?" Rapunzel raised an eyebrow. Ella noticed for the first time that Rapunzel's auburn tresses looked perfect. Her large braid was actually made up of hundreds of tiny braids woven together and then coiled around the back of her head like a bun. The end of the braid (she could never twist *all* of it into a bun) was tied off with a green ribbon that matched her dress. A few wispy curls framed her face. What had happened to the girl who seemed out of place in Looking Glass class? She had obviously been practicing more than communication signals with that hand mirror of hers!

"I think I have an idea," Rapunzel said, sitting Ella down on a hay bale and reaching for the hairbrush Rose had brought. She twisted and wove Ella's yellow tresses while Rose lazily pinched some color into Ella's cheeks, helped her with her gloves and jewels, and wove a satin ribbon through the bodice of her dress. Ella felt like royalty as her friends bustled around her.

"I think that's it." Rose stepped back, trying to hide another enormous yawn.

Rapunzel loosened a few strands of Ella's hair near her face and smiled at her own handiwork.

Standing up, Ella spun around to face her friends. The dress caught the light of the lanterns burning by the horse stalls. Ella's loosely swept-up hair revealed her happy face. She glowed.

Snow, Rapunzel, and Rose drew in their breath. They could not help but stare.

"What is it? What's the matter? Did I get it dirty?" Ella looked down at the shimmering skirts of her gown. "Do I look awful?"

"No. It's just that . . . it's just that you look so beautiful!" Snow exclaimed. Rose and Rapunzel nodded in agreement.

"Here." Rapunzel pulled the hand mirror back out of her pocket. "See for yourself."

Ella gazed at her reflection in the mirror for a long moment. From the curl on her forehead to the tips of her toes she felt beautiful — not just like a princess — like a queen. Like a queen on her way to a ball!

Ella's wet eyes sparkled as she looked gratefully at her three smiling friends. "Thank you," she said, choking up. She rushed toward them with her arms open for a hug. "I could never have made it here without you!"

Chapter Eighteen
The Ball

Smiling and holding hands, the four girls headed out of the stables and across the gardens to the castle.

"We have to go through the front," Rapunzel said, steering everyone around the low wall that separated the rose garden from the main entrance. "So everyone can see the beautiful princess." She winked at Ella, and all four girls giggled. Ella beamed. She really did feel like royalty.

The girls rounded the end of the wall, and the glorious sight of the illuminated castle overwhelmed Ella once again. The flags hanging from the turrets blew gently in the night breeze. The torchlights flickered, casting gentle shadows on the castle walls. The school was truly an enchanting sight.

Making their way across the bridge, the girls pulled Rose along with them. Ella noticed that she was practically sleepwalking.

"Are you all right, Rose?"

Rose yawned, but opened her eyes wide. "I'm completely fine," she replied blearily.

As the girls lifted their skirts to ascend the castle stairs, several of the pages stopped trumpeting to watch them pass. At first Ella thought they were looking at Rose. But some of them seemed to be staring in her direction.

They couldn't be looking at me, Ella thought shyly as they entered the castle. *Could they?* It was all too dreamy. Ella wondered what Kastrid would think if she saw her now. She smiled wider just thinking about it. For once her stepmother would be speechless.

Inside, the girls made their way to the ballroom. When they stepped through the carved double doors, all four of them stopped to take in the breathtaking sight.

The marble floor had been polished to a sparkling shine. Colorful silk streamers hung from the walls and pillars. At one end, a long banquet table was covered with delicious meats and pastries and punch. At the other, an orchestra played a lively waltz on a small raised stage. Just to the right was the ballot box, gaudily decorated with too many ribbons and bows.

That's Hagatha and Prunilla for you, Ella thought wryly.

"Let's dance!" Snow chirped, pulling the others

toward the dance floor, where several princes and princesses were already whirling about.

"I'd love to" — Rose yawned — "but I need to rest a minute first."

"I'll come with you," Ella offered.

"I can stay with Rose," a voice said from behind them. It was Val. Ella had almost forgotten he was with them.

"Of course you will," Rapunzel said, rolling her eyes.

"That would be wonderful!" Snow exclaimed, linking Rose's arm through Val's. "Come on, girls!"

Rapunzel looked a little irritated, but she let Snow lead her and Ella onto the dance floor. Right away the girls began to sway daintily to the music. Or at least, Ella and Rapunzel did. Snow seemed to have her own kind of dance style, which included a lot of leaping and flapping.

I wonder if the deer and the birds taught her those steps, Ella thought, smiling to herself.

"Nice moves," Rapunzel said slyly.

"Oh, do you like them?" Snow cried, hopping up and down like a rabbit. "The animals and I have been practicing!"

"Well, they're original," Rapunzel said, smiling affectionately at her friend. Ella had to laugh. Snow could be silly, all right. But she was also the sweetest person she'd ever met, and full of surprises.

"Excuse me," came a voice from behind them. "May I have this dance?"

Ella whirled around and found herself staring into the blue eyes of a handsome, dapperly dressed prince.

Ella was so surprised, she didn't say anything at first. Was he talking to her?

Next to her, Snow giggled. The prince held out his hand. "I am Allister," he said. "And I would be most pleased if you would dance with me."

Blushing, Ella nodded and took the boy's hand. As he whisked her away, Ella saw the smiling faces of her friends whoosh by. She felt light-headed, as if she might faint. Only she wouldn't, of course. If she did, she might miss something!

Allister was a wonderful dancer. He made Ella feel light and graceful on her feet as he turned her this way and that. Ella's head was spinning faster than her feet on the dance floor. In the Princess School ballroom, surrounded by her friends, she felt completely at home. Cinderella felt . . . right. She sighed as the music ended. She never wanted to lose this feeling. She happily agreed when Allister asked her to dance again.

Ella and Allister danced three times — until another boy cut in.

"May I have a turn?" he asked smoothly.

Allister nodded, bowed to Ella, and stepped away.

"I am Sebastian," the boy said. He was shorter than

Allister, and Ella guessed that he was in his first year at the Charm School. His dance steps were somewhat stilted and he kept counting to himself, but Ella didn't mind. She was having, well, a ball!

Sebastian only got one dance with Ella before another boy stepped in — and another, then another. Ella was grateful that she was wearing comfortable shoes. Her feet never would have survived all this dancing in glass!

Whirling atop the shining pink marble floor, Ella and her dance partner — a handsome, curly-haired boy named Ian — seemed to be in a private pocket of air. Several of the other dancers had stopped to watch them. They were murmuring and nodding approvingly. Ella couldn't recall ever getting so much attention! Peering around the crowd, Ella half hoped that her stepsisters weren't among the people watching. Hagatha and Prunilla were awful enough to ruin even this moment. But with a mischievous smile Ella changed her mind. She hoped Hag and Prune would see her! They would probably be too shocked to do anything.

Ella was just thinking she might need to take a rest when Rapunzel tapped her on the shoulder.

"Come quick," she whispered, sounding a little frantic. "It's your stepsisters!"

"Excuse me," Ella told her dance partner. "I have to attend to something."

His face full of disappointment, the prince nodded and bowed slightly. "Of course," he said.

"Those awful girls are stuffing the ballot box!" Rapunzel reported as she led Ella toward the stage. Sure enough, Hag was standing guard in front of the box. Behind her, Prune was stuffing scroll after scroll into the slot at the top.

"Hurry up!" Hagatha snapped at her sister. "We don't have all night!"

"I've just started. *You* try shoving all these scrolls in here," Prunilla snapped back. "My gown is so tight I can barely lift my arms!"

Ella knew she would get in trouble if her sisters saw her at the ball, but as she stormed forward, she didn't care. She was emboldened by her fancy gown and good friends. No one could tell her she didn't belong at Princess School — certainly not her awful stepsisters. It was time to put a stop to their torment. She would not allow them to rig the vote for Princess of the Ball!

"What do you think you're doing?" she asked, planting herself right in front of Hagatha. She glanced down at the too-tight bodice of her gown and tried not to smile. Her stepsister looked like a sausage!

"You!" Hagatha tried to sneer, but it came out more as a gasp. Her eyes narrowed but quickly widened again as she looked Ella up and down. Even nasty Hagatha could not hide her admiration.

"What are you doing here?" Prunilla panted over her sister's shoulder. Her gaze held on the lovely gown Ella wore.

"Attending the ball, of course," Ella said, gazing directly at Prunilla.

"Never mind that," Rapunzel cut in. "What are *you* doing to the ballot box?"

"Ah, yes, the ballot box," Headmistress Bathilde echoed as she approached the girls. The headmistress's stiff silk skirts swished with each step. The people in her path fell silent with awe and drew out of her way. Her willowy frame seemed to float over the ground, making her look taller than she actually was, and her face showed few of her numerous years.

Lady Bathilde cast her silvery eyes on the ballot box. "You must agree it's quite thoroughly decorated," she stated. Beside her, Madame Taffeta watched Hagatha and Prunilla closely.

Ella wasn't sure if the headmistress intended what she said to be a compliment or not, but she thought she saw an unusual sort of smile on Madame Taffeta's face.

"It's time to count the ballots," the headmistress added smoothly.

"Oh, of course," Hagatha said in a sweet but high-pitched voice as she and Prunilla stepped aside.

"We were just guarding it for you," Prunilla peeped.

"To make sure nobody tampered with the voting scrolls." She let out a puff of air and clutched her stomach.

"Yeah, right," Rapunzel said, glaring openly at the older girls.

"Are you all right, Prunilla?" Madame Taffeta asked Prunilla. "You look a bit . . . blue." She seemed to be eyeing the girls' gowns suspiciously, and Ella had a moment of panic.

"We're fine, of course," Prunilla replied. This time her voice almost sounded normal, but she still fidgeted in her golden gown.

"Yes. We were just going to get something to eat," Hagatha rasped.

As Hagatha and Prunilla limped away, Ella tried not to laugh. If either of them ate a single bite, she'd definitely rip a seam!

"Come on," Rapunzel said. "Let's go find Rose and Snow."

Disappointed, Ella nodded and followed her friend away from the ballot box. Part of her wanted to tell the headmistress and Madame Taffeta what Hag and Prune had been up to. But although their actions had looked totally suspicious, they didn't have any actual proof. And besides, why would the headmistress believe a couple of Bloomers? If the teachers didn't trust the older girls, they wouldn't have let them decorate the ballot box to begin with!

As she and Rapunzel crossed the ballroom, Ella struggled with what to do. Then, suddenly, she noticed that people were staring at her.

"What's going on?" she whispered to Rapunzel.

"They're gazing at the belle of the ball," Rapunzel replied with a grin.

Ella thought Rapunzel might be teasing, and whacked her playfully on the arm. But by then they had already reached their friends.

Rose was sitting with Val and Snow on the edge of the dance floor, her drooping head dipping dangerously low to the heaping plate of food she held.

"I'll take that," Rapunzel said, removing the plate before Rose's face fell into the meat pies. "I need to drown my sorrows at our defeat."

"Help yourself," Rose replied sleepily.

"What defeat?" Val asked.

"We think Ella's nasty stepsisters were trying to rig the vote. We caught them stuffing ballots into the box."

"How do you know they weren't real ballots?" Snow asked.

Ella sighed. Sometimes she wished she could be more like Snow — always trusting and expecting the best of people. But living with her stepmother and stepsisters had made that impossible.

"Because we're talking about Hagatha and Prunilla," Rapunzel said.

"Exactly," Ella agreed.

"Excuse me," said a prince as he approached. He stopped directly in front of Ella and stared down at the floor nervously. "Would you like to dance?"

"No thank you," Ella said as kindly as she could. "I'm spending a little time with my friends."

The boy looked crestfallen.

"But I would love to dance later," Ella added.

The boy looked up, grinning from ear to ear. "All right!" he said excitedly as he bounded away.

"I think you've put a spell on everyone here, Ella," Val teased. "Everybody keeps staring at you and whispering."

Ella blushed. "It's Rose's gown, Rapunzel's hairstyling talent, and Snow's shoes," she said modestly.

"Oh, no!" Snow said. "The elves made those shoes for you. They're for you to keep!"

Ella gave Snow a hug. She hardly ever got new items of clothing — and nothing as beautiful as these suede shoes. "Thank you!" she cried.

"And for the record, it's not the gown or the shoes — or your hair," Rapunzel said. "It's *you*, Ella. You're glowing."

"Princes and Princesses," called a loud voice. It was Lady Bathilde. "Please gather around the stage. It is time to crown the Princess of the Ball!"

"Come on!" Snow said excitedly.

Helping Rose to her feet, the girls and Val made their way to the stage. Ella saw Hagatha and Prunilla right up front, still fidgeting with their gowns.

Tapping the school scepter on the stage floor and holding a glittering crown aloft, Lady Bathilde stood with her back straight. Her mere presence demanded attention. The crowd quieted, and she slowly began to unroll an ornate scroll that held the winner's name.

"This year's Princess of the Ball is . . ."

"Move over!" a voice rasped out. Ella recognized it at once. Hagatha.

"That crown is mine," Prunilla hissed back.

There was a scuffle as the two girls tried to grab for the crown, nearly knocking over the headmistress. Then Hagatha tripped on the hem of her gown and fell over, dragging Prunilla down with her.

On the stage, Lady Bathilde was ignoring the scuffle quite successfully. Looking over the waiting crowd, she smiled as she announced the winner's name: Cinderella Brown!

Chapter Nineteen

A True Princess

Ella was so shocked when she heard her name that she didn't move. Beside her, her friends squealed with delight.

"It's you! It's you!" Snow cried, clapping her hands together.

Rose gave her a giant hug. "You deserve it," she said with a yawn.

Rapunzel nudged her forward. "You have to go up to the stage," she said. "Your tiara is waiting."

"No!" Prunilla shrieked. On her hands and knees, she was still trying to grab the tiara out of Lady Bathilde's hands.

"It's mine!" Hagatha screamed.

One of the older Charm School princes near the front unceremoniously pulled the girls to their feet. "It's not yours, or yours," he said firmly, eyeing each girl with disgust. "It's Ella's."

"But she, she —"

"She is the Princess of the Ball," the prince said flatly.

Several of the princesses in the crowd began to laugh at Hagatha and Prunilla, who were so dumbfounded by the prince's words that they were actually speechless. As the laughter grew, the girls slinked toward the ballroom door and their waiting carriage, wheezing and limping the entire way.

As Ella watched them go, she realized she would be in big trouble when she got home. But as she stepped onto the stage she didn't care.

Lady Bathilde smiled majestically as she placed the tiara on Ella's head. Then she put her hands on Ella's shoulders and turned her slowly to face the crowd. The ballroom erupted into claps and cheers. Looking down at her schoolmates and her new friends, Ella felt like a true princess.

When the coronation ceremony was over, even more princes were vying for dances with Ella. But after she danced her promised dance with the boy who had asked her earlier, she kindly declined them all. This was a moment she wanted to share with her friends.

"Do you get to keep it?" Snow asked, fingering the tiara on Ella's head.

"I don't think so," Ella said. "They need it again for next year's ball. But just wearing it is wonderful enough."

Suddenly the music was interrupted a second time

and a regal-looking woman in a black gown and flowing black cape took the stage.

"Who's that?" Rapunzel asked, her eyes wide.

"That's Malodora," Val whispered. "She's the headmistress at the Grimm School. Not someone you want to mess with."

Ella shuddered. Just the sight of this woman was enough to scare anyone. She made Kastrid look friendly! She glanced at her friends to gauge their reactions. Rose looked as sleepy as ever. Rapunzel looked wary. And Snow looked three shades whiter.

"Snow?" Ella put a hand on her friend's arm. "What is it? Are you okay?"

Snow's free hand squeezed the one Ella had placed on her arm, but her eyes never left the stage. "That's my stepmother," she said in a frightened whisper.

Waving her hand through the air dramatically, Malodora made an important announcement.

"The Grimm School and Princess School will be holding the annual Maiden Games exactly one month from today," she said in a booming voice. "Everyone will participate, and I myself, along with Lady Bathilde, will oversee the Games. The winners will receive the coveted Golden Ball."

"Wow," Ella breathed.

"Games!" Rapunzel cried excitedly, hopping up and down. "I love competition!"

Rose slumped even more heavily against Val, finally completely asleep.

"Oh, no," Snow said, her dark eyes wide with fear.

"Don't worry, Snow," Ella said comfortingly. "Whatever it is, we'll help you through it."

"That's right," Rapunzel agreed, coming to her other side.

Snow smiled, but Ella sensed that she was still afraid. Ella couldn't blame her. Malodora was clearly a force to be reckoned with. And she knew all about sinister stepmothers.

"Maybe we should move Rose to a corner and lay her down," Rapunzel suggested.

"Oh, I'm fine," Val replied, but he was clearly tiring from holding the sleeping girl up. He'd been doing it practically all night! "I don't mind, really." In a moment of chivalry, he reached down and lifted Rose's hand to his face, kissing it gently.

No sooner had his lips brushed her hand than Rose sat bolt upright, her eyes wide.

"What's going on?" she asked, looking around. "Did I miss anything?"

The girls all laughed — even Snow joined in — and began to fill Rose in on the evening's events.

"Ella is the Princess of the Ball!" Snow exclaimed.

"And Hagatha and Prunilla got laughed off the stage!" Rapunzel laughed.

"Wow," Rose said. "And I thought it was all a dream!"

"No, it was real," Ella assured her. "Val has been holding you up all night. When he kissed your hand, you . . . woke up."

Rose looked up at Val. "Thanks," she said.

Val blushed. "You're w-welcome," he stammered.

By the time the ball was finally over, it was very late.

"Anyone want a ride home in my carriage?" Rose asked. "There's plenty of room."

"Yes!" the girls chorused.

As they left the ballroom, Madame Taffeta approached Ella.

"I could not help but notice the interesting stitchery on your stepsisters' gowns," she said pointedly. Ella braced herself. She'd been sure she was going to get punished tonight, but not by a teacher!

Madame Taffeta leaned toward Ella slightly. "I can see you do extensive and, shall we say, creative stitching at home," Madame Taffeta went on, her eyes gleaming. "And your stepsisters seem to require careful watching."

Ella nodded, too surprised to say anything. Could it be that a teacher was on her side?

"In light of the situation, I believe it is only fair that you be excused from Stitchery homework for the foreseeable future."

For the second time that night, Ella could not believe her ears. But one look at Madame Taffeta's smiling face told her that her words were true.

"Thank you!" Ella said, giving the teacher a spontaneous hug. Then she hurried to join her friends and tell them the news.

Laughing together, the group traipsed outside to the waiting carriages. The pages were still lined up along the steps and the bridge, but several had fallen asleep.

Val escorted the girls to Rose's carriage, then bowed to them. I will leave you ladies here," he said. "My horse awaits."

The girls scrambled into the carriage. "Bye, Val," Rapunzel called. "See you tomorrow!"

Val waved while the carriage pulled away. Inside, Ella sat back on the lush maroon seat and looked around at her friends. Two weeks ago, she'd felt completely out of place at Princess School. Now she felt right at home. There was no doubt in her mind that with her friends around her, her future at Princess School was as bright as the sparkling tiara that graced the top of her head.

The
Princess School

Who's the Fairest?

For Brian and Nathan, our own prince charmings.

—JBM & SHS

Chapter One

Sleepless Beauty

"Pass the oatmeal," said a growly voice at the end of the table. It was Gruff, the crankiest of Snow White's seven surrogate fathers. His bushy eyebrows met in the middle of his forehead due to his constant scowl. And he wasn't grumpy just because it was early in the morning. Gruff was cranky *all* the time.

"Achoooo!" Wheezer let out a loud sneeze. Oatmeal flew off his spoon, landing with a splat on Nod's face. Nod, who had been drifting off to sleep, sat up straight and elbowed Gruff in the side.

"Er, please," Gruff added.

But at the other end of the long, low table, ten-year-old Snow White stared blankly into her bowl of already-cold hot cereal.

"Snow White," Mort said gently. Though he was barely as tall as the table they were eating at, Mort was essentially the dwarf in charge and happened to be sitting next to Snow. He put his small, pudgy hand on her pale-skinned arm. "Dear, is everything all right?"

Snow White looked up to see seven pairs of friendly but worried eyes staring at her.

"Is everything okay?" echoed Hap. He had a smile on his face like he always did, but his typically easygoing expression was full of concern.

Snow tried her best to smile back. "Oh, yes," she replied. "I'm just fine." She reached for the large spoon in the cast-iron pot of oatmeal. "Who wants seconds?" she asked.

Nearly all of the dwarves raised their colorful ceramic bowls in the air. "I do, I do!" they chorused, pounding their wooden spoons on the table in a musical rhythm. Then they began to sing merrily:

More oatmeal, more for me,
More for my tummy, yes, indeed.
Fill my bowl up to the top,
I'll eat and eat and never stop!

Snow couldn't help but smile at the little men who had become her family. Their woodland cottage was always full of laughter and music, and Snow loved it. But even the dwarves' silly breakfast song couldn't make Snow forget her troubles that morning. As she refilled their bowls with steaming-hot oatmeal, she forced herself to hum a few bars of the cereal song. The last thing she wanted was to make the dwarves worry.

After seconds — and thirds for Dim and Hap — the dwarves cleared the table, carrying the dishes to the sink. Then they each took a pail filled with a lunch Snow had prepared (roast venison sandwiches and berry tarts) and hugged her good-bye. After gathering up their shovels, axes, and picks and pulling their rough-spun shirts down over their round bellies, they headed off to the mine.

"Good-bye," Snow called as the dwarves scurried down the path whistling a work song. It was so early that the sun was just rising, but Snow and the dwarves had been up for hours. The woodland cottage was a place for early risers. Every morning the dwarves woke Snow with a rise-and-shine serenade. Then they scampered downstairs to set the table and get the fire going for breakfast.

Snow remembered those mornings when the merry singing would wake her from a peaceful slumber. But lately she'd been wide-awake even before the serenading began. In fact, she'd been up most of the night for almost a week, worrying about the upcoming Maiden

Games at Princess School. And on the few occasions that she'd been able to doze off, she'd had terrible nightmares!

When Meek, the shy dwarf at the end of the line, had disappeared down the forest path, Snow closed the cottage door and headed to the sink to wash the breakfast dishes. As she filled the basin with warm, soapy water, she remembered the Coronation Ball at Princess School just the week before.

Everyone at Princess School had been looking forward to the ball, and it was truly a magical night. Not only did Snow go to the ball with her new friends Briar Rose, Cinderella Brown, and Rapunzel Arugula, Ella had actually been crowned Princess of the Ball! It had been Snow's first ball, and it was better than she'd ever dreamed. There'd been dancing and food and boys from the Charm School . . . everything was perfect.

But then Malodora, her awful stepmother, had appeared onstage to announce the upcoming Maiden Games — the annual competition between Princess School and its archrival, the Grimm School. Grimm was the academy attended by all the young witches in the land, and most of the girls who went there were less than friendly. A prominent figure at the Grimm School, Malodora had come to make the announcement because she herself would be a judge at the Games.

And to scare me, Snow thought. If that was Malodora's intention, it had worked.

Until that night, Snow hadn't laid eyes on her stepmother since she'd run away from home. As she rinsed one of the bowls and set it in the carved wood strainer, she shuddered at the memory of living with Malodora. The woman made snakes and spiders flee in fear.

When Snow's father had first told Snow he was going to remarry, Snow had been ecstatic. Snow's mother had died when Snow was a tiny baby and she had always longed for a motherly figure to share things with and look up to. She'd had high hopes for her relationship with her father's new wife.

When Malodora first arrived at Snow's father's castle, she seemed content to be queen. She had a lovely castle to run and she herself was beautiful to look at. Everyone said so. Even Malodora herself couldn't help but gaze at her own reflection in the large looking glass she'd brought with her to the castle.

Snow liked to sit and gaze with her — until Malodora asked her to leave. "You make me nervous with your staring. Don't you have anything better to do?" the queen had said curtly. Snow had curtsied and left quietly. She'd only wanted to make her new mother feel welcome. But the next time she peeked into Malodora's chambers, hoping to sit with her, the looking glass was gone.

157

Snow kept trying. She did everything she could think of to please her new stepmother. But instead of warming to Snow, Malodora got colder. She looked at Snow with disapproving stares. The more Snow smiled, the more Malodora frowned. Snow's very presence seemed to make her unhappy.

Malodora began to spend most of her time alone in her attic chamber. Since the chamber was off-limits, nobody was sure what the queen was doing. But the strange lights and harsh smells made Snow suspect that her stepmother was concocting potions and casting spells. Sometimes Snow even heard voices.

The maid told her there was a magic mirror in the attic that Malodora spoke to, asking it questions. The mirror claimed to speak the truth, yet the more Malodora spoke to it, the angrier she grew. "There's something wrong with that looking glass," the maid confided to Snow. "I think it's cracked!"

Then something truly horrible happened. Snow's father disappeared. One evening he sweetly kissed his young daughter good night, and in the morning he was nowhere to be found. When Snow asked her stepmother where he had gone, she simply replied that he'd had to go to sea.

"Why didn't he say good-bye?" Snow had asked, her eyes full of tears.

"Perhaps he didn't think it was necessary," Malodora had replied icily.

Snow wiped her nose on her sleeve as she placed a freshly washed bowl with the others next to the stone sink. It had been so long since she'd seen her father, and whenever she thought of him, it was difficult not to cry.

With her father gone, life in the castle had changed utterly. Snow began to worry. The halls she had once skipped down now appeared dark and scary. The flowers withered in the gardens. Even the once-cozy fires burning in the grates hissed and popped, sending out sparks and frightening Snow away. The castle staff only dared to speak to Snow in whispers. They told her Malodora had taken a job as headmistress at the Grimm School. And in hushed tones they told her, "Beware!"

Snow was so lonely without her father she decided to reach out once more. Perhaps Malodora was lonely, too. Summoning her courage she'd climbed the stairs to her stepmother's attic room carrying a tea tray laden with cookies and pastries. When she reached the top she stopped. She didn't have a free hand to knock, but the door was standing open just a crack. Snow leaned against the door frame and was about to call out when she caught sight of Malodora.

Her stepmother was bent over in front of her mirror, stooped with laughter. Her cackles turned into howls. She was watching an image in the mirror, an image of Snow's father struggling on board a ship in a terrible storm! The image disappeared and a horrible face appeared in the glass. It, too, looked amused.

"Well done, my queen," the mirror said. "Your worthless husband is lost in your spell, sailing the endless sea. May he never see the shore again.

"The castle is nearly yours. Only that ridiculous cheerful child stands in your way."

Shocked by what she was seeing, Snow dropped the tray with a clatter and a hot splash. Malodora had certainly heard her, but Snow did not stop to look back or apologize for the mess. Snow fled the castle that very moment.

It was a terrifying journey. Snow had stumbled along the forest paths, her vision blurred by tears. She did not know where to go or what to do, and she felt completely alone. But when she stumbled upon the little cottage in the woods, it immediately seemed like home.

It was Meek whom Snow White met first — he was outside chopping wood. But he was so shy he wouldn't talk to her! He ran behind the woodpile and peeked timidly through a knothole. Luckily Hap came out to help with the stacking, and he chattered kindly with

Snow, saying nothing about her blotchy, tear-stained cheeks. In an instant Snow felt like they were old friends. Soon the rest of the little men — Wheezer, Mort, Nod, Dim, and Gruff — came out to see what the commotion was about. Gruff took one look at Snow and stormed back inside. The rest of the dwarves welcomed her with open arms. She had supper with them that very night and, after she told the dwarves her tale, they insisted she stay. Snow agreed to spend one night, and had lived in the woodland cottage ever since.

At first Snow had been nervous that her stepmother would come after her. With her sorceress talents and all-seeing mirror, Malodora most certainly knew where Snow was. But for whatever reason, she left Snow alone. Perhaps she was glad to be rid of her. One thing was certain: Snow was glad to be away. In the cottage she felt safe . . . at least until recently.

Ever since her stepmother's appearance at the Princess School ball, Snow couldn't shake the creepy feeling that Malodora was watching her in her awful mirror. . . . Sometimes Snow could swear she felt the sorceress's icy fingers on her neck! And if Snow did anything to draw attention to herself — like compete in the Maiden Games — it might enrage her stepmother. Snow knew that every Princess School student was expected to participate, but she'd have to find a way to get out of it.

Glancing at the carved wooden cuckoo clock, Snow realized that if she didn't hurry she'd be late for school. She grabbed her cape, books, and scrolls and rushed out the door.

Every tree and stone along the path was familiar to Snow, so it was easy to move quickly. The morning air was crisp but not cold, and the sky was cerulean blue. Usually Snow drank in the woodland beauty. Today she barely noticed it.

Stepping into the lane, she immediately spied the shadowy Grimm School. Its smoke-stained spires poked at the sky. Snow resisted the temptation to sample the school's gingerbread gate — doing so was a sure way to be ensnared by the nasty Grimm girls. Snow hurried past so quickly that she forgot to look where she was going and ran — *smack!* — into Lucinta Pintch, a fast-talking snoop of a witch from Grimm.

"What's your hurry?" Lucinta asked, eyeing Snow mischievously. "Care to rest for a spell?" Quick as a flash she raised her twisted black wand toward Snow. "Or are you worried your stepmother might see you showing your face in her territory?"

Snow gasped, horrified by Lucinta's words.

If all of the Grimm witches know I'm Malodora's step-daughter, they must also know she hates me! Snow thought. *The whole school is probably out to get me!*

Swallowing hard, Snow stepped around Lucinta without uttering a word. Up ahead, she could see Rapunzel in the distance. She hurried to catch up to her friend. Behind her, Lucinta's cackling voice echoed on the fall breeze.

Chapter Two
Confidence

When Snow caught up to Rapunzel and Rapunzel's best friend, Prince Valerian, they were deep in conversation.

"We've just got to win the Golden Ball," Rapunzel said, her brown eyes flashing.

Snow knew the Golden Ball was just that — a shimmering orb. But it was also the coveted trophy for the winner of the Maiden Games.

Rapunzel hitched up the skirts of her gown and strode down the path determinedly, as if getting to school first would guarantee her the prize.

"Slow down, princess," Val called to Rapunzel as she leaped over a fallen log and hurried ahead. Then he turned. "Hello, Snow," he said. He smiled charmingly and offered her a hand to get over the fallen tree.

Snow returned the smile and took Val's hand. He really was a nice prince. Snow could see why he was

Rapunzel's best friend. And being with *nice* people was just what Snow needed right now.

Val called out to Rapunzel again. "What's your hurry? The competition isn't for a week!"

Rapunzel turned to face her friends, her freckled cheeks flushed with excitement. "A week is hardly any time to prepare! We need a strategy if we're going to take back the Golden Ball. The Grimm School has beaten us three years in a row!"

Val seemed about to explain that sprinting to school wouldn't improve Princess School's chances, but Rapunzel had already whirled around again and was dashing up the path. He shrugged at Snow.

"Uh, how is Rose doing?" Val asked hesitantly.

Snow was about to answer when Rapunzel finally slowed down.

"Rose?" Rapunzel echoed, rolling her eyes. "As I've told you the last twenty-six times you've asked, she's fine."

Now it was Val's turn to flush. "I haven't asked about her twenty-six times. I just haven't seen her since the Coronation Ball. So naturally I was wondering how she is. Is she feeling . . . well-rested?"

"Hmmpphhh," Rapunzel said as she turned off the path onto the lane leading to Princess School.

Val was silent for several long moments. Snow

waited to see what would happen. But Val knew Rapunzel well enough to know it was time to change the subject.

"If you really want to win the Maiden Games, you'll need lots of practice and confidence," Val finally said, getting back to Rapunzel's topic of choice.

Once again Rapunzel turned to face him, this time so fast the end of her impossibly long braid nearly whipped him in the face. The braid was actually coiled into a gigantic bun on the back of Rapunzel's head, but the end of it could never be fastened properly and hung down her back past her waist. "Are you saying I lack confidence?" she asked huffily.

Val bowed low to his friend. "Absolutely not," he replied quickly. "I value my life far too much to make such a claim."

"Wise choice," Rapunzel acknowledged, turning back down the lane.

Though she would never say so to Rapunzel, Snow thought Val was right. It *would* take a lot of practice to win the Games. While she knew Rapunzel didn't lack confidence, she was not so sure about herself or the other princesses. Even the oldest girls at Princess School — the Crowns — hadn't seen a victory over the Grimms. And most of the princesses were, well, *princesses* — painfully poised and not very full of sporty gusto. Rapunzel seemed ready for the challenge, but Snow wished the Games weren't even happening.

Lost in thought, Snow did not notice that they were passing by a grove of huge gnarled fruit trees. And then — *thud!* — Val got hit square in the back with something orange, squishy, and rotten.

"Hey!" Val protested, whirling around.

Rapunzel whirled, too. Snow covered her head. But they didn't see anything . . . until they looked up. Leering down at them from high in a leafless persimmon tree hanging with overripe fruit was Hortense Hegbottom, a Grimm School witch.

"Still hungry?" she snickered nastily, swinging her gigantic black boots. "How about another?" She hurled a second moldy persimmon straight into the air. The orange mush-ball rose so high it almost disappeared, then barreled straight down toward Rapunzel so fast it whistled.

Rapunzel's eyes never lost sight of the squishy fruit, and a split second before it careened into the bodice of her gown she ducked. *Splat!* It hit the hard dirt lane and splattered her skirt.

Snow swallowed a scream.

"Thought I might help you practice — being a loser." Hortense's raspy voice reminded Snow of dry leaves. Her broad face and long, pointed nose contorted into a sneer. Tossing another piece of rotting fruit into the air, she casually swung her red-and-black-striped-stockinged legs. "And now I think I'll have a little practice myself . . . with that nest." She waved a fat-knuckled hand at Rapunzel's head and muttered a few words under her breath.

It only took Snow two seconds to figure out what Hortense was up to, but that was two seconds too long. She tried to call out a warning to Rapunzel, but before her long-haired friend could step backward, the branches of the persimmon tree bent dramatically, reaching for her bun. Within moments Rapunzel's reddish-brown coil was half undone. Twine-thick locks stuck out in all directions.

"Hee-hee-hee, and all from a tree," Hortense sang as Val and Snow untangled Rapunzel and pulled her away.

"Ugh, not again," Val complained. "That's two days in a row!"

"At least she didn't open a can of worms on top of *your* head," Rapunzel fumed, shaking a fist at the still-cackling Hortense. "It took me an hour to get this bun in place!"

"Want me to help you fix it?" Snow asked.

Val eyed Rapunzel's hair skeptically.

"No, thanks," Rapunzel said with a frustrated sigh. "I can do it in Looking Glass class."

Snow wished again that the Games were not happening. She felt defeated already. Two witches in one morning were too many! But Rapunzel was raging and even Val seemed energized.

The prince brushed hastily at the orange splotch on his waistcoat. His eyes were bright with excitement. "It's too bad the Charm School doesn't have anyone to compete with," he said. "We could use a little rivalry to shake things up!" He kicked at a pebble in the path. "There's nothing going on at my school but chivalry. I wish I were a girl!"

A Royal Rally

Though it meant they had to say good-bye to Val, Snow was relieved when the glimmering spires of Princess School finally came into view. It was good to be in the company of friends — and the more friends the better!

"Look, there's Rose and Ella!" she said, taking Rapunzel's arm. Maybe they were talking about something besides the Maiden Games!

Passing under the carved silver archway, Snow and Rapunzel joined their friends. Rose and Ella were looking down at the swans swimming gracefully in the moat. The Coronation Ball tiara still sparkled on Ella's head.

Ella turned to greet them and gasped when she saw the orange splotches on Rapunzel's dress.

"She got you again?" Rose asked. Her blue eyes were wide and her rose-lipped mouth agape at the sight of Rapunzel's hair.

"That ugly little witch has it coming to her," Rapunzel fumed. But even though she scowled, Snow saw another expression in Rapunzel's eyes: exhilaration. She *liked* the competition.

"Hortense's nasty pranks just make me want to win the Maiden Games even more. I'll show her — and all the bratty witches at Grimm!" Rapunzel said with a fiendish grin.

Snow admired her friend's courage and resolve, but as she listened to Rapunzel's words, her breath caught in her throat and she felt numb all over. The images from her nightmares still lingered in her head, along with Lucinta's and Hortense's taunts. Snow was afraid of the Maiden Games — and the Grimms. And for some reason she didn't want to tell her friends how she felt.

"Rapunzel, your hair!" Ella said, reaching up to tuck in a few of the renegade strands.

"Don't bother," Rapunzel replied, blowing a thick auburn curl off her face. "I'll fix it in Looking Glass."

"Good thing it's right after hearthroom," Rose said with a grimace. "No offense, Rapunzel, but it's a *mess*."

"I believe you, and I'm not offended," Rapunzel said flatly. "At least, not by you."

"Weren't you at all frightened?" Snow asked, her dark eyes wide.

"Of course not," Rapunzel replied. "It takes more

than a few rotten persimmons and an enchanted tree to scare me."

"Oh!" Snow said. "I thought it was awful." She saw Ella and Rose exchange smiles, but her face felt frozen as she stared into the moat.

"Is everything all right, Snow?" Ella asked. "You look shaken."

Snow nodded distractedly, her gaze never leaving the smooth, blue-green water below. Everything was not all right. In fact, it was feeling more wrong every minute. But she wasn't sure how to tell her friends. She opened her mouth to speak and closed it again as the two-minute trumpet sounded. Class was about to begin.

The girls climbed the polished marble stairs and the heavy doors to Princess School whooshed open as they approached.

"I'm sure you'll get back at Hortense at the Maiden Games, Rapunzel," Rose said as the girls made their way down the long, tall-ceilinged corridor to hearth-room. Their slippers padded along quietly on the pink-and-white stone floor. All around them golden sunlight glistened off the carved alabaster pillars.

Rapunzel nodded. "Believe me, I intend to," she said with an impish grin.

Behind her, Snow felt an icy chill run up her spine.

Malodora, she thought. Pulling her cape around her shoulders, she followed her friends down the hall.

When the trumpet signaled the end of Hearthroom the first-year Bloomers headed out to the gardens for a special Maiden Games rally. They were followed by the second-year Sashes, the third-year Robes, and finally the fourth-year Crowns.

Snow and her friends made their way past the gleaming statues of famous princesses past and present toward the large Princess School gazebo. Carved stone benches with purple velvet cushions circled an open area with a podium. Celebratory pink banners hung from the rafters, encircling the seating area. At the podium, Headmistress Bathilde stood with her trademark scepter, surrounded by several other teachers.

Snow and her friends found an empty bench near the back and sat down just as Headmistress Bathilde cleared her throat regally.

The gazebo was instantly silent as the princesses waited to hear what Lady Bathilde had to say. The headmistress was not only a beautiful and elegant ruler, she was also a wise and fair guardian of the school.

"Welcome, princesses," she said in her commanding but friendly voice, "to the Princess School Maiden Games rally.

"As those of you who have experienced them before know, the Maiden Games represent many things to our school — sportsprincessship, hard work, team spirit, and honor among them. I want each of you to do your best to be a worthy teammate and competitor at the Games. I'll now turn the proceedings over to our head coach and Self-defense instructor, Madame Lightfoot."

The princesses-in-training clapped delicately as Madame Lightfoot moved to the center of the gazebo. Ella nudged Snow in the side. "We're supposed to clap," she whispered.

Snow smiled weakly and clapped her hands together a few times before the crowd quieted to hear Madame Lightfoot's words.

"This year we are beginning a new tradition of naming four team captains — one from each year — who will help their fellow princesses prepare for the Games and bring all of you together as princesses and competitors. Being team captain is a great honor and also a great responsibility. A panel of teachers, including the headmistress herself, chose this year's captains based on athletic and leadership skills."

Snow looked at the excited faces of the girls seated nearby. Many of them fidgeted in their seats, obviously itching to be named the Bloomer captain. Snow felt nothing. She wished she were anyone in the crowd but herself.

"Per royal etiquette I ask you to please hold your applause until after I have announced all of the team captains.

"The Crown captain will be Astrid Glimmer," Madame Lightfoot read from a scroll. "The Robe captain will be Tiffany Bulugia. The Sash captain will be Antonella Printz. And the Bloomer captain will be . . . Rapunzel Arugula!"

The students burst into hearty applause, momentarily abandoning their proper princess decorum.

Ella let out an excited squeal and squeezed Rapunzel's hand.

"Congratulations!" Snow cried. For the first time all day she felt happy. Rapunzel was a perfect choice!

Rose gave Rapunzel a quick hug. "I knew it would be you!" she said.

"And now for the names of the judges," Madame Lightfoot said. "The Princess School representatives will be Administrator Ballus and Headmistress Bathilde. And from the Grimm School . . . Vermin Twitch and the headmistress, Queen Malodora."

There was a groan from the girls when Vermin Twitch's name was announced.

"He looks like a rat!" a Robe whispered.

"Those beady eyes give me the creeps," added a Sash.

Snow tried to control the shivers that overwhelmed her when the judges were mentioned. But it wasn't Vermin who was upsetting her. She liked rats.

"Practice will begin tomorrow!" Madame Lightfoot declared, ending the rally.

While the rest of the princesses clapped politely, Rapunzel let out a loud whoop and jumped to her feet. Ella and Rose stood to hug and congratulate their friend. In their excitement they didn't notice frozen Snow. Icy fingers gripped the back of Snow's neck and, rooted to her seat, she shook like a bowl of chilled vanilla pudding.

Chapter Four
The Tiara Twist

Perched on her stool in front of a giant mirror in Looking Glass class, Cinderella gazed at the tiara on her head. She had been wearing it for a week and it still took her breath away.

"It's soooo beautiful," said Lisette Iderdown, who was sitting next to her. "It's perfect for you."

Ella blushed. Until recently, she had never thought of herself as beautiful. And to tell the truth, she still didn't. Her blond hair was thick and shiny, and there was nothing really wrong with her face. But she wasn't striking, not like Rose, who was so stunning that more than half the people at school called her "Beauty." But since Ella had been crowned Princess of the Ball a week ago, she'd been getting a lot of attention. She'd gone from being invisible to being . . . well, kind of famous. Every princess in school knew who she was. Older girls — Sashes and even Crowns — stopped her in the halls to ask her opinion about everything from hairdos and gown adornments to how to dance with a boy (she'd done a lot of that at the ball). Even here in Looking Glass class, the teacher, Madame Spiegel, had designed an entire fortnight of classes around tiara hairdos.

Ella loved the attention . . . sort of. It took a lot of work to live up to the crowned princess expectations, and she already had a lot of work to do at home. Her stepmother, Kastrid, and her stepsisters, Hagatha and Prunilla, treated her like a servant. Being crowned at school certainly hadn't changed that. She still had to do all the cooking and cleaning and washing and sewing at home. And now she had to spend extra time on her own hand-me-down gowns, making sure they were clean and perfectly pressed. She was grateful for the honor her new school had bestowed upon her. But sometimes being the center of attention was exhausting. How did Rose do it?

At least Hag and Prune are leaving me alone at school now, Ella thought. They'd managed to make her first two weeks at Princess School simply awful — it was only with the amazing help of her new friends that Ella had made it to the ball at all. But since her steps had made complete fools of themselves in front of *everyone*, including the headmistress, they were now on their best behavior. And Ella had also noticed that Madame Taffeta, her Stitchery teacher, had been watching Hag and Prune closely. Ella was grateful for all of that, but knew better than to expect their silence to last forever.

"It's only a matter of time before they'll be tormenting me again," Ella whispered to her reflection. But then, maybe having things back to normal would be a relief.

"All right, girls," Madame Spiegel said, clapping her hands together and tearing herself away from her own reflected image. "It's time to get to work on our tiara twists." She handed each princess a tiara made of simple silver wire and polished pastel-toned stones. The girls had spent the last week perfecting hairdos that could be worn with crowns: the basic nape-of-the-neck bun, the slightly more advanced French braid tuck, and now the tricky tiara twist.

Once the tiaras had been distributed, Madame Spiegel went back to the giant looking glass at the front of the room. Picking up her comb, she began to divide her blond hair into sections.

"To properly create a tiara twist, you must divide your hair into six equal parts — three per side." She looked over at Rapunzel sympathetically. "Don't worry, Rapunzel," she said. "I'll come help you get your hair under control as soon as I'm finished demonstrating."

"Thank you, Madame Spiegel," Rapunzel said, untangling her massive mess of hair.

One by one, Madame Spiegel took each section of

hair and twisted and coiled it just so. She was so skilled at it that she only needed one hairpin to hold each coil in place.

"After twisting each section several times, you pin it to the side of your head very carefully, maintaining the delicate coil. There should be a curl falling on each side of your face, one over each ear, and one on either side of the nape of your neck. Together they make a complete circle of twists to surround the tiara." Madame Spiegel turned slowly so the princesses could see her hairdo.

"Lovely," said Rose.

Snow nodded blankly.

"My mother says the tiara twist is the perfect princess style," added another Bloomer.

The girls got to work, carefully dividing their long hair into sections. Now and then a frustrated sigh echoed in the tall chamber, but in general the girls seemed excited to try something new. Ella was grateful they didn't think having to learn this tricky style so early was her fault. Normally the tiara twist was part of the Robes' curriculum.

"Do you think we stand a chance at beating the Grimms?" Red, a small friendly girl who always wore a scarlet cape, asked as Ella completed her second twist.

"Definitely," Rapunzel replied as she tried to comb

several tiny twigs out of an auburn lock. "But it's going to take a lot of work — and practice — from all of us."

Ella felt a tingle run up her spine as she remembered the Maiden Games. They sounded so exciting! And she wanted to beat the Grimms as much as she had wanted to see her awful steps get what they deserved for all the trouble they'd caused when they'd hazed the Bloomers earlier in the school year.

Hag and Prune are such witches, they'd be better suited to the Grimm School, Ella thought. She smiled at her reflection as she completed her final twist. *If I'm lucky, they'll get recruited!*

As she began another twist, Ella spotted Snow at a dressing table behind her. Snow was staring wide-eyed at her own reflection and was sitting so still she almost looked like a statue.

Snow hasn't been herself all day, Ella thought as she pinned the twist to the side of her head. *Maybe if I can get her to myself after class I can find out what's bothering her.*

Satisfied with her plan, Ella got back to her tiara twist. She had just pinned the last coil into place when the end-of-class trumpet sounded. It was time for the girls to have their noonday meal in the dining hall. As the princesses spilled into the corridor, Sashes and Bloomers paused to curtsy to Ella. Even Robes and Crowns nodded respectfully.

"There's no need to do that," Ella insisted when Veronique, a popular Robe, momentarily halted her conversation to acknowledge her.

Ella curtsied to Veronique and her cluster of friends before stepping into the dining room. The large chamber was filled with round wooden tables covered with crisp white tablecloths. The gilded silver chairs were ornately carved with roses and ivy to match the pillars found throughout the castle. And the pink-flowered china was as delicate as the most poised of princesses.

Walking with Rose, Ella began to cross the room to get to Snow when a Sash curtsied just inches in front of Ella. Ella tried to return the courtesy, but tripped on the hem of her gown.

"Ugh!" Ella mumbled, steadying herself on a gilded chair just before she fell to the tiled floor. "How do you deal with this, Rose?" Ella asked, straightening up and adjusting her skirt.

"Oh, I suppose you just get used to it," Rose replied. She sounded odd, and didn't look Ella in the eye.

Ella was about to ask Rose if something was wrong when Rapunzel called out from the other end of the room.

"Come on!" she practically shouted. "I've saved us all seats!"

Chapter Five

The Same Path Twice

The trumpets sounded and inside the castle Self-defense class began. Outside, Snow heard the heavy doors close behind her as she raced down the stairs and away from Princess School.

"I'm going to get in terrible trouble for this," she said aloud as she hurried across the bridge. "But I can't bear to stay another minute!"

Snow had been worrying about Malodora and the Maiden Games all day. Ever since the rally she'd wanted to flee the castle. Though she'd almost made it through the day, all the excited talk about the Maiden Games among the other girls finally got to her in Frog ID class. She couldn't even smile when a little green guy had croaked a froggy song to her. As soon as class was over she'd made a dash for the door.

Snow knew she owed it to her school and her friends to do her best at the competitions. Rapunzel was one of the captains! But her stepmother was one of the judges — and Snow just couldn't face her! She was torn between fear and friends. What was she going to do? Perhaps she would be able to sort out her thoughts in her cozy cottage.

I'm not going anywhere near Grimm, Snow thought with a shudder as she followed the lane that led away from the smoke-stained castle. It was the long way home. *The very last thing I need is another encounter with awful Lucinta Pintch!*

As Snow walked down the path, she pictured Lucinta's face. Her beady black eyes reminded Snow of a weasel she once caught stealing eggs from a robin's nest.

"Nasty witchy weasel!" Snow said aloud, startling herself. It wasn't like her to say anything mean, even about a witch.

Snow tried to put the entire terrible day out of her mind as she picked her way along the shadowy path. She puckered her lips and tried to whistle the cereal song. She couldn't remember it. It was lost in her head. And suddenly Snow felt lost in the woods. She looked around for familiar landmarks. Though she knew she had chosen the safer route, an uneasy yet familiar feeling came over her . . . the feeling that someone was watching her.

Above her the sky was light, with a few clouds scattered here and there. But the forest was dark and the branches seemed to reach down to her.

Her heart thudded in her chest and Snow picked up her pace, moving more quickly through the forest. The path led deeper and deeper into darkness, and rocks and gnarled tree roots made the route treacherous. Still, Snow moved faster and faster until she finally broke into a run. Branches above and beneath her creaked and snapped, and the howls of forest animals echoed in the distance. Snow was dismayed to realize that even this normally comforting sound was now terrifying to her.

An icy finger snaked its way up her spine, and Snow turned, certain that someone was behind her. But the darkened path was empty. Turning back, Snow raced ahead, dark shadows swirling around her. As branches and leaves swiped at her face, she suddenly realized she was not lost. She had taken this path before . . . when she fled her father's castle.

With tears streaming down her pale face, Snow White stumbled out of the dense forest and fuzzily saw the dwarf cottage in a clearing before her. Sobbing, she ran toward it, burst through the door, and flew up the stairs. Her tiny alcove room was a welcome sight, but she was too distraught to do anything but cross to the wooden bed the dwarves carved for her when she'd moved in. Exhausted, threw herself across the sweet-smelling straw-filled mattress and fell fast asleep.

No sooner had her eyes closed than Snow White began to dream. There was the ocean, blue-green with lapping waves. Then a ship appeared and, with it, a howling wind. Rain poured from the sky, and waves began to pound the sides of the seemingly tiny boat. Then suddenly, Snow's father appeared on deck! He was calling Snow's name, Snow was sure, but the wind and rain were carrying the cries away as quickly as he uttered them. The tattered sails blew wildly in the wind. With a final desperate cry, Snow's father fell to his knees. . . .

Snow sobbed and turned in her sleep and the scene before her eyes shifted dramatically. Suddenly Snow was back at her father's castle — a little girl playing happily in the orchards. Apple blossoms rained down on her rosy cheeks, dusting her eyelids. Above her, she saw her father's face as he playfully shook the branches of the apple tree. But then the shimmering castle beyond the blooming trees transformed into a dark, soot-stained fortress.

Snow was instantly inside, following her stepmother up a darkened staircase to her attic workshop. Dim torches cast more shadow than light and the air was dank and stale.

Malodora's eyes shimmered with evil as she threw

open a door to another, smaller chamber. Heaped on the floor were dead rodents of all shapes and sizes — moles, squirrels, shrews, mice, and rats.

"Noooo!" Snow screamed, turning her eyes away from the poor dead creatures. Whirling on her heel, she raced down the stairs and out of the castle back to the orchards . . . the only place in the castle where she could still feel her father's presence, the place they walked together on many an afternoon, smelling the blossoms and picking the luscious fruit. And then Snow felt her father's strong, comforting arms around her waist as he lifted her high to pick a ripe and perfect apple. . . .

With a jolt, Snow sat up in bed. Tears streamed down her face. Looking around her small room, she felt lonely and relieved all at once. Her father was gone, but so was Malodora. Snow was in her cozy woodland cottage and safe . . . at least for the moment.

Chapter Six
Admiration and Envy

It seemed like an eternity before the final trumpet sounded, announcing the end of the school day. Rose didn't think she'd ever watched the hourglass on Madame Taffeta's desk so closely. At times it felt like the sand was running backward!

Rose was in such a hurry to find out what was going on with Snow that she rushed out of class and onto the steps at the entrance of the school without stopping to put her texts and scrolls in her trunk. It was a mistake. Now, as she stood alone, her books weighed heavily in her arms. And she had to wait for Ella and Rapunzel to catch up — they were probably stuck in the mobbed hallway putting *their* stuff away so they could travel light.

Sinking down to sit on the polished stone landing, Rose felt anxious. Her chest was tight. It felt like there was something caught inside it — a sigh maybe, or a sob. She was really worried about Snow. But there was something else wrong, too. Something she couldn't quite name.

With a rustle of skirts and the patter of slippers on stone, the landing at the top of the stairs was flooded with princesses. Rose could hear the excitement in their voices as they chatted about the Maiden Games, but at the moment she did not share it.

As a group of especially talkative girls began to flow past her, Rose realized they were all focused on someone in the middle of the swarm. Something shiny sparkled in the center of the girls. Rose recognized the glint. It was Ella's tiara.

As she watched Ella soak up attention from the other girls, the tightness in Rose's chest threatened to split her wide open.

What is wrong with me? Rose wondered, hugging her texts tightly. Only last week this same swarm of girls was buzzing around Rose. The attention had been annoying — exhausting even. But in some ways, Rose had to admit, it had been nice to be admired — or at least noticed.

Rose brushed her skirts and forced a smile in Ella's direction. Ella was her friend. Rose should be happy for her. If anyone deserved attention it was Ella. Didn't she have to put up with her horrible stepfamily? Hadn't she spent enough of her life being harassed? She could use a little admiration!

A hundred thoughts buzzing in her head, Rose leaned back on one hand.

"Ouch!"

Intent on what Ella was saying (something about the dress she'd made for Hagatha), a fawning princess stepped right on Rose's fingers. "Oh, sorry, Rose!" she said quickly. But an instant later she had turned back so as not to miss another of Ella's words.

Rose fumed, sucking on her crushed finger. Last week that same girl had been calling her "Beauty"! It was such a silly nickname; Rose always thought she hated it. But at the moment she actually missed it. A lot.

Rose got to her feet. "Don't you feel a little silly wearing that tiara *every* day?" she asked, speaking a little more loudly than she'd meant to.

Ella's face turned bright pink as the crowd around her fell silent. She touched the jeweled crown self-consciously. "It's traditional," she replied, looking hurt and a little confused. "The Princess of the Ball wears it until the closing ceremony of the Maiden Games. "I just . . ." she trailed off, too surprised and confused to go on. For a moment, Ella and Rose stared at each other in silence. Then Rose looked away.

At last Rapunzel burst out of the Princess School

doors and waved frantically at her friends. Rose met her on the edge of the top step, and as they waited for Ella to break free of her fans Rapunzel spoke to the rest of the students on the stairs.

"Don't forget to come to Maiden Games practice tomorrow morning! We'll start the warm-up at the cock's first crow!" Rapunzel said loudly.

Several of the girls groaned. It was barely light at first crow! But Rapunzel was unmoved. "We want to win the Golden Ball, don't we?" she asked with her arms wide.

"Yes!" the girls chorused as they headed down the stairs.

"Okay, then." Rapunzel planted her fists on her hips and gave a little nod. Then in a quieter voice Rapunzel spoke to Rose and Ella. "Now, let's go find Snow."

The farther they got from Princess School the better Rose felt. It was good to be with her friends. When she wasn't surrounded by adoring girls, Rose could see that Ella was still just Ella. Besides, it felt great to finally be on their way to Snow's house after worrying all through Self-defense.

"I don't know what would make Snow take off like that." Ella shook her head.

"I know she's nervous about the games," Rose said.

"But it's not like Snow to worry," Rapunzel put in. "She's *always* cheery."

Rose had to agree. Something was seriously wrong.

Moving quickly, Rose followed Rapunzel and Ella down a path she'd never been on before. Rapunzel knew all of the trails in the woods and insisted this was the fastest one. But it was dark and narrow and the trees grew close on either side, meeting overhead and almost completely blocking out the autumn sun. Rose usually traveled by carriage with about a dozen guards. It was a little creepy slogging through the forest this way. But seeing Rapunzel's massive reddish bun and Ella's shining locks and sparkling crown bobbing ahead of her was enough reassurance to keep her going.

"Look!" Rapunzel called as they approached a clearing. "It's Grimm!" Indeed, the back side of the towering black castle loomed over them.

Rose had never seen the Grimm School from this angle before. Her heartbeat quickened a little as she stepped off the path and peered past the ornate gingerbread fence surrounding the school. The Grimm castle was oily black with brackish moss growing on the square stone walls. Smoke belched out of smokestacks and even from the windows of some of the towers. Rose wasn't sure whether it was coming from wood fires, the kitchens, or spells gone wrong. Besides the sickly mosses on the castle stones, there wasn't a single patch of green on the Grimm School grounds. All of the grass was dry and brown — perhaps killed by the acrid smoke. And the only plant that dared to approach the tall, narrow building was a bloodred creeping ivy vine that circled one of the towers like a tightening rope.

Rose shivered.

"There's nothing we can't handle here," Rapunzel said encouragingly, not altering her course to avoid walking right past the gingerbread gate. "Besides, the witches have all gone home."

Rose was starting to relax a little when she heard a *whoosh* overhead. Ella grabbed her elbow and the girls looked up in time to catch a flash of black-and-red stocking as a nasty-looking witch swooped by on a ratty broom. Rose stole a look at Rapunzel. From the way she was glaring, Rose knew the girl had to be Hortense Hegbottom, the same witch who had messed with Rapunzel that morning, and the morning before. But Rapunzel didn't look scared, just mad.

"Three little princesses, pretty as can be . . ." The wide-faced witch cackled, circling over Rose and her friends, obviously enjoying herself. Then with eyes filled with scorn, Hortense raised a red-knuckled finger and pointed at the gate. The pretty gingerbread swung open so quickly it slammed into Rapunzel and knocked her over. Rapunzel landed on the damp dirt with a thud.

"One got wholloped and landed on her knees!" Hortense finished her rhyme and swooped lower to laugh in Rapunzel's face before she could pull herself back to her feet. "A perfect position for you," Hortense sneered. "I suggest you get used to it. You'll be begging for mercy at the Maiden Games."

Then Hortense turned to study Ella and Rose more carefully. Her broom hummed in one place — a hovering seat — and she casually swung her sturdy legs back and forth just inches above the ground. Hortense smiled wider, revealing large yellowed teeth.

"These must be your teammates," she cackled. "Aren't they lovely!" Then the nasty witch began to laugh so hard she nearly fell off her broomstick.

One look at Rapunzel and Rose knew they had to get her out of there — fast — or Rapunzel was going to make trouble. She pushed past Hortense and helped Rapunzel to her feet, keeping a tight grip on her arm to prevent her friend from launching herself at Hortense.

"Let's go," Ella said softly, taking Rapunzel's other arm and backing away. "We'll get our chance to retaliate at the Games."

Luckily Rapunzel was too angry to speak. She was casting daggers with her eyes, but they weren't penetrating Hortense's armor. With a heavy thunk, Hortense flipped off her broom and lay on the dirt, howling and pounding it with her fist.

The sound of her laughter followed them down the trail, and only after it had disappeared completely did Rapunzel find her tongue.

"Who does that witch think she is?" she asked, practically shouting. "And what does she mean saying we're 'lovely'? Lovely's got nothing to do with it!"

Rose couldn't have agreed more, but she knew better than to feed Rapunzel's fire. "Don't worry, captain. She'll see how lovely we are when we're holding the Golden Ball."

Rapunzel snorted, but seemed to calm down a little. By the time they made it to Snow's cottage she was almost her normal self.

"This must be it," Ella said, gazing at the small stone cottage in a grassy clearing. It was adorable and neat as a pin. The grass had been trimmed all around the house, and a large pile of carefully stacked firewood stood under a small lean-to along with a sturdy wheelbarrow and a collection of garden tools. Wildflowers and shrubs of all kinds grew in the garden in front of the house, and a few potted plants bloomed beautifully on the front porch.

Ella hurried ahead and knocked on the small door, which was painted bright red.

"Snow!" Rose called up to the eight round windows on the second floor. Each window had its own small window box bursting with flowers, and beneath the sod roof the rafters of the house were carved into the shapes of different animals.

"Snow!" Rapunzel echoed Rose's call, but didn't bother to knock. She opened the front door and strode inside, Ella and Rose at her heels.

At the end of a long but rather short dining table Snow sat, slumped over a giant bowl filled with applesauce. Empty jars were strewn everywhere, along with several sticky spoons. Snow looked up and a lump of sauce slowly slid down her face to drip off the end of her quivering chin. The poor girl's dark eyes were rimmed with tears and her usually lovely pale skin was red and covered in splotches.

Chapter Seven
An Apple a Day

Nothing was working. Usually when Snow was blue, a little bowl of applesauce was all she needed to sweeten her mood. She'd eaten seven and she was still miserable. Sniffing, Snow spooned up another bite. She couldn't let the dwarves see her like this — she just had to cheer up! Letting one last tear drip into her bowl, she closed her eyes and tried to picture Hap's face. Nobody could resist that cheerful dwarf's smile.

Suddenly the door to the cottage opened with a *bang*. Snow felt panic surge within her.

There in the doorway stood Snow's friends — Rapunzel, Ella, and Rose. Worry showed on their faces.

"Oh, Snow!" Ella rushed forward and threw her arms around the sauce-covered girl.

Seeing her friends should have made Snow feel better, but it only made her feel worse. A fresh flood of tears poured onto Ella's shoulder.

"What is it?" Rapunzel asked.

"Did something happen to the dwarves?" Rose wanted to know.

"Oh gosh, no." Snow sniffed. "Well, gee, I hope not." Now she had something new to worry about. But all she really wanted was to keep other people from worrying about her. Snow hiccuped.

"You have to tell us what's the matter," Rapunzel said gently, easing the large applesauce spoon out of her hand. "We can help, I know it."

"It's nothing, really." Snow watched Rose carry an empty applesauce jar to the sink along with her bowl. "I just . . . well . . ." She gazed at the floor. "I just can't face the Maiden Games. I can't go."

"Oooh." Rapunzel sounded relieved. "You don't have to worry about the Games! You'll be fine. Of course we all need to practice. But by game day —"

"No." Snow shook her head. That wasn't it. She knew she wasn't exactly the fiercest competitor — it was always so much more fun to see someone else win — but she wasn't afraid to try. She was afraid of something much scarier.

Snow hiccuped and felt Ella's arm across her shoulders. She hadn't realized she was trembling.

"You can tell us," Ella coaxed.

"We're your friends." Rose nodded, wiping a tear

from Snow's cheek with her sleeve. "You can always tell us anything."

With another hiccup Snow finally managed to say what was really bothering her. "It's my stepmother, Malodora. She's been watching me — I can feel it. And I've been having nightmares."

Rapunzel and Ella exchanged looks.

"It's that mirror," Snow went on between hiccups. "She sees me in it. It turns her against me!" Snow hadn't wanted to burden her friends with all this, but it felt good to finally tell somebody what was bothering her.

"I just don't understand. She is so mean to me. I think she's . . . jealous!" Snow finally put it into words. "She didn't understand that people were nice to me because I was nice to them." Snow slumped in her seat with a final hiccup, exhausted.

Her friends looked at her with big eyes, waiting to hear more.

"So I ran away," Snow said, wiping the applesauce off her chin. "I knew Malodora was going to put a spell on me like she did my father. So I ran, and ended up here — with my dwarves." Snow took a deep breath and let the sight of the peaceful cottage kitchen comfort her. She felt her breathing get closer to normal and the warmth of her friends' hands on hers. "I guess

I've been pretty safe here." She sighed. "I felt her watching me for a while, but then it stopped. Maybe if I'm not in Malodora's way, she doesn't hate me so much. But lately, ever since they announced the Games, she's been looking in that mirror again. She's been watching me. And I've been having nightmares." Snow shuddered. "Horrible nightmares!"

"Do you think Malodora sends them?" Ella asked. "My stepmother, Kastrid, is awful, but at least she doesn't have magical powers."

"Do you think she can see us now?" Rapunzel narrowed her eyes and glared around the room.

"When she's looking I can feel it," Snow explained. "It feels like a chill — like someone is sneaking up behind me. And sometimes I feel icy fingers on my neck."

Rose looked like she might cry. "How awful!"

"Hic!" Snow's hiccups returned. She picked up a nearly empty jar of applesauce from the table and clinked a stray spoon around the bottom, looking for a last bite. "That's why I can't go to the Games. She's already watching me. If I get in her way, she'll do something awful, I just know it!

"Hic. She might use a spell. Hic. She might never let my father come home. Hic. Or she might hurt the dwarves. Hic. Hic. Hic. Besides, I just freeze in front of her. If she's a judge at the Games, I won't be any help to anyone."

"You are always a help, Snow, to all of us." Rapunzel pried the applesauce jar out of Snow's porcelain hands.

Rose and Ella nodded as they quickly cleared away the remaining jars and spoons.

"We can get through this," Rose said.

"Together!" Ella added, starting to work the pump for the sink. "We can get through anything together."

Rose took over the pump, and Ella sat down on the low bench next to Snow. "Look how we got around *my* evil stepmother." Ella smiled.

"We won't let anything happen to you," Rapunzel said. "I promise." She shook out a flour sack towel with a snap. "And I promise you something else, too. We are going to beat Malodora and her Grimm girls. For Princess School, and for you!"

Feeling better than she had in days, Snow got to her feet and hugged her friends. Maybe she *could* face her stepmother if she didn't have to do it alone — if she had Rose, Ella, and Rapunzel beside her.

While Snow helped Rose and Ella finish washing and drying the applesauce dishes, Rapunzel got comfortable by the hearth scratching out game plans on the slate with a charred stick.

In the cozy firelight, Snow didn't notice that it was getting dark outside. And over the happy chatter of her friends, she didn't hear the low humming of the dwarves' voices as they made their way home.

"Ho, ho!" exclaimed Mort as he threw open the cottage door. "Where's our Snow?" he called. But he stopped short when he saw the four girls in the kitchen. Then his already-cheerful face broke into a wide grin.

Hap clapped his hands together and danced around excitedly, catching Wheezer's hands and pulling him into the jig. "Company! We have company!" he cried.

"More mouths means more dishes!" Gruff groused.

Peeking over Gruff's shoulder, Meek waved a single stubby finger at Snow and her three friends before disappearing again behind Gruff's huge backpack.

Taking charge like he usually did, Mort gently elbowed Hap and Wheezer out of the way and stepped up to Ella.

"Introductions!" he declared out of the corner of his mouth. While Mort took Ella's hand and bowed, Hap and Wheezer fell in line behind him, followed by a reluctant Gruff and, finally, Meek.

"Oh." Ella giggled when Mort kissed her hand. "I'm not really royalty. Not yet, anyway."

Mort looked at the tiara on Ella's head and raised his eyebrows.

"This is Ella," Snow jumped in.

"Oh, yes, the belle of the ball." Mort nodded. "And this beauty must be Briar Rose." Mort kissed Rose's hand next before moving on to Rapunzel. "And you are the maiden in the tower, I presume?"

"Rapunzel," she said, introducing herself. "We've heard all about you, too."

"Ah . . . ah . . . ah'm Wheezer," Wheezer managed to put in before burying his face in a handkerchief.

"And this is Gruff and Hap and, behind that chair is Meek," Mort added.

"That's only five," Rose counted. "Aren't there seven of you?"

Crash! A sturdy wooden wheelbarrow suddenly plowed into the room and rolled onto its side, spilling a sixth dwarf onto the floor, but not waking him.

"Nod," Rose said knowingly.

"And you must be Dim." Ella put out her hand to the dwarf driving the wheelbarrow. The little man looked at it blankly for a moment and then handed her his backpack.

The four girls burst out laughing, and Snow felt warm all over. She hadn't expected to be introducing her friends to the dwarves today. Now, with the cottage filled with so many of her favorite people, thoughts of her stepmother felt far away. And everyone seemed to be enjoying one another.

Rose helped Nod find a comfortable chair to doze in while Rapunzel loaded Dim into the wheelbarrow and pushed it back out of the kitchen. Mort and Ella looked like they were deep in conversation. Hap was still dancing with a sneezing Wheezer, and Gruff's wrinkled forehead looked a little smoother than usual as he took a seat at the table, ready for his evening meal.

"Oh." Snow put her hand to her mouth. She had forgotten all about supper.

"Don't you worry about supper," Mort said, patting Snow on the shoulder. "You haven't been yourself lately, my dear, and time with friends is just what you need. Besides," he added, placing a chubby hand on his round belly and giving Ella a sideways look, "you might even say we're a little *too* well fed. We'll get our own supper."

"Hmph." The furrow in Gruff's brow returned as he slid back off the bench. "And do our own dishes, too, I suppose," he muttered. But the rest of the dwarves seemed thrilled to dip into the larder and come up with something to eat.

"Stay for supper!" Hap called to the girls as he scooped flour into a big wooden bowl.

"Ah-chood." Wheezer nodded, seconding the motion and spraying flour all over Nod.

"Please?" Meek said faintly from under the bench where he'd been drumming out a rhythm with a pair of forks.

"I wish I could," Rapunzel said. "I have to get back

to my tower before Madame Gothel suspects something."

"And I have chores," Ella moaned.

Snow thought she saw Ella's eyes following Hap as
he gleefully tossed two apples, a potato, and a half a
loaf of bread into the pot of water hanging over the
fire.

Rose glanced at the setting sun and bit her lip. "It's
getting late. My parents will be worried sick," she said.
"I told them we might have practice for the Games,
but they'll be expecting me now. And they might send
out a search party if I don't show up soon."

"Yes, yes." Mort nodded like a teeny grandfather.
"Mustn't worry the parents." Mort walked the girls to
the door, bowing and kissing their hands again. The
rest of the dwarves had erupted into a raucous song
about hasty, tasty vittles. They yelled good-byes, blowing kisses between verses.

Snow couldn't keep a smile off her face as she
stood beside her funny family and watched her good
friends disappear down the path. Maybe everything
would be all right after all.

Chapter Eight
A Less-Than-Perfect Practice

The sky was pink with morning sun as Ella trotted onto the large field where the princesses were holding their practices. A quartet of pavilions — two for each school — had already been set up on the field to house equipment and the official rule scrolls of the Games. Though the Grimms practiced on the same field, they were scheduled to use it at different times.

Ella had gotten up and started her chores before the rooster had even rolled out of his nest that morning, but she was still late. The field was already bustling with princesses crowded around scribes scribbling names on sign-up scrolls. Ella gave a quick wave to Rose and a pale, but smiling, Snow, and hurried over to Rapunzel, who was directing traffic. She hoped she wasn't too late to put her name on the list for something good.

"Once you have signed up, please report to your

captains for warm-ups!" Rapunzel barked. "We have to get in some playtime before hearthroom." She turned to Ella. "So, what are you going out for? Unicornshoes? Spinning Straw into Gold? Maze to Grandmother's?"

Ella wasn't sure what she wanted to do.

"Spinning is out for you, Rose," Snow said gravely. Her skin was still a little splotchy around her mouth, but she looked a lot better than yesterday. The others agreed Rose should stay away from sharp objects — especially spindles. Ever since the pinprick that brought on Rose's sleepy episode before the Coronation Ball, her friends were nearly as protective of her as her parents.

Ella knew she didn't want to do Spinning, either — it was too much like the drudgery she had to do at home. The Delicate Touch competition might be okay, or the Gingerbread Man Chase. Surely she could catch a cookie. But could she catch it before a Grimm girl? Ella wanted to be sure she could do more than just play. She wanted to win.

Ella was sure that her classmates had the talent. And she was sure they could win without the terrible cheating tactics of the Grimm girls or the help of Hagatha and Prunilla, who had gotten a decree from home excusing them from participation.

Good riddance, Ella thought. *The Princess School team is better off without them.*

Lost in thought, Ella almost fell over when Rapun-

zel nudged her toward a page holding a large feathered quill. "You and Rose should do the Lace Race,"
she said. "We need a strong team."

The Lace Race! That will be perfect, Ella thought. She
imagined running beside Rose with their inside legs
tightly bound together with several pieces of delicate
lace. *We'll be a great team. All we have to do is work together.*

"Oh, I wish I was on Ella's team," a nearby princess
said quietly to her friend. Ella waited for the admiring
girls to step aside politely so she could sign up.

She smiled at Rose as she gave her name to the
scribe. But Rose didn't smile back.

She must be nervous about the Games, Ella told herself. She couldn't blame her. There was more than just
the trophy at stake now. They needed to win for Snow.
While Ella truly believed they could win the Games,
she had no idea how it was going to happen.

The competition was going to be tough. The princesses would have to deal with elbowing and tripping
and cheating, but Ella could only imagine what the
Grimm girls would have to face from their headmistress
if they lost. Malodora looked like she would revel in
doling out punishments, and after what Snow had told
them last night . . . Ella shuddered. Even if they didn't
win, Ella was grateful she would be playing on the
Princess School team.

"Oh, Ella, are you going out for Lace Race, too?"

An elegant Sash sidled up to Ella, looking admiringly at her tiara.

Wow. Ella smiled back at the other girls, unsure what to say. She had never had so many people trying to be her friend! Luckily Rapunzel intervened.

"We only need one more team for Lace Race. But I'm looking for a few princesses who are good at guessing. Who wants to play Guess the Little Man's Name?"

"I can do that," the Sash replied.

"And we need some hearty souls to join me on the team for Full Contact Maypole." Rapunzel pointed the way to another scribe, and seven well-postured princesses followed her orders. Enough for a team.

"Maypole is one of the toughest events of the Maiden Games." Rapunzel shook her head and talked in low tones to Rose, Ella, and Snow. "It almost always goes to the Grimm side. But this year *I'll* be playing." Rapunzel winked and scurried off to make sure her team got signed up properly.

"What are you going out for, Snow?" Ella asked, trying to distract her friend. The pale girl hadn't hummed a note yet that morning. Though she put on a brave face, Ella knew she was still nervous.

"I guess I'm doing Ball Fetch. Rapunzel says all I have to do is ask a frog to retrieve a ball from the bottom of a spring. The Grimm witches use threats. But Rapunzel says I have a way with animals."

"You do." Ella nodded. Ball Fetch was the perfect game for Snow!

"Animals love you," Rose added.

"Well, I love them, you know." Snow smiled for the first time all morning, then pulled her cloak tighter around her neck.

In the center of the field, Astrid Glimmer, the Crown captain, put a large horn to her lips and produced a most undignified sound. All the girls scattered on the field looked up as she began an announcement. "My royal teammates. We have a full roster for each of the events." Several girls applauded politely. "Let the practice commence!"

Each captain held up a large banner on a pole, indicating which event she would direct. The princesses walked in orderly fashion to their various groups. Ella and Rose's event wasn't up yet, so they stood on the sidelines watching the other girls.

She was no expert, but Ella could tell things were off to a rocky start.

The Unicornshoe throwers were awful. The first girl to try a toss couldn't get the U-shaped shoe even close to the spiraled horn sticking out of the ground. The second girl spun around for speed and ended up throwing the shoe behind her, whacking one of the Maypole players in the shin. As the Maypole player limped off the field with the back of her hand held to her forehead, trying not to swoon, the thrower fell to her knees and begged forgiveness.

On other parts of the field, things were even worse.

"I'm exhausted," one of the Maze runners complained. She'd barely made it halfway to Grandmother's House when she fell to the ground in a heap and yelped as she landed on a tiny toadstool.

"I'm hungry," Gretel cried, watching the Gingerbread Man run into the woods.

"Princesses, please!" Rapunzel yelled so loudly that every girl on the field stopped and looked at her.

If Ella didn't know better, she would have been frightened of her friend. Rapunzel stood with her hands on her hips. Her coiled hair made her appear taller than most of the older girls. And the look on her face said quite clearly, "Don't mess with me."

"Heed my words. We must all do our royal best. While we will always demonstrate good conduct and sportsprincessship, we will never get anywhere if we give up before we begin. We need practice! Practice is the key to winning. I want to see you all working harder and doing your best. Yes, your gloves will get dirty and your dresses will get stained. But we must endure if we want to win!"

Everyone stared at Rapunzel. Ella knew her friend

had the best of intentions, but this drilling wasn't doing any good. The princesses looked like cornered kittens. No one made a sound.

Suddenly the silence was broken by a loud buzzing and crackling. Ella looked up and gasped. In the sky above the field, two smoky messages slowly appeared behind a pair of Grimm witches riding broomback: BEAT THE BLOOMERS! DOWN WITH CROWNS!

Chapter Nine
Smoke Choke

Thick green smoke drifted down and settled over the stunned princesses on the field. Rapunzel coughed. Ugh! As if the sky taunts weren't bad enough, the smoke they were written in smelled *horrible* — a cross between rotten eggs and kitchen slop.

The satin sleeve covering Rapunzel's nose didn't keep her eyes from watering. On the sidelines Snow, Ella, and Rose breathed into their capes. Through her tears Rapunzel saw the two witches who had left the messages howling on their broomsticks.

"You think you're crying now — just wait until Game day!" one of them spat. As the smoke cleared, the witches flew away, growing smaller and smaller in the distance until they looked like tiny, irritating gnats.

Rapunzel uncovered her face and looked around the field. Everywhere novice princesses were coughing into lacy handkerchiefs and dabbing their eyes. It was clear that practice was over even before the ten-minute trumpet sounded, alerting them school would soon begin. The girls rushed off the field, relieved.

"After school we'll pick up where we left off," Rapunzel called. "Meet right here!"

Watching her classmates flee, Rapunzel suddenly had an awful thought. *What if it's the practice they're trying to get away from and not just the stench?*

Lost in thought and oblivious to the smell, Rapunzel walked slowly behind the others. She had to find a way to get her classmates to enjoy practice, to try harder, to want to win as much as she did. Reaching inside her pocket she felt the small, smooth hand mirror she always kept with her so she could communicate with Val over at the Charm School for Boys. That was it! She would flash Val a message to meet her in the stables at lunch. He would have some good ideas for inspiring the princesses. Feeling decidedly better, Rapunzel skipped the rest of the way up the steps.

Whatever was in the nasty green smoke seemed to have colored the mood at Princess School. Unlike yesterday, the girls were quiet. They were not passing small scrolls or whispering excitedly about the Games. In fact, nobody was talking about the Games at all — it was as if they thought that if the competition wasn't mentioned, it might just disappear. Not even Snow and Ella were talking. Rose seemed positively wilted.

Maybe the smoke was a spell, Rapunzel thought. If it was, it was a good one. Princess School didn't stand a chance at the Maiden Games without any enthusiasm. The closer lunch got, the more anxious Rapunzel was to talk to Val.

It felt like a lifetime before the trumpeters finally sounded the horns. When they did, Rapunzel was off like a fox fleeing a hunting party. She raced down the hall, slipping on the polished stones and sliding out the front door and down the steps. She arrived at the stables out of breath.

Since it was lunchtime, she and Val would have the stables to themselves.

"I'm so . . . glad . . . you're here," Rapunzel panted at Val.

He was sitting on a bale of hay in their regular stall. When he saw Rapunzel, his mouth spread into a grin. "I told you I would be! Have I ever let you down?"

"Not yet." Rapunzel slumped down next to the prince.

"Tell me everything," Val said. "We smelled something over at Charm. Everyone's saying it's the Grimms' choke smoke!"

"Yep." Rapunzel finally caught her breath. "They wrote us a few messages this morning."

"On broomsticks?" Val's eyes were wide.

Rapunzel nodded and told him all about the terrorizing witches. Val's eyes got bigger and bigger. He was enjoying the story so much Rapunzel couldn't help laying it on a little thick. "We could barely see to get off the field," she finished, shaking her head. Then she remembered the real trouble — the pouting princesses.

"But that's not the worst of it," she said, getting serious. "Even before the Grimms came around, the practice was terrible! No matter how much I yelled, nobody wanted to work harder."

"So you have your work cut out for you." Val said.

"I'm pretty sure we can take the Delicate Touch competition," Rapunzel said. "Princesses have it over witches in that category every time, if you ask me."

Val nodded as Rapunzel went on. "Grimms can't seem to touch that lace tapestry softly no matter what tricks they try. They tear the ancient fabric practically every time. Snow's going to do the Ball Fetch, so that's in the bag. And even though we haven't practiced it yet, Lace Race should be all sewn up." Rapunzel was beginning to ramble, but Val was listening intently.

"We don't have anyone to compete in the Apple Bob. We didn't even put it on the roster. There is just no convincing a princess to willingly get her head wet.

And we might as well just give Grimm the Guess the Little Man's Name and the Gingerbread Man Chase. Oh! If you could have seen the mess around the Maypole!"

Talking even faster, Rapunzel described the tangle of streamers and the toppled girls that were the result of Full Contact Maypole practice. "We were supposed to just walk through it — to get the feel of it. All we need is to get one member of our team to circle the pole ten times without losing hold of a ribbon attached to the top. During the actual Games, another team will be trying to wind their ribbons in the other direction — and keep us from winding ours. But we can't even get it right when we're all alone. I was yelling so loud I'm surprised you didn't hear me." Rapunzel rolled her eyes. "And I practically lost my voice trying to get a few girls to pick up the pace during the Maze to Grandmother's House run-through.

"Honestly, if I don't get this team going, we are going to stink worse than the choke smoke!"

When Rapunzel finally finished ranting, the stable fell silent except for the occasional horse blowing breath or pawing the straw-covered floor. Val squinted a little and tilted his chin toward the peak of the vaulted ceiling. It was a look Rapunzel recognized — he was thinking *hard*.

"So?" Rapunzel said impatiently.

"I think you need to tell them they're doing great," Val said slowly.

"But they're not!" Rapunzel cried, exasperated. Hadn't Val listened to a single word she'd said?

"Listen to me," Val said calmly. "They need encouragement. Tell them they are fantastic — better than you imagined. Tell them the Golden Ball is as good as yours."

"I would be lying." Rapunzel scowled. Obviously Val was not going to help her out on this one.

"Rapunzel," Val said, putting a hand on her shoulder, "you know you are my best friend. But once in a while you are too tough, even on me. Imagine how the princesses feel. They are used to a certain amount of pampering. You can't force them to get better. You have to make them believe they can. And you have to make them want to do it . . . for Princess School and for you."

Rapunzel wasn't sure what to say. She hated when Val used his kingly speech voice on her. But she couldn't really argue with what he'd said. For a long moment she looked up at the rays of sunlight slanting through the rafters and watched the dust motes settle. "I better get back," she said at last, heading out of the stall.

"Just think about it," Val called after her. "Okay?"

"Okay," Rapunzel replied, pushing open the stable door.

"Promise?" Val said, coming after her.

Rapunzel sighed. Val was a good match for her, sometimes too good. "Promise!" she yelled, breaking into a run. She was already thinking about it, and by the time the doors to Princess School whooshed open to greet her, she knew what she would do.

Chapter Ten
On the Right Path

When the trumpeters sounded the end of the day, the lump in Snow's stomach suddenly felt bigger. She gathered her texts and scrolls together and made her way through the crowded corridors to her velvet-lined trunk to drop off her things and get her practice pantaloons. Then she headed into the princess powder room to change.

Inside, it was crowded. The lace-curtained changing compartments were all occupied, and the girls who already had on their pantaloons and short gowns were bustling in front of the dressing table mirrors, pinning their hair up. The girls moved slowly. Nobody seemed eager to get onto the practice field.

"I wish we didn't have another practice," said Genevieve, the Goose Girl, as she secured a final strand of hair. "My eyes have just stopped watering from that horrible smoke. My handkerchief is filthy!"

"Ready to go, Snow?" said a voice beside her. It was Rose, already in pantaloons and practice-appropriate hair. Ella appeared a moment later from behind a compartment curtain.

"I still have to change," Snow said, slipping into the compartment Ella had just come out of. As she pulled her high-collared gown off over her head, she took a deep breath.

Everything is going to be fine, she told herself. But her words didn't help. She was grateful to her friends for trying to help her get through this. But her heart was still filled with dread.

Ella peeked behind the curtain. Her hair was already in a neat bun, and her tiara sparkled beautifully. "Almost done?" she asked. "We don't want to be late!"

"Our captain says it's our job to set a good example," Rose said with a mock-serious expression.

"Indeed." Ella sighed.

Flanked by her friends, Snow followed the other princesses out onto the practice field. Snow spied Rapunzel on the other end of the playing field, in a huddle with the other coaches.

"Let's gather over here!" Astrid Glimmer called, motioning the princesses toward the Maypole. Slowly the reluctant group of girls moved toward the pole.

"I know this morning's events were a challenge,

and, uh, kind of smelly," Rapunzel began. "But you are a great bunch of princesses with a great deal of talent." She looked over the group in front of her.

"Lisette, the straw you spun this morning may have turned into butterscotch and not gold. But butterscotch is the right color . . . and it was delicious! And even though you didn't catch the Gingerbread Man, Gretel, you got back up after you tripped on the button he lost, and that showed determination!"

Snow noticed some of the princesses looking at one another — this was not the speech they expected, especially from Rapunzel.

"I just know that if we keep practicing and work together, we can win the Golden Ball!"

The girls were silent as they looked at one another doubtfully.

"We can do it!" shouted Antonella Printz, the Sash captain.

"Let's hear it for Princess School!" Astrid Glimmer added, clapping her hands over her head.

Tiffany Bulugia patted several of her fellow Robes on the back.

"Maybe we can," said a Sash quietly.

"I suppose it's possible," said a Crown.

Murmurs of hope began to move through the group. The princesses were finally ready to practice.

Within minutes, mock competitions were being played out all over the field. Josephine Crest made it through the Maze to Grandmother's House on her second try. Vishalia Lith actually hooked a unicorn-shoe around the spiral stake without hitting anyone. And Lisette Iderdown spun three pieces of straw into solid gold!

Rapunzel and the other captains moved from event to event, offering words of praise and encouraging the girls to keep practicing. Snow could tell that their new strategy was working. The teams were working hard, but also laughing and talking together. Snow sighed. She wished she felt like laughing, too.

"Okay, Hoppy," Snow said quietly to her Ball Fetch practice frog. "I would really love it if you could hop over to that spring and retrieve that ball for me."

"Ribbit, ribbit!" Hoppy replied. Then he quickly hopped off toward the water.

"How's your frog doing?" Ella called. She and Rose were at the next event over, tying their legs together with delicate ribbons of lace.

"Just fine!" Snow called back with a wave. But as she watched the small frog with a large wart on one side of his face hop back toward her, she felt a familiar icy chill run up her spine.

Snow looked around in alarm. She didn't expect to

see anything. She never did. But just then the sky darkened and a swarming flock of Grimm girls swooped down to the ground. They were here to practice!

No sooner had the witches landed than the cowering princesses from the morning returned as well. A group of Sashes huddled together on the edge of the Unicornshoes course, and a few Robes even ran into the maze to flee.

"Just ignore those nasty bats!" Rapunzel shouted. But nobody seemed to hear her — the princesses were too busy staring at the black-clad, pointy-hatted girls whose faces showed nothing but scorn.

"That's Hortense Hegbottom," Snow heard Rose whisper to Ella. Sure enough, Hortense was making a big show of stomping all over the field in her giant black boots, smashing every buttercup and dandelion.

"Are those cleats?" Goldilocks whispered to a girl next to her.

Snow shivered. Lucinta Pintch was staring at her through narrowed eyelids, and a chilling wind blew over the field.

Am I the only one who feels those cold gusts? Snow wondered. As she watched a large group of witches set up for Full Contact Maypole, she heard a whooshing sound overhead. A witch dressed from head to toe in silver and white was still flying in the sky. The hem of her dress was cut in jagged points that resembled icicles.

When she swooped low, Snow could see her strange, light-colored eyes, shiny like the blade of a sword.

"That's Violet Gust!" Eugenia Oak whispered, unable to keep the fear out of her voice. "She's won the Apple Bob for the last three years. When she's finished retrieving her apples, the water in the tub is like ice, and the drops on her face actually freeze!"

Snow wasn't sure if Eugenia was exaggerating or not, but just looking at Violet sent a whole new set of shivers up her spine. Though she hadn't said anything to her friends, the Apple Bob kept popping into her head. She was fascinated by it and knew there was no princess signed up to compete. But if Violet was involved, Snow knew she had better steer clear.

"Snow, you're shaking!" Rose said gently, coming up beside her and taking her friend's hand. "Don't worry. We're here with you."

Snow nodded, only slightly comforted by her friend's words. The princesses *were* standing together against the Grimms, but Malodora was only after *her*!

"Come on, everyone, back to practice!" Antonella called, herding the girls back to their various mock competitions. Still looking over their shoulders at the Grimms, the princesses resumed what they were doing before the witch flock landed.

Overhead, Violet swooped by again and again. Suddenly snow began to fall on the field!

Mayhem erupted almost immediately. The girls practicing Unicornshoes slipped when they threw, landing hard on their bustles. The princesses chasing the Gingerbread Man were sliding around so much they had no chance of catching the speeding cookie. Even Ella and Rose, usually a sure-footed Lace Race pair, tripped often on the icy ground.

Madame Garabaldi, the Bloomers' strict hearthroom teacher, emerged from one of the Princess School pavilions and crossed her arms over her chest. "Violet Gust!" she bellowed. "Come down here this instant!"

To Snow's surprise, Violet landed in front of the strict hearthroom teacher in less than two seconds.

"You know very well that magic is allowed neither at the Games nor the practices." Madame Garabaldi looked around at several other witches. "If I see any additional signs of magic or spells, you will forfeit the Golden Ball, per the rules set forth in the Maiden Games Regulations scroll."

Madame Garabaldi looked pointedly at both Violet and Hortense, who glared right back but remained silent.

"Now, I suggest you busy yourselves practicing," Madame Garabaldi finished. "The Games will be upon all of us shortly."

Snow watched as her teammates returned to practicing for the third time. Since Hoppy had already retrieved the ball for her, she decided to watch her friends for a few minutes. Rose's and Ella's legs were securely bound together with five pieces of lace, yet they moved around the course as gracefully as a single princess. Even in the face of a pair of heckling Grimm girls — one with a tremendous hooked nose and another with a humped back — they maintained an amazingly serene composure.

"I'd like to see the two of you *fly* with your legs tied together," Hooknose guffawed as she and her teammate tied their legs together to practice.

Rose and Ella ignored the taunt, but a moment later Ella's tiara started to slide off the top of her head. She caught it just in time, but reaching for it threw the girls off balance and they tumbled to the grass. Hump and Hook broke into a new fit of cackles.

"Can't you just take that thing off for practice?" Rose asked a little huffily.

"Uh, sure, I guess," Ella replied with a shrug. She took the tiara off and handed it to Snow. Without the distraction of the tiara, Ella became even more graceful, and she and Rose practically ran through the course. But before they got back to the finish line, a hoarse whisper echoed in Snow's ear.

"You must be Snow White," the voice hissed. "Headmistress Malodora is correct, as usual. You *are* as pale as ice."

Snow was so startled she nearly dropped Ella's tiara. Whirling around, she found herself face-to-face with Violet Gust herself.

"But you don't seem nearly as hard, or as sharp," Violet continued with a leer.

Snow was desperately searching for a reply when her friends were suddenly by her side, flanking her and forcing Violet to take a step back.

"Don't you have some practicing to do?" Ella asked.

"You must, since you won't be allowed to use your nasty magic," Rose added, looking Violet in the eye.

Violet's strange, sharp eyes glinted, and she turned up her pointed chin before flouncing off toward the Maypole.

Just before the end of the princesses' practice, the witches hopped on their broomsticks and swooped away like a murder of startled crows, leaving the princesses in peace. With the field to themselves, Astrid Glimmer and Antonella Printz brought out a giant tub from the equipment pavilion. It was filled with water, and several red apples bobbed on the surface.

"The Apple Bob has never been our competition," Antonella admitted to the group of girls that Rapunzel had gathered. "Princesses do not usually enjoy submerging their heads."

A low grumble rumbled through the crowd, and Snow knew why. *Usually* was an understatement. She had never met a single princess who would bob for an apple. Since the announcement of the Games, princesses had been gossiping about who might be willing to do it.

"Do we have a volunteer to try the first bob?" Antonella asked sheepishly.

"You love apples," Ella whispered to Snow. "Why don't you try it?"

Snow didn't respond. Her eyes were fixed on the round copper tub. She had to admit, the shiny fruits bobbing on top of the water were appealing. Slowly she got to her feet. Kneeling in front of the tub, she dove right in, soaking her entire head. A few seconds later she emerged with a shiny red apple in her teeth.

The princesses erupted with a rousing cheer. Snow was a natural. For the first time in years Princess School had a competitor for the Apple Bob!

Chapter Eleven
Games Day

The day of competition finally dawned. As Rose made her way to the stables, she admired the beautiful arena set on the grassy field beneath the pale morning sky. Over the past few days, school groundskeepers had transformed the practice field in honor of the Games.

There were now more than a dozen pavilions, each with colorful flags flying from its peaked corners. A long row of food booths took up one end of the field — some pink, gold, and purple, others gray, black, and a putrid green. While the novice princesses handed out fruit drinks and sweet and savory pastries, the Grimms offered newt stews and mud cocktails. The playing field was marked with lines showing where each competition would take place, with the Maypole at one end and the Maze to Grandmother's House at the other. The Gingerbread Man Chase took place on a trail that ran through and around various parts of the arena, and the judges' thronelike seats were lined up in a booth along the center of the field, where the more portable competitions would be held. Finally, at the edge of the field, looming over everything, was the Hall of Mirrors, a spooky exhibit prepared by the Grimm School each year.

Though some of the meeker princesses were too afraid, most dared to enter the Hall of Mirrors, and secretly enjoyed it. More or less like a maze, the Hall consisted of all kinds of mirrors that could make you look bigger, smaller, fatter, or taller . . . and multiplied visitors' reflections so that they appeared in several places at once. A few of the mirrors were even rumored to be enchanted.

Rose shivered as she walked past the Hall of Mirrors. She wasn't as spooked as she was excited. The entrance was shaped like the mouth of a giant, mythical beast — its jagged teeth nearly skimmed the heads of the girls who nervously stepped inside. Ever since she'd heard about the Grimms' tradition of setting it up for the Games, Rose had wanted to go see it for herself. But at the moment she didn't have time. She had promised Snow and Ella she'd meet them in the stables as soon as she arrived.

In the stables, Ella sat with a pale and shivering

Snow in a maize-colored stall. Rose tried not to frown when she saw that Ella was wearing her tiara. Didn't she *ever* take that thing off?

"She's here, and she knows I am, too," Snow said, her dark eyes brimming with tears.

Rose sat down and took Snow's hand. "There are loads of people out there," she said soothingly. "Malodora won't hurt you in a place this public."

"We'll stay with you the whole time," Ella added.

Snow wiped her cheeks and sighed. "I suppose I can't stay in here forever," she admitted. "Even though I'd like to." She looked at her friends, took a deep breath, and got to her feet.

Linking arms, the three girls headed out of the stables and onto the playing fields. Snow seemed a little shaky, but she put one foot in front of the other alongside Rose and Ella, and they made it to the arena.

"Did you see the Hall of Mirrors?" Rose asked as they walked past a row of food booths.

"I think it might be a good idea to steer clear of it," Ella said, gesturing with her head toward Snow.

One look at Snow's white-as-a-ghost face and Rose wanted to smack herself for even mentioning it. The last thing her friend needed was something else to scare her!

The girls approached the field just as the opening ceremony was ending. Rose would have liked to see it, but knew it would not have done Snow any good to hear her stepmother introduced. Now the Ginger-bread Man Chase was about to begin. It was the first event to start, and often lasted the longest. Rose saw Rapunzel with the rest of the student captains at the starting line. She looked totally focused.

I just hope all our practicing pays off, Rose thought. Stepping between Snow and the judge's seats, Rose glanced toward the thrones. She spotted Malodora and Vermin Twitch immediately. Even at this distance, Rose noticed that Vermin's beady eyes and twitching nose made him look like a rodent. But he was nearly invisible next to Malodora. The woman commanded attention, and not in a pleasant way like Headmistress Bathilde. Malodora was dressed in a high-necked, long-sleeved black gown, with a full-length black cape that billowed behind her in the breeze, glinting purple in the sun. Her steely gaze studied the crowd intently, as if she was looking for something . . . or someone.

Rose steered her friends into a throng of princesses. The less visible Snow was, the better.

"Let's go see what's going on at Unicornshoes," she suggested.

"That's way at the end of the field!" Ella protested. "We don't want to be late for the Lace Race."

"We'll be back in plenty of time," Rose said as trumpeters blasted, announcing the beginning of the

Gingerbread Man Chase. While the wily cookie raced ahead, three witches and three princesses gave chase.

"I heard Rapunzel tell Gretel she couldn't have any sweets for two days before the competition," Ella giggled. "So she'd *really* want to catch him."

Indeed, Gretel was in the lead as the girls dashed after the elusive cookie. But the Gingerbread Man was notoriously fast.

"Go, Gretel!" Rose shouted.

The three girls cheered for their teammate until she disappeared into a thicket of trees. Then they headed over to Unicornshoes. Rapunzel was already there.

"You can do it, Ariel!" Rapunzel shouted loudly from the sidelines. The Grimms and the Princesses were neck and neck, with two shoes left to throw. If Ariel got both of them around the spiral horn, Princess School would win this competition.

A group of Grimms stood on the other side of the course, hissing and spitting at Ariel. Rose had to admire the way Ariel seemed to be ignoring them. If she was bothered by the witches' unsporting manners, she didn't show it. Her gaze never left the spiral horn as she swung her arm, tossing the heavy shoe into the air.

Ca-lunk! It ringed around the horn, then fell to the ground.

The cheering princesses clapped loudly while the witches hissed and booed.

Rapunzel jumped up and down. "Regal!" she shouted. Only one more to go!

Ariel's face showed intensity as she picked up another shoe. The Grimms snickered and hissed even more loudly, but Ariel seemed too focused to hear them. She stared at the spiral horn for a full minute, then threw the shoe.

"Too high!" Rapunzel whispered as the shoe left Ariel's hand. But at the last second the shoe dropped almost directly toward the ground, landing — *CLANK!* — around the horn. Princess School had won Unicornshoes!

The cheering was deafening as the girls congratulated one another with hugs. But a moment later trumpets sounded again. The next event — the Lace Race — was on deck.

"Let's get over there!" Rapunzel said, ushering Snow, Ella, and Rose toward the Lace Race.

"Okay, girls," Rapunzel said to Ella and Rose when they reached the starting line. "I know you're going to win this. Just don't lose concentration."

Rose helped Ella tie the ribbons of lace around their legs. Then, to Rose's relief, Ella handed her tiara to Snow. At least she wasn't going to let the tradition of wearing it ruin their chances of winning.

Ready to compete, Rose and Ella strode over and took their place at the starting line next to sneering

Humpback and Hooknose. The trumpet sounded three short blasts. They were off!

Like a seamless pair, Rose and Ella moved up the course, taking a fast lead. They were such a good match they didn't even need to pause to get in sync — they simply were.

Rose beamed as they slowed their pace a tiny bit to curve around the halfway marker. "We're doing great!" she whispered to Ella. But when she turned, something caught her eye: a group of cheering princesses, including many of the girls who were constantly crowded around Ella.

"El-la, El-la, El-la!" the girls cheered, jumping up and down.

Rose felt her face grow hot. Ella was only half of the team. What about her?

Anger bubbling up inside her, Rose couldn't take her eyes off the girls. And when her foot came down on an uneven section of grass, her ankle turned.

Rose had a split second to recover, but she was so angry, she didn't. She let herself — and Ella — fall instead.

Cackling madly, Hooknose and her teammate scuttled by and crossed the finish line.

While the Grimms chortled and cheered, Rapunzel scowled down at her friends.

"What happened?" she demanded. She glared at Rose. "It looked like you did that on purpose!"

More furious than ever — and partly at herself — Rose struggled to untangle her leg from Ella's.

"I don't know," Ella replied, sounding uncharacteristically angry. Her green eyes flashed at Rose. "Ask *her*."

"I guess you can't win all the time," Rose replied hotly.

"Neither can you, Rose," Ella snapped.

"And you!" Rose practically shouted, turning to Rapunzel. "Can't you think about anything besides winning? We could have been hurt!"

A long trumpet blare echoed across the field, signaling the next event: Ball Fetch. Rose finished untying herself from Ella and stood up.

"I don't have time for this," Rapunzel announced. "I need to get Snow ready for her event." For the first time the girls looked around for their friend.

Snow was nowhere to be found!

Chapter Twelve
Hide-and-Seek

Snow watched Ella and Rose gracefully stride forward, heading down the course with their legs tied together. Next to her, Rapunzel cheered loudly. Snow knew she should be cheering, too. But without Rose and Ella surrounding her, she suddenly felt exposed. She shuddered as the icy-cold feeling snaked up her spine — the fourth or fifth time since she'd woken up that morning. Malodora was watching her. Snow was sure if it. Snow stood stock-still, waiting for the awful feeling to pass. But it just kept getting stronger and stronger, until Snow was shivering in spite of the warm autumn sun.

"You can do it!" Rapunzel shouted, moving up the sidelines of the course. "Keep it smooth. And fast!"

Snow wrapped her cloak tightly around her with the hand that wasn't holding Ella's tiara. Nearby, a group of princesses began to chant Ella's name. "El-la,

El-la, El-la!" In the judges' booth, Malodora suddenly turned her attention toward the Lace Race.

Snow didn't waste any time. As soon as Rapunzel was a reasonable distance away, she fled toward the food booths. Shivering and with her heart racing, she searched for a place to hide.

"Would you like a little newt stew?" hissed a tall, thin witch with a crooked mouth.

Snow ignored her and rushed ahead, desperately searching for a tucked-away corner. Finally she spied a small space in between two booths.

Slumping down on the soft, green grass, Snow dropped the tiara and took a deep breath, waiting for her heartbeat to slow. Her head throbbed, and the memory of last night's nightmare roared through her mind.

She'd been trapped in Malodora's castle, in the dungeon, surrounded by jars of animal body parts and strange herbs. As she sat grinding frog bones into powder, her father's voice called out to her. The voice was everywhere at once, but Snow could not see him. Then Malodora's evil laugh echoed in the dim dungeon, and her father's voice disappeared altogether.

Snow gathered her blue cape around her, covering the sides of her head as she lay her forehead on her knees. She wished more than anything that she could disappear. Her head throbbed mercilessly, and the screaming crowd made her eyes ache. She heard the awful sound of Grimm girls roaring with excitement. Snow lifted her head to listen. Could the Grimms have won the Lace Race?

Snow was barely aware of time passing as she sat between the food booths, wishing the Games were over. And then familiar voices — friendly ones — were suddenly moving in her direction. Looking up, Snow saw Rose, Ella, and Rapunzel standing over her.

Ella sat down immediately, throwing her arms around Snow. "We're so glad you're all right," she cried. "What happened?"

Snow's dark eyes glistened as she gazed at her friends. "I just felt so awful, so exposed out there," she said. "And then that icy feeling came over me. I just had to . . . to get away," she sobbed.

"We lost the Lace Race," Ella said, shooting a not-so-friendly look at Rose.

Snow wiped away a tear. "I thought I heard the Grimms cheering," she said. "How did it happen?"

"We don't have time to talk about that now," Rapunzel said. "We need to get you to your first event, Snow. The Ball Fetch is about to start."

Just then the trumpets sounded, and the girls heard the last call for the Ball Fetch.

Snow's eyes widened. "I . . . I can't," she said. "Malodora will see me."

"We'll stay with you the whole time, Snow," Rose said softly. "We're finished with our event, so we don't have to leave your side for a second."

"I know it's a lot to ask," Rapunzel admitted. "But your team really needs you. We have to win the Fetch if we're going to have a chance at winning the Golden Ball."

Snow was silent for several long seconds.

"Please, Snow?" whispered Ella as she picked up her tiara and placed it on her head.

Snow sniffled, then looked up. "All right," she said. "I'll do it for the three of you."

"That's the spirit!" Rapunzel crowed, already backing away. "I have to get back to the field. But I'll see you over at the competition."

Snow nodded and tried to smile as Rapunzel sped off. Rose and Ella helped Snow to her feet. Snow steeled herself as her friends led her out onto the open field.

Just one step at a time, she told herself as they began to cross the arena. But she could not keep her eyes from darting toward the judges' booth, where Malodora sat surveying the field like a hungry hawk. Her eyes swept the field in one direction, then moved back toward the area where Snow and her friends were.

Snow inhaled sharply and stopped in her tracks like a mouse trying to avoid capture.

"What's wrong?" Rose asked, trying to lead Snow forward.

"Keep moving, Snow," Ella encouraged. "When my stepmother is mean to me, I always try to keep moving."

Snow allowed her friends to pull her forward, but it took every ounce of her will to do so.

I promised, she told herself. *I said I would do the Ball Fetch.*

Finally the girls reached the Ball Fetch area, where Rapunzel was offering a few words of encouragement to the other competing princesses. Half a dozen frogs were lined up, croaking excitedly as they waited for the race to begin.

Rose and Ella led Snow to her position at the starting line. Rapunzel was by Snow's side in a minute.

"Okay, Snow," she said quietly. "They held the start. Now all you have to do is ask Croaky to fetch the ball from the spring for you."

Snow gazed down at Croaky, who seemed to be smiling up at her. Usually such a sight would make Snow feel better. It didn't.

"Why is this taking so long?" boomed a voice from the judges' booth. Malodora. This time the icy shiver sank into Snow's shoulders like talons and snaked its way down her spine, overtaking her completely.

I can't do it! Snow screamed in her head. With one last fleeting look at Croaky, she scrambled to her feet and tore away from the starting line.

Chapter Thirteen
A Slim Victory

For a moment Ella was too surprised to move. She just stood there watching Snow disappear into the crowd, leaving her, Rose, and Rapunzel at the Ball Fetch starting line.

Finally Ella snapped out of it. "I'm going after her!" she announced.

Rapunzel put her hand on Ella's shoulder. "Let me," she said in her serious coach voice. "I need you and Rose to stay here and take Snow's place in the Fetch. Somebody's got to convince Croaky to get that ball."

Ella shook Rapunzel's arm off. Snow had run off faster than a spooked horse, and Ella was really worried.

Besides, she thought, stealing a look at Rose, who avoided her eyes, *the last thing I want to do after the Lace Disgrace is another competition with Rose.* Ella had no idea what the problem was, but Rose was all thorns.

Ella was about to say something when Rapunzel

stopped her. She put one hand on each of her friends' shoulders. "You and Rose are the perfect team — or at least you *can* be. I'll find Snow, then I have to get ready for Maypole. You two can do this."

"Ella doesn't need me," Rose said as she got to her feet. "I'll go look for Snow." Without waiting for a reply, Rose slipped out from under Rapunzel's hand and disappeared in the crowd.

Ella was speechless again. What was going on with her friends?

For a second, Rapunzel looked as shocked as Ella felt. Then she turned, and without a word gave Ella a look before taking off after Rose and Snow. There was no mistaking Rapunzel's meaning. Somebody had to stay and do the Fetch. And that somebody was Ella.

Sighing, Ella looked at the dampish green frog and wished she was the one who had to coax Snow out of hiding instead of this amphibian into fetching. Croaky nabbed a fly with his long, sticky tongue. He had a big belly and looked more interested in a nap than a swim in the spring. Sure, any frog would swim to the bottom of the spring for Snow White. There was just something about Snow that made every creature want to do its best for her — its very best. Well, her best was all Ella could do now.

Lined up at the starting line were five other frogs with girls standing behind them. Suddenly a trumpet blasted, startling Ella, and the other girls crouched down to start convincing their frogs to do their bidding. Ella got on her hands and knees and looked into Croaky's yellow eyes.

"Okay, Croaky," Ella tried to sound firm like Rapunzel and sweet like Snow at the same time. "It's just you, me, and the ball. Let's get it together."

The frog looked back at Ella blankly. He definitely did not look inspired. But then, to Ella's surprise, he leaped off — in the *right* direction!

Croaky was first off the block! Soon the rest of the frogs started hopping, too. Most of them were faster than Croaky and the gap between them narrowed. In no time Lucinta Pintch's large frog was taking the lead, but Croaky took a big leap and landed just ahead of the beefier bullfrog.

On the sidelines a particularly grungy witch furiously scratched at her tangled hair, sending a shower of tiny bugs and moths raining down on the grass. Her friends snickered and nudged her with their sharp elbows. She was trying to distract the frogs with the little insects. And it was working!

Croaky paused to gulp down a mealworm. Another frog competing for Princess School took off in the wrong direction. Lucinta's frog, Bump, was in the lead!

Satisfied with his snack, Croaky hopped back into the race, but he was at least two leaps behind Bump.

"Go, little green guy! You can do it!" Ella encouraged him even though her own hope of winning was fading. Bump's leaps were nearly twice as long as Croaky's. But who knew what would happen when Croaky got to the spring? Maybe he could swim better than he could hop.

It looked like the race was over when Bump suddenly slowed. He was tracking a moth that had fluttered over his head.

Beside Ella, Lucinta jumped up and down on her stick legs, screaming angrily. "You lumpy, bumpy sack of warts! Get in there and get that ball or I'll use your tongue in my next batch of brew!"

Lucinta's frog snapped the moth out of the air and chewed slowly.

"Go!" Lucinta screamed. "Or your tadpoles are toast!"

Bump didn't seem to hear or care. Satisfied with his moth meal, he stayed just where he was, closing his eyes for a little rest.

The Grimm girls' jeering cheers turned to hisses when Croaky hit the water. It looked like he was going to be the winner. Ella looked around for a moment, wishing her friends could see this. Across the field she saw Rapunzel getting ready for Full Contact Maypole. Rapunzel looked back at Ella and shook her head. She hadn't found anyone. *Where was Snow?*

Ella used the time Croaky was submerged to scan the crowd. She saw hundreds of faces, some gnarled and some lovely. But Snow's sweet, pale face was not among them. Not even in the bleachers . . .

Ella looked at the stands again and felt a fleeting hope. All seven of Snow's dwarves were there, waving pink-and-purple Princess School banners. Nod was asleep, his head hanging over the back of his seat. His banner fluttered each time he exhaled, tickling Wheezer's nose and making him sneeze even more uncontrollably than usual. Meek spotted Ella and waved shyly. Ella's heart sank again when she realized for certain that Snow was not with them.

Then Ella noticed something else. In the judges' booth someone was missing. Malodora's throne was empty!

Ella's heart raced. She was terrified for Snow. She had to tell someone, but couldn't leave her spot. Croaky was still diving and more frogs were hitting the water.

Finally Croaky's green head broke the surface. He held a golden ball firmly in his mouth. Proudly he flopped out of the water and spat the ball toward Ella's feet. They'd won! Princesses were jumping up and down all around Ella, circling her and cheering. They didn't understand that she didn't have time for celebrating, and she wasn't in the mood. She was too scared for her friends . . . all of them.

Chapter Fourteen
True Reflections

How do you find someone when you feel lost yourself? Rose wondered. All around her, girls were hurrying toward the noisy crowds already swarming around the Ball Fetch and the Maypole. Rose searched for signs of Snow's dark hair and red lips. She didn't see her, but suspected Snow would be headed in the other direction, anyway — away from the crowd.

Away, she thought. *That's where I'd like to be, too.*

Rose could not remember a time when she'd felt so confused. Usually she knew just what was going on and what to do next. Right now she felt like giving up completely. Girl after girl pushed past her. Grisly Grimm girls sneered at the perfect-looking princess. Some of Rose's classmates smiled. Still there was no sign of Snow.

This is useless! Rose's feelings of defeat turned to

rage in her head, then back to desperation. *What is wrong with me? Even if I find Snow, how will I be any help?*

When she reached the edge of the field, the sound of cheering girls started to fade into the background. Before her stretched an open grinning mouth: the Hall of Mirrors. Rose was drawn closer toward the entrance.

I just need a minute to think, she told herself as she stepped inside.

Though the light within the cavernous pavilion was dim, the reflections in the many mirrors were dazzling. Multiple Roses gazed back at the true Rose, reflecting her lost expression again and again.

"You don't look like you have any answers!" Rose told one image. "And you!" She turned to scold herself in another mirror. "What are you looking at? You aren't helping anyone by just thinking of yourself, you know." Rose stared at her reflection as the words she had just spoken sank in. Their unvarnished truth stung Rose and tears sprang to her eyes.

Following the path toward larger and more distorted images, Rose let the tears come. She felt sorry for herself, but most of all she felt foolish. At last she understood what she was feeling. It was jealousy. She was jealous of Ella! She was so accustomed to getting all the attention and feeling annoyed with it, that she never expected to be upset when the spotlight shone on someone else.

Am I really so shallow? Rose wondered. She gazed at herself in a huge gold-framed looking glass that made her appear as flat as a carpet. *Am I really going to let this stupid jealousy ruin one of the best friendships I've ever had, and the whole school's chances of winning the Golden Ball?*

Rose stared steadily into a new mirror. She did not like what she saw and she was ready to do something about it. She'd thrown the Lace Race and deserted the Ball Fetch. Even if Princess School still managed to win the Fetch, winning the Maypole *and* the Apple Bob would be crucial.

I'll find Snow, Rose thought. *I'll stop thinking about myself and be a good friend.* But first she had to find her way out of the mirrored hall.

It didn't seem like she had walked very far into the Hall of Mirrors, but as Rose turned corner after corner she didn't see any shafts of light to indicate that the edges of the canvas pavilion were near. Her heart was beginning to race when she came around another bend and saw something that made it stop beating altogether. Malodora!

Rose flattened herself against a wall and peeked around the corner to make sure she hadn't just seen another mirror trick.

She hadn't. Malodora was real.

The evil queen was standing in front of a huge mirror with her arms raised. Her midnight-purple sleeves hung so low they nearly touched the floor. Malodora was murmuring something to herself.

Slowly Malodora lowered her arms. Rose watched as the image in the mirror swirled and changed. Clouds bloomed and disappeared. Lightning flashed. No, wait. That wasn't lightning. It was flashes of light reflected in a tiny fissure crack.

In the mist that swirled on the mirror's surface, Rose thought she could make out a face.

Then a voice boomed, "What may I show you, my queen?"

Malodora's throaty voice echoed eerily in the chamber.

> *Magic mirror before me,*
> *I sense Snow White, but cannot see.*
> *Tell me true where she doth dwell*
> *that I may cast my evil spell.*

When she finished speaking, Malodora held her chin high and waited impatiently for an answer.

Rose shook her head. She felt like she was waking from a nightmare. Only this nightmare was real. Snow was in serious danger. If Rose didn't find her before Malodora did . . .

Rose gasped. She couldn't imagine what would happen!

There was no time to waste. Not waiting to hear what the magic mirror would say, Rose turned as quickly and quietly as she could. She ran two steps, and then — *CRASH!* Her petticoats caught on the mirror behind her, pulling it over. It shattered into a million shards and exposed her to the witch!

Frozen in her tracks, Rose cringed, preparing for the worst. Malodora spun once. Glaring at Rose, she silently lifted her hand. She pointed one daggerlike fingernail directly at Rose. With her other arm, she raised her cloak and brought it swooping down over her head. In a puff of smoke she was gone.

Rose didn't wait for the smoke to clear. She ran full speed, unsure of where she was going. The Hall felt darker, and all around her, figures loomed. She could hear the cackles of Grimm witches echoing everywhere.

Suddenly she came to a dead end. When she turned around, the path she had come down was gone! Mirrors closed her in on all sides. Her reflection was distorted infinitely in every direction.

Awful pinched faces danced in the glass — Lucinta and Violet! The witches taunted her in the smooth glass, sticking out their tongues, wagging their knobby fingers, and cackling maliciously. Rose turned again and again, trying to escape their gaze.

Their faces were too awful to look at — cruel, drawn mouths, green-tinted skin, and nasty eyes. With a jolt, Rose realized the hideous faces in the mirror had changed. Now she was looking at her own green reflection. *She* was a witch!

Rose screamed. A crack zigzagged down one of the mirrors and a new image appeared. It was Snow! She was okay! Rose felt relief wash over her as she watched an image of herself standing with Snow in the sunlight. Holding a juicy-looking apple, Snow smiled sweetly. She opened her mouth for a bite, but the moment the apple touched her mouth Snow fell to the ground and lay completely still.

Rose sank to her knees and hid her face in her hands. "No!" she screamed.

But there was no answer, only silence and reflections she was too frightened to look at.

Chapter Fifteen
Finding Courage

Snow cautiously peeked out at the playing field from underneath the shiny white bleachers. She could see Rapunzel gripping the satin Maypole ribbon tightly in her hand. Rapunzel crouched low to the ground and gave the Grimm witch in front of her a look that Snow recognized: Rapunzel meant business.

Snow couldn't blame her. Even in her terrified state she knew the Maiden Games competition had been fierce. Princess School was still in it to win, but Snow knew if they didn't take Full Contact Maypole, it would all be over for the royals.

"Sprat!" a humpbacked witch snarled at her long-nosed teammate. "You take 'Sparkly' over there and I'll get 'Moldylocks.'" The stooped witch motioned with her pointed chin — first to Astrid and then to Rapunzel.

Snow felt her stomach turn, but Rapunzel didn't even acknowledge the witch's words.

She's probably focusing every bit of her energy on winning, Snow thought admiringly. Rapunzel was the bravest person she knew, and an amazing competitor. Snow, on the other hand, was a coward. She'd run away from Ball Fetch, letting her whole school down!

When the trumpets blasted, Snow could tell that Rapunzel was ready. Eight witches holding ribbons began their counterclockwise charge toward Rapunzel and the other princesses. Snow winced as she witnessed the toughness of the game. This was not like Delicate Touch!

The princesses did not shrink or cower. They stepped lightly and quickly around the witches with their heads held high. But the Grimms were playing dirty.

On one side of the pole, Hortense Hegbottom heaved herself up to stomp on Tiffany's ribbon, shredding and grinding it into the mud. Tiffany was out. A second witch lunged past a princess and then turned and hissed, scaring the princess so badly she dropped her ribbon. It fluttered limply to the grass. That princess was out, too.

Snow could tell that the Grimm strategy was to intimidate the princesses, while the princesses were going for speed. Snow remembered Rapunzel coaching the girls to stay away from the Grimms as much as possible and to focus on circling the pole. "Avoid direct confrontation," she'd told them. But Snow could tell Rapunzel's strategy wasn't working.

Quickly Rapunzel stopped circling the pole and stayed in one place, blocking witches and helping the other princesses make it around. She was thinking on her feet, Snow realized, changing the strategy.

For a moment Snow thought the new plan was really helping. With a leap, Rapunzel jumped over a Grimm girl who had tucked herself into a cannonball aimed right for Rapunzel's legs. Reaching out, Rapunzel hooked the witch's ribbon and pulled it from her grasp. Hump was out.

But so were five princesses! Everything was coming unraveled. Snow could see Rapunzel quickly sizing up the situation and deciding what to do. A second later she started moving again. She met Sprat with a classic skip-trip. Rapunzel made it past, but Sprat kept her ribbon, too.

Dodging and weaving like a jackrabbit, Rapunzel made it four times around the pole without looking up. Snow held her breath. Rapunzel and Astrid were the only princesses still in the game, pitted against four witches!

Make that five. Snow spotted Hortense and her monster boots barreling full speed at Rapunzel. Rapunzel spun to the inside and crashed headlong into Sprat, taking a bony elbow to the shin. Sprat sniggered, but Astrid was there, catching the witch off guard and slipping the ribbon from her hands with a small curtsy.

It was a majestic move, but there was no time for compliments. Side by side, Rapunzel and Astrid wound their way around the pole, facing each new assault as a team. It looked as though they would *both* finish when Rapunzel saw Hortense coming at them like a speeding boulder with teeth.

Rapunzel stepped ahead of Astrid to bear the brunt of Hortense's assault, but the witch stepped aside at the last moment. Astrid stumbled. And just as she fell, Hortense raised a massive boot to stomp on her competitor.

There was nothing Rapunzel could do. You could not turn around and go the other way in Maypole. Luckily, Astrid rolled away just as Hortense's spikes came down. The princess was spared, but her ribbon was lost.

Snow could barely watch. Alone on the field Rapunzel picked up speed. She only had to make it around the pole one more time to win the game. But it wouldn't be easy.

The four remaining Grimm girls focused their evil sneers on Rapunzel and formed a wall of witches. They stopped moving and stood waiting to rip Rapunzel's ribbon from her hand.

Smiling back at them, Rapunzel rounded the pole. She may have been just one girl on the field, but she had grace and agility on her side. And she had something else. Nearly every girl in Princess School was watching, cheering her on. Snow felt sure she was the only princess not yelling!

Snow could almost see the cheering bolster Rapunzel's courage. She stood taller and looked Hortense straight in the eyes. Watching her, Snow felt full of pride. Her friend would not be intimidated!

With a final burst of speed, Rapunzel feinted right, crouched low, and jumped! The witches tried to move as one and tripped. When they attempted to leap and block they all went in different directions, bumping heads and tangling themselves in a mass of ribbons and limbs.

While the Grimms lay on the field hissing and spitting at one another like a ball of writhing snakes, Rapunzel skipped the rest of the way around the pole and finished her lap with a twirl and a bow to the judges. The crowd went wild.

In the judge's box, Vermin Twitch held a megaphone to the end of his quivering snout. "Full Contact Maypole goes to Princess School," he announced flatly in his nasal voice, clearly not very excited. Beside him, a scowling Malodora took her seat.

Snow longed to run from her hiding place and give Rapunzel the hug she deserved. But Malodora was so close she dared not move.

Snow watched Rapunzel look around, searching

for her friends. But before she could spot them she was swept up in a giant hug by her Maypole team-mates.

"We won the Ball Fetch!" Snow heard Astrid yell over the cheers. "If we can just win the Gingerbread Man and the Apple Bob, the Golden Ball will be ours!"

Rapunzel smiled back at Astrid, while under the bleachers two tears trickled down Snow's frozen face. Princess School was so close to taking the Maiden Games — but they would not. And it was all her fault.

Chapter Sixteen
Searching for Snow

"You did it!" Ella joined the pack of princesses hugging Rapunzel. She had run from the Ball Fetch to the Maypole as quickly as she could and had managed to see Rapunzel's victory lap.

"So did you!" Rapunzel was flushed with excitement. She hugged Ella back. "We won!"

"You trounced those witches!" Val appeared out of nowhere. He clapped Rapunzel on the back and tousled her bangs as if she were his jousting steed.

Rapunzel shook him off. "Thanks." She grinned. "It's about time you showed up. Where have you been?" she teased.

"Some of us attend classes during the school day. We don't have time for silly games." Val clicked his heels together, stood up straight, and lifted his nose in the air as if he was trying to smell something distant and not at all pleasant. But he couldn't hold the snobbish stance for long. His smile returned and he leaned closer to Rapunzel and Ella. "Actually, I let Hans Charming best me in fencing so I could sit out and sneak away early. It wasn't easy — Hans can't fence his way out of a coach!"

Ella laughed. Val's eyes were shining. Obviously he was enjoying the win as much as Rapunzel. And even Ella.

Ella had to admit it felt good to win the Fetch — much better than it had losing the Lace Race with Rose. But the thought of Rose — and Snow — brought Ella back to reality.

Rapunzel seemed to read Ella's mind. "The Games aren't over yet," she said, getting serious.

"Do you know where Snow is?" Ella asked.

"I was hoping she was with Rose," Rapunzel replied.

Ella pinched her lips together. "I suppose she could be, but I don't know where Rose is, either."

"Rose is missing?" Val asked, sounding alarmed.

Rapunzel ignored the prince and scanned the crowd. The swarms around the Maypole were beginning to drift away to other parts of the field. "They should be back by now." Rapunzel squinted into the distance. "Unless something happened . . ."

"Malodora wasn't in her box during the Fetch," Ella said, suddenly remembering. Fear shook her voice.

"We have to find Snow. Now." Rapunzel was getting good at giving orders. And Ella was happy to follow them.

"Let's split up," Rapunzel continued. But before she could point Ella in a direction, the Robe captain, Tiffany Bulugia, made a quick curtsy and cut in.

"Rapunzel! Rapunzel! We need you over here!" Tiffany pulled Rapunzel by the arm. She was talking fast. "It's the Gingerbread Man. The competition has been going on for hours. The princesses are running and running as fast as they can, but two of them have fainted from exhaustion!"

Ella watched as Rapunzel was pulled away. Rapunzel glanced back. The look in her eyes was pained.

"Go help the team," Ella yelled. "We'll take care of Snow!"

"And Rose!" Val added with a wave.

Now it was Ella's turn to give orders. "You take that side, I'll take this." She pointed. "Snow won't want to be found, so check *everywhere*."

Val nodded and bowed. Ella didn't wait to see him flourish his hat before she started peeking into every dark corner she could find in the arena. Snow wasn't anywhere. Ella was beginning to lose hope when, crouching low and peering under the bleachers, she heard a sniff. She ducked lower and spotted a pale white elbow. Snow!

Ella crawled beneath the bleachers to join her frightened friend. "Are you okay?" she asked gently.

"They need me." Snow sniffed. "I'm the only one who can do the Apple Bob." The pale girl shook and talked in a whisper. "I want to do it, Ella. But I just can't stand to have my stepmother's eyes on me. I just . . . freeze."

Ella laid her arm across Snow's trembling shoulders. She knew what it felt like to be frightened, but she had never been so scared she couldn't move. "You don't have to do anything, Snow. These are just games. You matter to us more than winning." As she spoke, Ella knew her words were true.

Snow sniffed. "I want to do it, Ella. I really do."

Ella smiled weakly at Snow. She wanted to help her, but how could she give her friend courage?

Suddenly she spotted some familiar red shoes walking past the bottom row of seats. She stuck out her hand and grabbed Red's ankle. Red shrieked.

"Shhh!" Ella hissed.

Red crouched down and looked into the shadows under the seats. "Ella!" She smiled. "Snow!"

"Shhhh!" Ella and Snow hissed in unison, and Ella pulled the cloaked girl under the bleachers with them.

"What is it?" Red whispered. "Are you in trouble? Is it a wolf? Do you need me to call a huntsman?"

"No, nothing like that," Ella explained. "We just need to borrow your riding cape."

"This old thing?" Red asked, shrugging off the large, hooded cloak she always wore. "Gladly! My mother makes me wear this thing everywhere. My real name isn't even 'Red,' you know. It's Scarlet. People started —"

"Thanks," Ella interrupted, taking the cape and pulling it around Snow's shoulders. Red was really nice, but boy, could she talk!

"Oh, that looks good on you!" Red cooed when Ella pulled the hood around Snow's face. "Red is your color! You look totally different. I almost don't recognize you!"

"Perfect," Ella said softly.

Snow managed a weak smile. Beneath her hands Ella felt Snow stop shaking.

"Ready?" she asked.

From deep in the hood, Ella heard Snow's soft, sweet voice.

"Ready."

Chapter Seventeen
Bobbing for Apples

Snow took one small step at a time as she and Ella made their way toward the apple-bobbing area. The Bob would take place right in front of the judges' booth since it was the final event. As they approached, Snow could feel the icy fingers grasping her neck, and her feet slowed. It was only because of Ella's reassuring hand on her arm and the cloak disguise that she kept moving at all.

This hood may not keep Malodora from seeing me, Snow thought, *but it keeps me from seeing her.* Peeking out cautiously, Snow spotted Rapunzel by one of the copper bobbing tubs. At first Rapunzel didn't recognize Snow. She kept glancing around the field with a worried expression. But as they got closer Snow saw a smile spread across Rapunzel's face and she stepped away from the tub to meet them.

"I'm so glad you're all right," she whispered to

Snow. "And that you're here. You can do this, Snow. I just know it."

Snow wished she felt as sure as her friend sounded. As Ella led her over to her apple tub, she seemed to be looking around for someone. It didn't take Snow long to figure out who — Rose. Where was she?

A moan from the Princess School side of the crowd interrupted Snow's thoughts.

"They must really think you're Red," Rapunzel whispered excitedly. "And if they can't tell it's you, the witches won't be able to, either." A sly smile spread across her face. "This could be our biggest secret weapon yet!"

Snow wanted to share in her friend's pleasure, but for some reason she didn't. Unable to help herself, she stole a glance at Malodora. The queen's piercing light blue eyes ran over her like an icy shower, causing Snow to shiver. But a moment later her gaze fell on something else in the stands — the dwarves! They were holding handmade signs, and some of them were waving them like banners in the air. GO SNOW! read Nod's. Only Nod was fast asleep, leaning against a very put-out-looking Gruff. Only the letters OW in the SNOW of Nod's sign were actually legible.

Snow giggled. Her surrogates must have taken the afternoon off to come and cheer her on. And they had even made signs! Meek and Wheezer were laughing and pointing to the Gingerbread Man, who had been caught by a princess but was now being chased again by a very hungry Gretel.

POUNCE, PRINCESSES! declared the sign held in Hap's stubby fingers. Hap and Dim watched the apple-bobbing area with great interest. Mort held his hand over his eyes and peered intently at the field.

Are they looking for me? Snow guessed that they were. And she felt terrible for not really being there . . . even though she was. She watched Hap lift his sign as high as he could, which was barely above the heads of the spectators in front of him. The dwarves may have been small of frame, but they had huge hearts. And they loved her.

"You can do this, Snow," Ella whispered. "We'll be right here with you."

Snow felt the icy feeling drain from her limbs, replaced by a wonderful warmth. It spread from her torso to her fingers and toes. Suddenly Snow knew that she really *could* do it. Her head no longer ached, and for the first time in weeks she felt sure of herself and of what she needed and wanted to do. And no one was going to stop her. Not even Malodora.

Taking a deep breath, Snow stepped away from her supportive friends and lowered the red hood. She was tired of hiding.

"It's Snow White!" came the whispers from the

crowd. And within seconds the whispers were replaced by resounding cheers. The dwarves cheered louder than anyone. "Hey, ho, there's our Snow!"

"Go, Snow!" princesses shouted.

The Grimm girls hissed loudly, glaring at Snow White. From her judge's throne, Malodora continued to stare at Snow coldly. But the edges of her cruel mouth twisted upward in the tiniest hint of a smile.

Snow ignored Malodora completely as she stepped up to her bobbing tub. Thirteen shiny apples danced on the surface.

Her heart racing, Snow waited for the trumpet to sound. She was ready when the blast came, lowering her head toward the water's surface with lightning speed.

Snow pulled out her first apple in fewer than five seconds, then her second and her third. Every ounce of her being was focused on the apples in the tub in front of her. Her whole body tingled with exhilaration. Next to her, Violet the bobbing Grimm witch was retrieving apples just as quickly. The two girls were neck and neck.

Faster, Snow told herself. *You've got to get them faster.*

Behind her, the crowd was cheering like crazy. She heard Hap's voice as she threw herself forward again, trapping an apple against the bottom of the tub almost immediately. After sinking her teeth into the crisp flesh, she came up for air. When she pulled her head out of the bucket, cold water splashed down the front of her dress. Snow ignored it.

"Hey, ho! Go, Snow!" the dwarves cheered in singsong unison.

Snow smiled to herself when the sound of their cheerful voices reached her ears. She was still stunned that they had taken a day off from work to watch the games — to watch *her*. But she had to stay focused on the apples. . . .

Suddenly a strange feeling came over her. The dwarves' voices seemed to fade, and her gaze fell on one particular apple bobbing on the side of the bucket — an apple with one white side and one red one that Snow hadn't noticed before. The apple glinted in the sun. Snow could not take her eyes off it. She had to have that apple.

Chapter Eighteen
Mirror, Mirror

Rose slumped against one of the mirrors that made up her mirror cage and let out another sob. Everything seemed so hopeless. Snow was in trouble, and she was trapped in some kind of cursed reflective cage. Images swam before her — Lucinta's and Violet's sneering faces, Malodora's gnarled, daggerlike fingernail, Snow falling lifeless to the ground, her own desperate face. Malodora's chant echoed in her head, again and again like a broken gramophone.

> *Magic mirror before me,*
> *I sense Snow White, but cannot see.*
> *Tell me true where she doth dwell*
> *that I may cast my evil spell.*

Rose pulled her knees to her chest and lay her head upon them, hoping to shut out the horrible images.

But they played over and over again behind her closed eyelids. There was no escaping them.

Another sob escaped Rose's chest. How could she warn her friend if she couldn't even get out?

Lucinta's high-pitched cackle rang so loudly in her ears Rose thought her skull would shatter. She was about to scream when something caused her to look up instead — a noise.

Was that the screaming crowd? Were those princesses cheering, or witches? Rose couldn't tell.

I have to be calm, Rose told her reflection as she wiped away tears with the sleeve of her gown. *If I don't, I definitely won't be able to help myself, or my friends.*

My friends, she repeated, closing her eyes. She could still hear the jeering laughter of Lucinta and Violet, but she ignored it as she pictured the smiling faces of her friends. The straightforward, headstrong Rapunzel. The warm, friendly Ella. And the sweet, always cheerful Snow. Before she came to Princess School, Rose had never really had friends, only admirers. Now there was a group of girls she could trust and confide in, count on for anything.

Rose looked at the mirror before her again. Her distorted reflection was still there. But this time Lucinta and Violet were gone. Rose was surrounded by her friends and they were all smiling at her, giving her strength.

Reaching out, Rose placed both hands on one of the mirrors that made up her cage. She pushed — hard — and it fell backward to the floor, smashing to a hundred pieces. And as the last shard of reflective glass landed on the floor with a quiet ping, the voices of Lucinta and Violet were silenced.

Carefully Rose stepped over the shattered glass and quickly made her way down the exposed corridor. She could hear the sounds of the Maiden Games coming from the arena. She walked toward the noise, letting it guide her. The sound was initially reassuring. She felt hope building. She could still make it out in time! But then she heard a chorus calling Snow's name, and she realized that the Apple Bob had already begun. Panic filled her heart and she started to run. Left, right, left. The Hall of Mirrors seemed endless. There had to be a way out!

At last she spotted a sliver of light through a flapping tent door. Gasping for breath, she raced toward it as the sound of the crowd got louder. By the time Rose surged into the daylight it was roaring in her ears, along with her own single thought:

Please don't let me be too late!

Chapter Nineteen
The Enchanted Apple

"Hey, ho. We love Snow!" cheered the dwarves in the stands.

Snow shook her head, and water drops flew from her dark locks. She ignored the red-and-white apple on the far side of the bucket and dunked her head to retrieve another apple nearby. All around her, her friends and family were cheering madly. The noise was deafening, but she was focused on the task in front of her.

Snow went after each apple like a cat chasing a scurrying mouse. She'd pulled out so many apples she'd lost count — eight, maybe nine — at least as many as Violet Gust beside her. Snow's brow furrowed as she imagined the icy witch beside her. She would not let Violet beat her. She was out to win.

But as she leaned forward, again her attention was drawn to the strange apple she'd noticed before.

It's on the edge, Snow told herself. *Get the others first and then go for that one.*

Still it pulled at her. Gritting her teeth, Snow ignored the odd apple and dove in, pinning an all-red one in less than three seconds.

"Hey, ho, that's our Snow!" the dwarves whooped in the stands, getting to their feet to dance a little jig. With Rapunzel and Ella leaping like gazelles behind her, Snow retrieved another apple, pulling ahead of Violet.

"You can do it, Snow!" Ella screamed at the top of her lungs.

Snow's entire body was filled with exhilaration. She was doing it! She was going to win! And she was standing up to Malodora, something she never thought she'd have the courage to do!

Snow stole a glance at Violet and could almost taste victory. Violet's apple pile looked smaller than hers! But as she lowered her head to dive again, Snow's stomach lurched with sudden hunger, and her eyes locked on the strange apple bobbing enticingly at the tub's edge. All of a sudden it seemed to be the only one that could satisfy her appetite. Her head spun, and everything shifted out of focus. She felt dizzy. Confused. But more than anything else, she felt hungry. She had to have that apple.

Snow dove, chasing the strange apple straight to

the bottom of the copper tub. Where was it? She could feel its presence, but couldn't find it with her mouth. She opened her eyes under water, but the water was so churned up it was impossible to see clearly. She raised her head.

"Snow!" Rapunzel shouted. "Hurry! She's catching up!"

"Come on, Snow!" Ella screamed desperately.

Snow heard her friends' words, but could not pull her focus away from that apple. Hunger was gnawing at her stomach — at the very core of her being. And then there was another voice, even louder than Rapunzel and Ella, and more frantic. The voice screamed a single word: "NOOOOOO!"

Diving deep, Snow pinned the half-red, half-white apple to the bottom. She sank her teeth into the crisp flesh. She felt a moment of complete victory. But an instant later she seemed to lose control of her body. She felt her torso and limbs jerk up mechanically, sending water flying everywhere. Staring at but not seeing the confused crowd, she stood for a second with the apple clenched in her teeth. Then she crumpled to the field in a heap as the apple rolled to the sidelines, and everything went black.

Chapter Twenty

Fairest in the Land

The next few minutes felt like an eternity. Rapunzel watched it all happen in slow motion. Snow jerked upright, flinging her drenched head back on her shoulders and spraying water everywhere. For a second she stood and seemed triumphant. The trumpets blasted, signaling the end of the Apple Bob just as Rose raced into the center of the Bob arena, screaming.

"Nooo!" Rose's scream nearly drowned out the trumpets. All eyes were on her. Then Snow crumpled to the grass, lifeless.

Rapunzel was too stunned to move. She and Ella stood like statues, watching as Rose knelt beside Snow, cradling the girl's head in her lap. Snow's eyes were closed. She wasn't breathing.

"We have to get the piece of apple out!" Rose said, looking up into Rapunzel's eyes. "It's poison!" Rose struggled to lift Snow's limp body. That was when Rapunzel started to move. In a flash she understood everything. Snow had been tricked.

Before she even thought about what she was doing, Rapunzel had her arms around Snow. Ella was beside her. Together the three girls got Snow to her feet and Rapunzel adjusted her arms, squeezing her fist sharply under Snow's rib cage.

Snow coughed, dislodging the tainted apple. The pale girl opened her eyes and looked at her friends, dazed. "Hi-ho," she said softly, seeming surprised to see them there. "Why, I feel a little funny."

Rapunzel, Ella, and Rose collapsed into Snow, enveloping her in a huge hug.

"Oh, Snow!" Rapunzel breathed in relief. "I think you're going to be all right."

After a few moments of relieved and nervous giggling, Rapunzel pulled out of the embrace.

"That was close," Rose said, keeping an arm around Snow.

"Rose, how did you know?" Rapunzel asked.

"I saw it all in the Hall of Mirrors," Rose said somberly. "Malodora was there, and the magic mirror, too. It was cracked, Snow."

Snow sat down on the grass with a bump. "You mean . . ."

"That apple was from Malodora? She was trying to get Snow? Right here?" Ella asked with wide eyes. "I don't believe it."

"She's jealous," Rose said sheepishly, sitting beside Snow. "And, oh, Ella! So was I! I'm sorry. I'm sorry I've been acting funny, and I'm sorry about the race. I didn't fall on purpose, but it wasn't a complete accident, either. I heard those other princesses chanting your name and . . ."

Ella didn't let Rose finish. "*You* were jealous of *me*?" She laughed, plunked down on the grass, and hugged her friend. "I'm sorry, too. I should have realized I was neglecting my real friends."

Rapunzel shook her head as she stared at the three girls on the ground. "Wow. I knew something was going on," she said. "I guess I was too wrapped up in the Games."

"I'll say," said a familiar voice behind Rapunzel. Rapunzel didn't know how long Val had been standing there. In fact, she had pretty much forgotten that they were still on the field in front of the grandstand! She was just so glad that her friends were together, and okay.

"I can't believe Malodora tried to cheat," Val said. "She's a judge!"

Grabbing Val's hand, Rapunzel pulled him down into the small circle on the grass. "Let's put this all behind us," she said somberly, using her best coaching voice. "We must stick together in the face of Grimm reality."

Val groaned. He knew Rapunzel's puns seldom traveled alone.

"We all know Malodora is far from the fairest in the land." Rapunzel kept joking, finally managing to coax a smile, then a full-fledged laugh out of Snow.

The five friends sat in a circle, oblivious to the chaos on the field. Officials were rushing to see if Snow was okay, but hadn't made it through the crowds.

Suddenly the laughing stopped. A shadow fell across the grass and Rapunzel felt instantly cold.

"Snow White," Malodora hissed. She stood over the group of friends. Hortense stood behind her, peeking around the queen's flowing purple-black robes.

The smile disappeared from Snow's face. For an instant she looked paler than Rapunzel thought possible. Then she stood and flashed a winning smile. "Oh, hello, Stepmother," she chirped. "Have you met my friends?"

Val and the girls scrambled to their feet to stand beside Snow. They bowed politely, but Malodora didn't acknowledge them. Her glare never left Snow White.

And, Rapunzel noticed proudly, Snow White never looked away or stopped smiling. The silence was interrupted when all seven dwarves finally ducked through the crowd to circle Snow.

"You were amazing," Mort chirped.

"Stupendous!" Hap added.

"Wow," Meek whispered.

"I don't think you've met my dear *family* yet, either," Snow cooed to Malodora. "That's Mort and Hap and Nod and Meek and Dim and Gruff and Wheezer."

Malodora's glossy red lips twitched. Her shoulders trembled in rage.

Snow stood still and tall, waiting for her stepmother to speak. Rapunzel thought Snow looked ready for anything.

But no one expected what happened next. The crowd parted and Lady Bathilde walked silently up behind the girls to place a hand on Snow's shoulder.

"Snow, I am so glad to see that you're all right," she said in her soft regal voice. "And Mal," she said, turning to the evil queen and speaking familiarly, "you must be so proud. Your Snow so easily captures the loyalty of her peers." Lady Bathilde smiled at Rose, Ella, Rapunzel, and Val. Rapunzel had never stood so close to the headmistress before and felt almost as if she were under a wonderful spell.

Lady Bathilde's voice alone was enough to inspire awe and royal respect as she went on. "Snow effortlessly gains the adulation of every creature around her.

As I recall, that was what you struggled with most at Princess School, was it not?"

Rapunzel's jaw dropped. Malodora went to Princess School? Looking at Snow, she saw that this was news to her, too. But instead of looking simply shocked or even angry, Snow suddenly gazed at her stepmother with *sympathy*.

Leave it to Snow to be understanding of someone so awful! Rapunzel thought. *Although*, she supposed, *I guess we all want to be liked.* Rapunzel watched Malodora's face as Lady Bathilde continued. She was striking, and would be truly gorgeous if she weren't so cruel. . . .

"Of course we are all so pleased to have Snow here at Princess School. I myself have been personally keeping an eye on her." Lady Bathilde smiled at Malodora as if she were doing the evil queen a personal favor. Malodora could only nod.

When Malodora turned to leave, she had to steady herself on Hortense's head, flattening the young witch's hat.

"You have all performed admirably today," Lady Bathilde said after Malodora had gone. "Whether we win or lose, you should be proud."

Rapunzel *was* proud, she suddenly realized. She smiled and Val elbowed her in the arm.

"Don't try to tell me you don't care if you won or lost," he said, disbelieving.

"I wouldn't say that I didn't care. . . ." Rapunzel admitted. Actually, she was dying to know!

Near the judges' stand the apples were still being counted. Rapunzel watched Vermin Twitch whisper something in Malodora's ear. Malodora smiled slightly, but her eyes narrowed before she raised her hands to silence the crowd. "It appears," she announced, "that the Apple Bob is tied. In light of this, the victory and Golden Ball will go to the Grimm School."

"Wait!" Ella shouted. Rapunzel turned to see Ella lunging for the last apple that had fallen out of Snow's mouth. It was sitting by the sidelines and hadn't been counted!

Lucinta Pintch must have spotted it at the same moment. Ella's and Lucinta's heads banged together as they grabbed for the fallen fruit. Lucinta was jabbed by Ella's tiara and Meek, who was standing nearby, shyly plucked the apple from the ground and handed it to Rapunzel.

Rapunzel marched up to Malodora and looked her in the eye. "Don't forget this one!" she said, sweet as Snow.

Chapter Twenty-one
Sweet Victory

As soon as he saw the red-and-white apple Rapunzel held, Fistius Ballus took the podium from Malodora. Rapunzel wasn't sure, but he almost seemed . . . smug. "The Apple Bob and the Maiden Games victory go to Princess School!" he proclaimed.

The field erupted into a chorus of cheers and applause. Snow felt ready to burst. She could not remember ever feeling so happy or so proud. She was proud of her school for fighting back against the Grimms. She was proud of her friends for helping her overcome her fears. And most of all she was proud of herself for finally standing up to Malodora. She knew she never could have done it before, not without her friends and not without the dwarves. And in the end she had done it with them, and for them, too. Even Lady Bathilde had been there!

Every princess in the school marched together

around the whole arena. Music played behind the procession and flower petals rained down over everything.

The Grimm witches stood under their own dark cloud, muttering and grumbling and shaking off the delicate petals as if they would be burned by them. Snow *almost* felt bad for the witches. Almost.

After the procession, Snow and Rose settled into the bleachers. With a minimum of fanfare Ella returned her tiara, holding out a delicate but calloused hand to quiet the applause. When she joined her friends in the stands, the three girls grinned as they watched Rapunzel take the stage with the other Princess School captains for the presentation of the Golden Ball.

Vermin and Fistius held the orb aloft. Glowing almost magically in the slanted sunlight, it was one of the prettiest things Snow had ever seen.

"It gives me great pleasure to award the Golden Ball to the winner of the Maiden Games — Princess School!" Fistius announced. Vermin twitched, and together they handed the ball to Rapunzel, who was first in line for the Princess team.

In the stands Snow leaped to her feet. She, Ella, and Rose jumped and cheered as Rapunzel held the ball over her head. It almost looked like an egg in her nest of hair.

Snow watched Rapunzel search for her friends in the grandstand, then looked at each one of them and lifted the ball higher before passing it to the Sash captain, who passed it to the Robe captain, who finally handed it to the Crown captain.

Snow sat back down but kept her eyes on Rapunzel. Rapunzel, though, was looking at someone else. She was watching Val, and her victory smile was fading. Snow followed Rapunzel's gaze to Val, then followed Val's gaze . . . to Rose. Feeling a familiar twinge in her stomach, Snow swallowed hard and looked away. She'd had enough of jealousy, and nothing was going to ruin her mood.

The sun was beginning to set as the presentation ceremony ended. The princesses politely waved goodbye to the Grimm witches as they skulked into the forest with their brooms between their legs. It was clear the Grimms would be counting the seconds until the next Maiden Games and their chance for revenge. But they could not change the fact that Princess School had won, fair and square. Malodora led the Grimm group out without a backward glance.

"Who wants to come to the cottage for supper?" Snow asked, clapping her hands together when Rapunzel had rejoined the group.

"What a wonderful idea!" Mort said as he jumped off the last grandstand seat.

"Jolly good," said Hap.

"Nobody will miss me at the tower." Rapunzel shrugged.

"I think it's worth a few extra chores." Ella grinned.

"Just a moment. I have to get permission." Rose hurried to the edge of the field where carriages and coaches were starting to line up. She poked her head inside one and a few minutes later she was back with seven fairies fluttering all around her face, putting out a soft glow. "I can go if I take my bodyguards." She smiled and tilted her head toward the fairies.

"Ooh, they're lovely," Snow cooed. "We can collect some dew and nectar for them on the way."

The walk to the cottage felt like an extension of the victory procession. The dwarves hummed, the fairies made tiny chiming sounds, and the girls recalled the most exciting moments of the day as they made their way through the darkening forest. The last rays of pink sun glinted on the damp leaves, and the tree branches made lacy patterns on the sunset sky.

The party at the cottage was no less glorious. The food was a little strange (the dwarves cooked), but the music was wonderful and Rose's fairies even provided some fireworks.

It was late when Snow finally hugged her friends good-bye. Sleepily she walked up the stairs to her room. Then with a yawn she fell into the bed the dwarves had carved just for her. That night she slept soundly with a small smile on her face and had nothing but sweet dreams.

Let Down Your Hair

For Emmett, Elliot, and Oliver,
our knights in shining armor.

—JBM & SHS

Chapter One

A Narrow Escape

Rapunzel Arugula swung herself over the gray stone windowsill of her tower. She had done it so many times, she barely had to look to see where her feet went. But today she was moving slower than usual. She'd woken up with a sore neck.

Maybe the weight of Madame Gothel's daily descent from the tower on her braid was getting to her. *Or maybe Princess School is making me soft,* Rapunzel mused as she lowered her leg to the next foothold.

In spite of the ache in her neck, Rapunzel grinned. On her first day of Princess School she had been sure the other students were nothing but silly, frilly girls. Now she knew better. A lot of the girls were interesting and fun. And her friends Snow White, Cinderella, and Briar Rose were the best. They were smart, funny, and always there for her.

Ella, Rose, and Snow weren't Rapunzel's only friends, of course. She and Prince Valerian had been pals for years. But Rapunzel got something different from her girlfriends. They understood how life was. They made her feel, well, like she was a part of something.

Rapunzel grabbed hold of the pointy reddish rock a few feet above the ground. Then with a little kick she swung her body away from the stone wall and jumped to the ground. Another successful descent.

Brushing off her hands, Rapunzel looked up at her small, round tower. It was utterly familiar. She'd lived there for as long as she could remember — ever since Madame Gothel took her from her parents when she was just a baby.

Rapunzel couldn't remember her parents at all. She had no idea what they looked like or who they were. Madame Gothel never mentioned them and Rapunzel didn't ask. She didn't want the old witch to know she cared. She used to daydream about them all the time, imagining what life would be like if they were bringing her up instead of Madame Gothel — if you could call what she was doing "bringing her up." It often felt more like holding her down.

But in the past few months Rapunzel hadn't been thinking about her parents. She had been focusing on other things — on school, on her friends, on the reflective flash code she'd invented to communicate with Val while she was at Princess School and he was at the Charm School for Boys.

Rapunzel leaned against the gnarled trunk of a giant oak. She rubbed her neck and looked around for Val. Where was that prince, anyway? Rapunzel tapped her foot on the ground. Late, as usual.

All of a sudden a dark cloud covered the sun, casting a shadow across the tower. Shivering, Rapunzel pulled her cloak around her shoulders. What was going on? She stood perfectly still and listened. All was silent — even the birds had stopped singing.

Rapunzel's heart beat quickly. Only one thing silenced the birds.

Charging the tower and ignoring her stiff neck, Rapunzel leaped as high as she could and began to climb. Her hands and feet found their regular holds as she vaulted her body upward. A moment later she hurled her leg over the windowsill and threw herself onto her lumpy bed. She barely had time for a single breath before Madame Gothel appeared in her room in a puff of greenish smoke.

"Lizard's leg!" she screeched. "How can I search for good potion roots without my basket?" Her steely gray eyes glinted at Rapunzel, looking her over carefully. Pretending to stretch, Rapunzel quickly tucked her feet under the skirt of her gown. She didn't want the witch to spot her muddy shoes. She let out what she hoped was a convincing yawn.

"Now where is that basket?" Madame Gothel looked toward a small side table where the basket lay on its side. But Rapunzel was already on her feet, reaching for the willow container.

"It's right here!" Rapunzel held it toward the witch and did her best to keep her breath even.

I can't believe I didn't notice it was here, she scolded herself. *What if she had come sooner?* Madame Gothel's visits were almost always predictable. She appeared in the tower twice a day — once to deliver breakfast and again to deliver supper. She always arrived in a green cloud and always departed out the tower window using Rapunzel's braid as a rope. And she never left anything behind without Rapunzel noticing. At least not until now.

"I see it," Madame Gothel snapped, snatching the basket. "I'm not blind."

Rapunzel shuddered. That was what she was afraid of. If Madame Gothel had come a moment earlier, she would have been caught for sure. Madame Gothel had no idea Rapunzel was going to Princess School. And if she found out, Rapunzel wouldn't be able to go any longer. As it was, the witch seemed slightly suspicious. Her gaze fell repeatedly to the bottom of Rapunzel's gown. Rapunzel felt sure she was trying to get another look at her shoes. And she seemed in no hurry to leave, which was unusual. She didn't normally linger in the tower.

Rapunzel uncoiled her braid and made her way to the tower window. She couldn't remember the last time she'd felt so nervous. And not just for herself. "I can lower you whenever you are ready," she said loudly. She quickly stole a glance at the oak tree and the path below.

Please let Val be hiding behind that tree, she thought. *Or be even later than usual!*

Chapter Two

Through the Woods

Leaping over a fallen tree trunk, Rapunzel grabbed her l-o-n-g braid and slung it over her shoulder for the third time. It kept falling out and was driving her crazy. But there had been no time to re-coil it.

Madame Gothel had lingered in her room for what seemed like ages, describing in great detail the cackle syrup and wart-growing potions she'd been concocting. She'd gone on so long Rapunzel and Val would be lucky if they made it to school on time.

"I think she might suspect something!" Rapunzel shouted as she pushed aside a wayward branch.

Val was right behind her. "Don't worry," he said, panting. "You've been getting out of that tower for years and she's never even guessed. You're probably imagining it."

"I know," Rapunzel groaned. "But if she ever finds out I've started going to Princess School . . ." She swallowed hard. Princess School was the best thing to happen to her, well, *ever*. She couldn't possibly give it up now!

Val's green eyes looked serious. "Well, maybe you should be more careful," he advised.

Just then the sparkling towers of the giant castle school came into view. It was a beautiful sight, one Rapunzel would sorely miss if her witch caretaker found out what she was up to.

"See you after school!" Rapunzel called. She lifted her skirts higher and charged across the Princess School bridge, startling the swans in the moat. She bounded up the steps, two at a time, and the doors whooshed open as she approached. Rapunzel loved that. It made her feel royal.

Clusters of princesses lingered in the hall, chatting. A group of fourth-year Crowns was laughing lightly over a shared joke. Several third-year Robes were gossiping about a boy from the Charm School. Some second-year Sashes marveled over a classmate's new dress. Rapunzel scanned a group of first-year Bloomers as she let out a sigh of relief. Obviously the final trumpet had not yet sounded. Rapunzel slowed to a walk and quickly tried to make a proper bun with her ropy hair. It wasn't easy, but she'd learned a lot in Looking Glass class and from Rose, who really knew her way around a head of hair — even an unwieldy one like Rapunzel's.

"Rapunzel!" called a voice from up ahead. It was Ella. Snow and Rose were with her. "We were beginning to worry about you. You know how rigid Madame Garabaldi is now that exams are coming up!"

Rapunzel rolled her eyes. "Madame Garabaldi is nothing compared to what I had to deal with this morning. Madame Gothel showed up just as I was leaving," she explained. "I barely got back in my tower before she appeared!"

Snow shivered. "I can't believe she silences the birds," she said. "The poor little things!"

Rapunzel waved a hand through the air. "The birds are fine," she said. "But I'm a little worried that Madame Gothel knows I'm getting out. She's never paid me extra visits before." Her breath caught in her throat. "If she figures it out, I . . . I . . ."

"She won't," Rose said firmly. Her lovely blue eyes looked determined as she tucked a stray lock of hair behind Rapunzel's ear and smiled reassuringly.

Ella linked an arm through Rapunzel's. "We've got to get to hearthroom," she said. "And after that we're off to our first class in Cordial Correspondence! We're going to be paired with boys from the Charm School. I can't wait!"

Rose and Snow both giggled, and Rapunzel rolled her eyes again. But truth be told, she had been looking forward to Cordial Correspondence class, too. It sounded much more fun than all the girly things they had to do in Looking Glass, and less impossible than Stitchery. It would be nice to start something completely new — especially if she could figure out how to be paired with Val. Their light-flashing code was great, but there was only so much you could say with light and mirrors. Letters would be a lot more detailed — and fun.

The final trumpet blasted, echoing off the alabaster walls and carved arches. Ella, Snow, Rose, and Rapunzel hurried down the hall together, their slippered feet padding softly on the pink-and-white marble floor. They made it through their hearthroom door and into their high-backed, velvet-cushioned seats seconds before Madame Garabaldi strode into the room.

Rapunzel stopped rubbing her neck and sat up a little straighter. Madame Garabaldi had a way of making you do that.

"Good morning, princesses," the teacher said briskly. She picked up a large parchment, unrolled it, and immediately began scroll call. She rapped out names like a king commanding troops, looking up over her half-spectacles as each girl replied. When she was finished, she set the scroll down and began to pace back and forth across the front of the room.

"Beginning next week you will all be alloted time to study during hearthroom in recognition of the more vigorous academic schedule you must follow to prepare for the impending exams," Madame Garabaldi announced. "They are closer than you think. You will also begin a new unit today: Cordial Correspondence. You will improve your pen-princessship. You will refine your royal language skills. In short, you will begin to learn how to communicate regally." Madame Garabaldi raised her sharp nose into the air slightly. "I hope all of you will take this new unit seriously. I do not want to find myself disappointed in any of you. And it is not an excuse to neglect your extra exam studies." She gazed at several of the princesses in turn, finishing with Rapunzel.

Rapunzel bristled. She knew she was not as princessy as the rest of her classmates. And she didn't always take her classes seriously (it was hard to think of Stitchery as a serious subject!). As Madame Garabaldi stared, Rapunzel shifted in her seat. Something in the teacher's eyes made Rapunzel feel suddenly nervous, as if Madame Garabaldi could see right through her. She wondered if Madame Garabaldi knew what made Rapunzel different. Maybe Madame Garabaldi could tell that Rapunzel had been raised by a witch.

Lost in thought, Rapunzel jumped when the end-of-class trumpet sounded. She followed as the princesses spilled into the hall, stopping at their velvet-lined trunks to get their materials for Cordial Correspondence. Rapunzel joined her friends at Ella's trunk.

Rose held up a beautiful rose stamp she had brought to seal her scrolls. "My parents just gave it to me," she explained.

Snow had some old scrolls her mother had written to her father during their courtship. "My stepmother ordered a servant to destroy them, but he gave them to me instead," she whispered, her eyes wide.

Even Ella had a lovely silver calligraphy pen. "It was my mother's," she said with a glowing smile. "My stepmother doesn't know my dad gave it to me."

Rapunzel bit her lip. She hadn't brought anything for her new class. As the girls made their way to the Cordial Correspondence classroom on the top floor of the castle, her friends chattered excitedly. Rapunzel was silent.

"My goodness," Snow said breathlessly, stepping into the class chamber.

"It practically glitters!" Ella said, looking around the room. Light poured into the room through the diamond-paned, floor-to-ceiling windows. Silver platters lined with seals and colorful candles sat next to stacks of pastel-colored parchment on polished marble tables.

Rapunzel sat down at a carved wooden desk. An ink-well and a pen with a fluffy pink feather sat before her.

Just then their teacher, Sir Spondence, ambled into the room. Rapunzel grinned as soon as she saw him. His thinning silver hair was perfectly groomed, as was his wide, curved mustache and pointed goatee. He wore puffy short pantaloons with stockings and a short waistcoat with tails — neatly tailored and starched. They suited him perfectly.

"Potential royals," he said warmly. "My first order of business is to communicate to you the name of the young prince with whom each of you will correspond for the duration of the course." He unrolled a large, cream-colored scroll.

Rapunzel crossed her fingers under her desk. *Please let me get Val,* she thought. *Please, please, please!*

"Snow White will have the privilege of corresponding with Hans Charming," Sir Spondence announced. Snow giggled, her pale face turning slightly pink. "Scarlet Riding Hood shall be paired with Hector Velveteen. Cinderella Brown shall exchange pleasantries with Allister Arlington."

"The best dancer from the Charm School," Rose whispered. This time it was Ella's turn to blush.

Rapunzel was already working on a new secret code to use in her letters to Val.

"Briar Rose will be expressing her royal thoughts to Valentine Valerian."

Rapunzel looked up. What was that?

"And Rapunzel Arugula shall correspond with Oliver Eggert," Sir Spondence finished.

Rapunzel's jaw dropped.

As Sir Spondence lowered the scroll, murmurs echoed through the room.

"Hans Charming!" Snow said with an excited giggle. The Charming boys were famous throughout the kingdom for their good looks and fine manners.

"I get to write to Val!" Rose said. Her always-pink cheeks looked a little extra flushed.

Rapunzel scowled. She did not want to write to Oliver Eggert. And even worse, she didn't want Rose to write to Val! He always acted so goofy about Rose. All of the boys did, and most of the girls. It drove Rapunzel crazy the way people fawned over Rose and called her "Beauty."

"Kindly make your way to the front of the room and choose an unsullied paper," Sir Spondence instructed. "Today you shall be writing a simple letter of introduction."

Rapunzel felt as though she were weighted to her desk. First Madame Gothel practically catches her outside her tower, and now this! She watched as the other girls chose parchments and returned to their seats. Stifling a groan, she did the same.

Rapunzel watched Ella dip her mother's silver pen in the inkwell and begin to write. Snow's old scrolls lay on her desk next to the paper she was writing on. And Rose's stamp was ready to be used for the first time.

Rapunzel had a knot in her stomach. Her friends had all brought something special — a piece of home, of family . . . the one thing Rapunzel didn't have.

Gazing out the window, Rapunzel let her mind wander. What *would* it be like to have a family? To be surrounded by people who loved her all the time, like the way the dwarves doted on Snow, or how Rose was adored by . . . well . . . everyone. Rapunzel was grateful for her friends, but families were different. More permanent.

I don't even know when my birthday is, Rapunzel thought miserably. *Or what my mother looked like. Or if she would even like me.*

Without thinking, Rapunzel picked up her pen, dipped it in the inkwell, and began to write. But she wasn't writing to Oliver Eggert. Or Val. She was writing to her mother.

Dear Mother,

I know it is strange, me writing to you. But so many things seem strange to me lately. I feel as though my whole world is changing before my eyes, and I can only watch. I love Princess School and my new friends. For the first time I feel connected to something. But sometimes I feel so different from everyone else. My friends all seem to have things that I don't. We are taking a new class called Cordial Correspondence, and I had hoped to be able to write to my good friend Prince Val. You'd like him. But my friend Briar Rose will be writing to him instead. It just doesn't seem fair. I need Val right now. He knows me better than anyone. But now he'll be busy writing to Rose. I wish you were here, Mother. Then I would have someone to talk to.

Love,
Your Daughter, Rapunzel

Chapter Three
Cordial Creations

Ella dipped her silver pen into the inkwell and paused to examine her letter. So far she had introduced herself and thanked Allister for their dances at the Coronation Ball.

She ran her finger lightly over the thick paper. It was lovely. And the personalized seals and colorful waxes they'd use to seal their communications were enough to make any letter seem regal.

Sir Spondence cleared his throat. "In this class you shall compose communication masterpieces so lovely that their recipients will keep them tucked inside the pockets of their royal waistcoats."

Ella and several other girls giggled. A look of surprise from Sir Spondence silenced them, but he soon broke into a grin. Ella smiled back at him. Cordial Correspondence was turning out to be as wonderful as she had hoped. And thanks to her mother's lessons years ago, her calligraphy wasn't too embarrassing.

Ella gazed around the room. Most of the princesses were writing busily, but Rapunzel was staring out the window, seemingly lost in thought. Her paper was partially filled. Ella tried to catch her friend's eye, but Rapunzel looked over at Rose, who was bent low over her paper. The quill in Rose's hand danced over her paper, and she was smiling broadly. Rapunzel glowered.

"Sir Spondence," asked Ariel, a petite princess with flowing red hair. "How will we send our correspondences once they are written?"

"Hear this, clever students," Sir Spondence replied. He tugged at his waistcoat and lowered his voice, as if he were about to tell them a great secret. "Composing the correspondence is but the beginning of a letter's grand journey. Once completed and sealed, your perfect post must find its way to its intended recipient via one of three royal methods: wing, willow, or woodland creature."

The teacher straightened and opened a window. A gust of wind blew into the room, ruffling his perfectly coiffed hair. "Though the breeze is brisk," he said, "I am inclined to advise that today we should send by . . . willow! You shall each have an additional turn of the time-glass to complete your missives. Then, after the initial sealing ceremony, we shall venture forth together to the enchanted postal tree."

Only one turn of the glass! Ella looked down at her note. There must be something more to say — she just wasn't sure what. After rejecting several ideas she simply wrote: "I am very much looking forward to communicating with you. Your Royal Friend, Cinderella Brown."

"And now for the seals!" Sir Spondence crowed. "Each of you may come forward and select a seal. Choose carefully, for your seal is the mark you will leave on each and every epistle you send forth this term."

All at once the princesses leaped from their seats and rushed to the front of the room. By the time Ella reached the marble table, several girls had already made their seal selections. Rose had her rose, of course. Snow was exclaiming with delight over a tiny hummingbird. Rapunzel had a tight grip on a seal with a knot impressed in it. Ella looked through the remaining seals. There was a daffodil, a perfectly tied bow, a unicorn, a crown . . . all lovely, but none of them just right.

"What about this one?" Snow asked, holding up a seal. "It's perfect for you!"

Ella leaned closer and her eyes widened. It was a slipper!

Snow slid the seal into Ella's hand. The silvery

metal was cool to the touch, and the weight of it took Ella by surprise. It was heavier than she thought it would be. But Snow was right. It was perfect.

"Ladies, ladies," Sir Spondence said from the sealing table a few feet away. "Gather 'round and I shall demonstrate the art of sealing a royal missive."

The teacher stood before a large marble table. A polished silver tray sat in the middle, heaped with candles of every imaginable color. Behind the tray was a single white taper, already burning.

Sir Spondence chose a dark blue sealing candle and lit it using the white taper. Ella held her breath as, carefully holding the blue candle over the thick parchment, he allowed several drops of melted wax to fall onto the rolled paper.

Sir Spondence let seven drops fall, then quickly blew out the blue candle. Placing his feathery quill seal over the hot wax, he pressed firmly but gently, uniting the two ends of parchment.

"Voilà!" he said, blowing lightly on the wax to help it harden. "A perfectly cordial, perfectly sealed correspondence. And now, ladies, it is your turn."

The girls excitedly chose their colors and began to practice their sealing.

"Ooops!" Snow cried as she dripped a few too many drops of yellow wax on her parchment. She pressed her hummingbird seal onto the warm liquid. "Poor thing! He looks like he's stuck in a mud puddle!" she giggled.

Next to Snow, Gretel's wax was falling onto the white marble table.

"Here," Rapunzel said, handing her a lace cloth to wipe it up.

"Wow, Rose," Ella said admiringly. "Your rose looks perfect."

"It does," Snow chirped.

"Thanks," Rose said.

Next to Ella, Rapunzel pressed her knot seal hard onto her melted wax. And, Ella noticed, she was frowning again.

Clutching their letters so they wouldn't blow away, the princesses followed Sir Spondence to the postal tree.

"I must say this breeze is unseasonably brisk," the instructor said over the howling wind. "But we shall not be deterred in our delivery!"

He led the way to the huge, gnarled willow that sat on the edge of the Princess School grounds.

"It doesn't look enchanted to me," Snow whispered as they approached the tree.

"Each of you may slip your missive into the knot-hole," he said.

Ella stepped forward eagerly and dropped her rolled parchment into the tree. She moved aside to make room for Snow, who gave the tree a funny little curtsy before slipping her roll through the hole. She was giving the trunk a thank-you pat when Rose placed her correspondence in the hole in a single, graceful motion. The other Bloomers sent off their scrolls, too. Only Rapunzel, Ella noticed, seemed to hesitate. She clutched her letter to her chest and remained several feet away from the tree.

"Rapunzel," Ella said, approaching her friend. "It's your turn."

Rapunzel's eyes were full of uncertainty. Ella was about to say something encouraging when the willow suddenly snaked a tendril over Rapunzel's shoulder and snatched the letter. A moment later the giant tree stuffed the scroll into its knothole as if feeding a hungry mouth.

Rapunzel stared up at the tree, horrified.

"Mr. Willow!" Snow scolded. "How terribly rude!" She strode over to Rapunzel and placed a comforting hand on her friend's shoulder.

"Are you all right?" Rose asked.

Rapunzel's eyes flashed. "I'm fine," she snapped.

Ella was taken aback by Rapunzel's harsh reply. Rose was only being nice.

The knothole was now sealed, and the tree's branches blew carelessly about, as if mocking the girls.

"Don't worry, Rapunzel," Ella said. "I'm sure your letter will be delivered just fine."

She must be upset about her near run-in with Madame Gothel, Ella thought. She turned to their instructor. "How *do* the letters get delivered, Sir Spondence?" she asked, hoping for an explanation that would console her friend. Rapunzel was usually so unflappable, but she seemed pretty shaken. And it was just a scroll.

Sir Spondence looked a little perplexed by the question and paused before he began to speak. "Ah, the delivery of royal missives is, um, a long-lived tradition. Each letter must . . . ah . . . travel the distance, short or vast, reaching its destination only when the passage has been successfully navigated," he finally replied.

While Snow nodded eagerly, Ella gave Rose a confused look. *What was that supposed to mean?*

"Eventually, the letters will reach the Charmed Cherry, the ancient fruit tree at the edge of the Charm School grounds," Sir Spondence finished somewhat meekly.

Just then a cold gust of wind caught the group by surprise, and Sir Spondence stumbled. Frowning slightly, he looked up at the sky. "All's well!" Sir Spondence clapped his hands together. "Back to class, my ladies," he said in his cheerful voice. But his eyes registered concern, and Ella saw Rapunzel turn back to the tree, glaring fiercely.

All was not well.

Chapter Four

Blowup

Rapunzel kicked a stone along the path while she waited for Val to catch up. He could be such a slowpoke! But she wasn't really annoyed about having to wait for him. She was used to that. She was annoyed about the willow tree stealing her letter.

"That dumb tree stole my personal thoughts right out of my hand!" she said to a squirrel munching on an acorn nearby. His fur was standing on end from the gusty wind that had been blowing hard all day. "And then it ate them!" This wasn't entirely true, of course. The willow had actually stuffed the letter into its mail slot so that it could be delivered to the proper place. But that was just the problem. Since the letter was to Rapunzel's mother, there *was* no proper place.

Rapunzel wasn't exactly sure why she had written the letter. She knew her mother would never get it. But writing out all her thoughts and feelings had felt pretty good.

Until that nasty willow stole it away. Now her letter could end up anywhere! What if her innermost thoughts wound up in the hands of some Charm School boy — or, worse, a witch at the Grimm School!

Rapunzel pictured Hortense Hegbottom cackling madly as she read all about how Rapunzel missed her mother. Ugh! What a nightmare!

Shifting her book satchel and picking up a rock, she threw it as hard as she could into the stream that ran next to the path. But the wind tossed it farther than she'd intended, and it bounced off a tree on the other side of the brook.

"Nice throw," called out a voice. It was Val. He ran up and stopped right in front of her to catch his breath. Rapunzel was grateful to see a friendly face. She was about to tell him everything that had happened when Val started in about the Charm School's Correspondence course.

"I thought it would be totally boring," he admitted as he started down the path. "I mean, what's interesting about writing letters? But having Rose for a correspondent is going to be great! I'm sure her pen-princessship is terrific. And the other princes are all jealous I got Beauty."

Rapunzel's jaw dropped. Was he kidding? Since when did Val give a crown about pen-princessship? She felt a surge of jealousy. He didn't care about calligraphy. What he cared about was Rose.

"Did you have to do your introductory notes today?" Val asked.

"Of course. That's how you always begin the class," Rapunzel replied flatly, like she was an expert.

"Professor Insignia told us we'll be writing our introductions tomorrow. But he seemed surprised when your letters hadn't arrived in time for our afternoon class."

"How fascinating," Rapunzel said sarcastically. Val didn't seem to notice.

A gust of wind stirred up a layer of dust on the path, and Rapunzel shielded her eyes. What was with the weather? It had been so weird today.

"What a wind," Val said, echoing Rapunzel's thoughts.

"Uh-huh," Rapunzel replied dully. She did not want to encourage him to go on about anything. Especially Correspondence and Rose.

Val looked back at Rapunzel. Confusion showed in his eyes. Lowering his head, he hurried up the path in silence.

Rapunzel sighed. She hadn't meant to be mean. It wasn't Val's fault he'd been paired with Rose. But couldn't he have said he'd have liked to have been paired with Rapunzel just as much? That it would be great for them to correspond, too?

The wind unraveled a few strands of Rapunzel's braid and they flew across her face. Halfheartedly she tucked them back in and followed several paces behind her friend. She wished her girlfriends were there. They would listen to her. They would understand her worries about her letter.

When their paths split off, Val waved good-bye but didn't call out. The wind was howling now, and Rapunzel knew she probably would not have heard him anyway. But she also knew that wasn't why he was silent, and a fresh wave of guilt washed over her as she watched him walk away. She shook her head and began to climb the tower, grabbing hold of the familiar stones and cracks. A few minutes later she hoisted herself over the windowsill. Glad to get out of the wind, she was about to shutter the window when she heard something behind her.

"Newt's nostrils!" shrieked an angry voice.

Rapunzel whirled around. Madame Gothel stood in the middle of her tower room, her gnarled hands balled into fists.

"I see you have been deceiving me, Rapunzel," she hissed. "Escaping the protective haven I've so carefully created for you." She eyed Rapunzel's heavy satchel.

"And going to . . . to . . . Princess School!" She spat out "Princess School" as if it were rancid cheese. Then she stepped forward, her gray eyes as sharp as daggers. "But I swear on my best possum potion, you are not a princess. You are the abandoned daughter of poor, *thieving* parents!"

Rapunzel stepped forward, her face hot with fury. "I was not abandoned. And my parents aren't thieves! I was stolen — by you, you evil witch!"

"Stolen?" Madame Gothel screeched. "Stolen? Snake's spit! I granted your parents their fondest wish. How many times I heard your mother cooing in your ear when you were a babe — every night, always the same wish."

The old witch picked up Rapunzel's lumpy pillow and rocked it like a baby. "'Please, keep this child safe,'" she said in a sickeningly beseeching voice. "'Don't let the world harm a single hair on her beautiful head.'"

Madame Gothel dropped the pillow onto the bed like a soiled diaper. "And, by my wart, that is exactly what I have done."

Rapunzel longed to lunge forward and scratch out the old woman's eyes. But she knew better than to try. Madame Gothel was crafty, and she knew a lot of icky spells.

"You haven't kept me safe," she said, forcing her

hands to be still at her sides. "You've kept me imprisoned."

"Safe," Madame Gothel hissed.

Rapunzel stepped so close to the witch that their noses almost touched. "Imprisoned," Rapunzel said.

The two stood nose to nose for several seconds. Outside, the wind howled around the tower. Then Madame Gothel stepped back. "You shall not escape your tower again," she announced, her eyes glinting. "Now, lower your hair and let me out of here."

Anger still burned in Rapunzel like a bonfire, but she knew she had no choice but to obey. Uncoiling her hair, she allowed Madame Gothel to lower herself to the ground. Then she threw herself onto her straw mattress and squeezed her eyes shut to hold back a torrent of unspilled tears.

Chapter Five

Thick as Pea Soup

Snow tugged the last wrinkle out of the cover on Dim's tiny bed and gave the pillow a pat. "There!" she said, satisfied. The dwarves had already left for the mines, but Snow didn't like to go before the house was tidied up. It was so much cheerier to come home to a clean house.

Grabbing her cloak, Snow dashed downstairs. It was still early. She knew she should probably spend the extra time studying, but decided to meet Rapunzel and Val so they could all walk to school together instead. After all, the exams were still weeks away. Looking over her shoulder, Snow smiled at her cozy cottage and waved good-bye. It didn't matter that nobody was there. Snow felt sure some of the field mice and birds were watching her depart.

Skipping blithely down the path, Snow slowed down when she got to the dogwood tree where the path branched. She glanced at the three arrow-shaped signs on the trunk. A fine mist swirled around the tree, making the signs hard to read. But Snow knew what they said. The arrow that pointed right read TOWN. The arrow that pointed left read GRANDMA'S HOUSE. And the arrow that pointed the way Snow had come read ENCHANTED FOREST.

Snow took the path toward Grandma's House. It was also the way to Rapunzel's tower, but her home was supposed to be a secret. Only Rapunzel, her friends, and the witch who locked up Rapunzel knew how to find it.

As she bounced toward the tower, the mist grew thicker around Snow's feet, hiding the trail. She stopped skipping and felt her way slowly along the path in her thin slippers.

"Oh, my," Snow said softly as the fog grew even more dense. "It's as thick as pea soup!" she chirped to nobody in particular.

Though Snow sounded like her cheerful self, the fog was making her feel unsettled. Turning, she looked back the way she had come. She couldn't see a thing! The fog blanketed her path completely.

"Oh, my, my!" Snow said again. Then she began to hum. Humming almost always made her feel better. When it didn't work, she pursed her lips and whistled, practicing her best birdsongs — but not even the finch's chipper song was helping. Snow felt as though the fog were seeping into her. She was lost and damp and frightened. Panic rose in her chest. She opened her mouth to sing and —

"Oh!" Snow stumbled on a fuzzy rock in the path and pitched forward onto a mossy bank. What was that? Snow reached out to clear the rock from the path and pulled her hand back in alarm. It moved! It was warm and soft, too. Snow stretched her hand out again.

"Why, you're not a rock at all!" Snow picked up a rabbit and held it close to her face. Two more rabbits jumped into her lap. "Bunnies! Have you come to rescue me?" Snow asked. She felt better already. "What darlings!"

While Snow rubbed noses with the rock rabbit, a sparrow sailed through the low-lying cloud, landed on her shoulder, and whistled softly.

"I feel ever so much better now that you're here," Snow told the animals.

She stroked the bunnies and whistled with the sparrow. Suddenly a crash in the thicket startled Snow and the animals. They turned as a young buck with tiny nubs for antlers stepped up next to them. He nuzzled Snow's elbow, and she leaned on him to stand back up. "Oh, what a deer!" Snow giggled.

Surrounded by her woodland friends, Snow felt

more confident. They were all a bit jumpy, and the fog still swirled around them, but they made their way down the path together. Snow followed the white tail of the young deer ahead of her, while the bunnies darted around her feet and the sparrow crooned his sweet song on her shoulder. Now and again, Snow thought she heard something else, too. Familiar voices — Val! And Rapunzel!

"We must be close!" Snow told the animals. The buck walked onward and soon, though she could not see it, Snow sensed that they were in the clearing around the tower.

"Rapunzel!" Snow called.

"Snow? Is that you?" a voice replied from the whiteness above her head. "I can't see to climb down. And I think Val is lost!"

"You can do it, Rapunzel. I just know you can," Snow called up encouragingly. "You've been doing it for years." The first time Snow had watched Rapunzel scale down her tower, her jaw had dropped. She had climbed the wall like a lizard!

"I feel dizzy. I can't see my feet," Rapunzel shouted. The fog was so thick it even muffled her voice, but Snow could still hear her friend's worry.

"You don't need to see your feet. Just close your eyes and follow the sound of my voice." Snow began to sing a simple song the dwarves had taught her. It did the trick. A moment later, Rapunzel was standing at her side.

"Thanks!" Rapunzel said. She spoke softly now and leaned in close to see Snow's face. "We had better get out of here quickly. And we'd better find Val before he wanders into the swamp — or worse!"

Rapunzel walked quickly even in the fog. And she seemed sort of . . . nervous. *It's probably just the fog,* Snow thought. *Or the blind descent she just made.*

"The deer knows the way," Snow said. She hoped her words would be reassuring.

"I know the way," Rapunzel replied a little shortly. "I mean, I've been on this path a zillion times before. It's just —"

Rapunzel was interrupted by the sound of rustling leaves and breaking branches.

"By my sword!" a voice cried just off the path to the left. "Yowch!"

Val.

"Over here, your highness." Rapunzel held out a hand and pulled a rather bedraggled prince onto the path. Val had a branch wrapped in his dark curls and a leaf sticking out of his vest. He was rubbing his forehead.

"Um, hi," he said, smiling. "I guess I sort of lost my way."

"It's the fog," Snow said.

"But I found this!" Val pulled the thorny branch out of his hair and offered the girls a few berries from it.

"We don't have time for a snack now," Rapunzel said. She was still speaking more softly than usual. "We're late. And Madame Gothel might be looking for me."

"Don't be ridiculous!" Val said, popping a berry in his mouth. "Why would Madame Gothel look for you?" Val teased. "You're always right where she left you."

"Listen. She knows I get out," Rapunzel said gravely. "She saw me yesterday. And if she catches me doing it again I don't know what she'll do." She paused and took a deep breath. "This could be my last day of freedom."

Snow gasped. This was terrible news! She couldn't imagine Princess School without Rapunzel! Snow's mind spun with questions and worries. How did the witch find out? What had she said to Rapunzel? And most important, what were they going to do now? Beside her, Val was speechless. And Rapunzel was already marching down the path toward school.

Chapter Six
Signed, Sealed . . . Delivered?

Rose shifted in her seat, waiting for Sir Spondence to speak. Instead the instructor peered out the tall classroom windows and gave his well-trimmed goatee three quick tugs. His swooping eyebrows sat low over his eyes as he looked into the fog.

"Alas, my ladies. In all the days it has been my pleasure to instruct fine, unformed royals in the art of courtly communication" — he paused dramatically — "I have never waited such a prolonged period to receive a return communiqué. I cannot believe that the Charm School has lost its charm. No, I simply cannot."

"Neither can I," Snow whispered to Rose. "Hans Charming is just, well, too charming!"

Not hearing her, Sir Spondence sank into his well-upholstered chair and looked with worry at the girls sitting expectantly before him, each at her own carved writing desk. "I greatly fear something is awry," he confessed. Then he sat up straighter, as if pulling strength from a hidden inner wellspring. "Yet, we shall not be deterred! We need not a missive in hand to compose another!"

Rose couldn't hide the small smile that played on her lips. Sir Spondence was *so* serious. He spoke as if he were trying to inspire an army to battle, not a group of princesses to write! She picked up her quill, gently wiping the tip on the inkwell so it would not drip on the thick parchment.

My Dear Prince Valerian, Rose began. Suddenly she felt something tap her knee. Snow was handing back a small scroll under the desk without turning around. Rose carefully took the scroll in her left hand without moving her quill from the paper. If Snow was passing scrolls, it must be important. Scroll-passing was seriously frowned upon in Princess School. Royals used pages and courtly communications — not notes on scraps — to convey their messages. Rose unrolled the tiny parchment in her lap and read:

We need to talk about Rapunzel's tower trouble. Soon!

Rose glanced at Rapunzel. She was hunched over her scroll, dripping ink onto her desk, parchment, and sleeve. She didn't look like she was in trouble. She just looked like Rapunzel — feisty and independent, with no princess pomp. It seemed to Rose that Rapunzel always had it together. And she didn't have any meddling parents to deal with or spying fairies "looking out for her," like Rose had. And even if she did, Rapunzel probably wouldn't care. That girl could handle anything!

Rose glanced down at the scroll on her lap. She knew Rapunzel was worried that Madame Gothel would find out about Princess School. But since Rapunzel had made it to school, Rose assumed the secret must still be safe.

Still wondering what exactly the trouble could be, Rose continued her letter to Val. Maybe she would ask him what was going on with Rapunzel. He certainly knew her well enough. But who knew if he would ever even get her letter, or if she would get a reply. She decided against it.

While the girls signed and sealed their notes, Sir Spondence peered through the diamond-shaped panes of glass. He pushed open the window just as Rose pressed her seal into the melted wax.

After licking his index finger, Sir Spondence poked it outside. A moment later he pulled it back in with a shiver. He banged the window shut and whirled to face the class. "Whether the weather will cooperate or not, we shall endeavor to deliver our impressive epistles!" he declared, pounding a fist into his open hand. "If it please Your Princesses, the latest letters will be

sent by the most courteous of couriers — the woodland creatures!"

That will cheer up Snow at least, Rose thought. Snow
White loved animals more than anything.

Rose followed Ella and Rapunzel out into the hall
and down several flights of stairs. The princesses spoke
of exams and correspondence and Charm School boys
in hushed voices as they wound their way past ivy and
rose-carved pillars and arches. When the doors to the
school whooshed open, Rose shivered. The misty air
was cool and they hadn't stopped to get their cloaks.
Crossing the garden, Rose leaned over to whisper to
Ella. "What's going on?" she asked. Rapunzel was walking up ahead.

Ella shrugged and showed Rose the tiny scroll in
her palm. She'd gotten a note, too.

On the other side of the misty garden, Sir Spondence held up his hand. The princesses stopped and
gathered around him, huddling close to hear and to
keep one another warm.

Sir Spondence pulled a tiny silver whistle from his
waistcoat and blew a quick tune. The whistle sounded
surprisingly like Snow's whistle — the one she used to
call the animals and birds when she scattered seeds
and nuts at her cottage. Rose looked at Snow, smiling,
to see if she noticed, too. But Snow — who would
normally have been dancing a jig at the chance to

combine her two loves, school and animals — looked worried.

Breaking out of the circle, Rose started toward her long-haired friend. She simply had to find out what was going on.

She stopped in her tracks when something caught her eye — a figure in a dark cape and striped stockings disappearing into the woods. Rose couldn't be certain, but it looked like a Grimm School witch. And it looked as though the witch was carrying a pink scroll! Rose was about to call out when Sir Spondence shrieked shrilly. The animals had arrived.

A raccoon with ruffled fur staggered close to the girls. He looked tired and wet. The dark circles around his eyes were extra dark, but his eyes were open star-tlingly wide. A moist badger, three wet foxes, and a shivering warren of sopping rabbits followed the rac-coon.

"Whatever is wrong?" Snow asked. She dropped to her knees and began to dry the creatures with her skirts, singing softly to them. A few of the other princesses awkwardly followed suit.

Clearly flustered by the disheveled and shivering animals, Sir Spondence wrung his hands in a most un-royal manner. Rose thought someone should comfort him, too.

"Never," he said, "never have I seen such disorder, such dampness. The woodland creatures look deeply distraught!"

Rose was thinking the exact same thing about Sir Spondence. The mist curled his hair and beard, and the worry gave his eyes a wild look. Just when she thought he would not be able to finish the lesson at all, the stocky teacher took a deep breath and steadied himself.

"Before we can go further you must each select a messenger," Sir Spondence said. The teacher gained confidence as he walked among the princesses handing out ribbons. "When you have secured your scroll you must announce to whom the post shall pass. Speak clearly and kindly."

Rose stooped and chose the closest animal, a dazed-looking porcupine. She quickly stuck her scroll onto the creature's prickly back. She wished she could pet it or something, but its whole body was covered in quills.

"Prince Valerian," she said softly, forcing herself to smile into the animal's face. "Please take this scroll to Prince Valentine Valerian."

The porcupine stared at her blankly. He didn't look like he'd understood a word. Rose wished she had Snow's way with animals, and even thought of asking

Snow for help. But the porcupine, whether it understood or not, had turned and was waddling back into the woods.

Rose watched as the fog swirled around the small creature. The scroll disappeared first in the white mist. And before the tiny porcupine had gone the length of a pink carpet it had completely disappeared, too.

Chapter Seven
Correspondence Chaos

Rapunzel watched as the silver fox carrying her scroll to Oliver Eggert trotted into the woods.

Somehow the fox's departure reminded her of the willow tree gobbling up the letter to her mother.

"Another missive duly swallowed," she said when the fox had disappeared. The missing letters gave her an uneasy feeling. So did the strange misty fog that surrounded Princess School. Rapunzel almost felt as if it were following her.

Brushing away her gloomy thoughts, Rapunzel got to her feet. Suddenly hailstones as big as teacups began to pound down around the girls.

"What in the world?" Rapunzel muttered, looking up. That was a mistake. A quail-egg-sized hailstone landed with a thunk on her forehead.

"Ouch!" Rapunzel scowled and rubbed her head. Compared to the hail, fog seemed pleasant. The chunks were icy and sharp and fell mercilessly from the sky. Bloomers and animals ran in all directions.

"Owie!" cried a princess who had been assailed on the arm. She held the sore spot as she ran toward a large oak tree to take cover.

"My gown!" shouted another, not sure which way to go. "It's been torn!"

"We must make our way back to the castle posthaste!" Sir Spondence called over the din.

Suddenly Snow appeared at Rapunzel's side. Rose and Ella were right behind her.

"Come on," Snow whispered. "We're going to the stables."

"Fine with me," Rapunzel replied. She and the other girls stole away from the chaotic group and made their way through the hail to the grass-roofed structure that housed the school's horses. Ella pulled open the heavy wooden door and the girls ducked inside.

Rapunzel led the way into their favorite empty stall — one that had been painted a washed lavender — and slumped down on a bale of hay. The smell of fresh straw and saddle soap met her nostrils, and she began to feel a little better.

"I have never seen anything like that," Ella said, pulling stray bits of icy hail from her hair. "It was awful!"

Snow nodded gravely. "I just hope they make it to shelter!"

"They will," Rapunzel said. She rubbed her forehead. "The castle is only a little farther than the stables."

Snow turned toward her friend. "I was talking about the animals!" she cried. "I mean, the poor creatures were soaked to the skin when they arrived. And then to have to deliver scrolls in this awful weather. . . . It just doesn't seem fair!"

"The weather *is* awfully strange," Ella said thoughtfully.

"Something is going on," Snow stated. "Something . . . spooky."

Rose sat up straighter. "Oh!" she said. "I'm almost positive I just saw a Grimm girl stealing into the woods with one of our scrolls!"

"Really?" Rapunzel asked. "Who?"

"I'm not sure," Rose admitted. "It was so foggy I couldn't really see."

"Those Grimms are trouble," Ella said.

Snow nodded in agreement. "I know," she said. "But we have something even more important to discuss." Snow's big, dark eyes were serious as she nudged Rapunzel. "Tell them," she encouraged.

Rapunzel let out a big sigh. "It's just that Madame Gothel knows for sure I've been escaping from my tower," she said.

Ella and Rose gasped simultaneously.

"She said that I'm no princess, that my parents were poor thieves. And she vowed not to let me escape again!"

Ella looked thoughtful. "Maybe the fog was Madame Gothel's way of trying to keep you in today," she said.

"That makes sense," Rose admitted.

Snow nodded. "That terrible witch said she's not going to let Rapunzel come to school anymore." Her voice was full of alarm.

"She can't do that. Maybe you ought to write *her* a letter," Rose said angrily. "Though she certainly doesn't deserve anything cordial."

The girls laughed halfheartedly, then fell into a worried silence.

"We have to make sure Rapunzel can keep getting out," Snow said. "Val meets her at the tower every morning, but he can't do it alone. It may take more than one person to foil that bad witch."

Rose and Ella nodded solemnly. They were taking it all so seriously! Rapunzel suddenly felt overwhelmed. She knew the trouble brewing with Madame Gothel was bad, but she could handle it, right? She looked at her shoes.

"Don't worry, Rapunzel," Ella said comfortingly. "We won't let Madame Gothel keep you all to herself.

Princess School just wouldn't be the same without you!"

"I can come tomorrow morning," Rose volunteered. "I'll tell the fairies I have curtsy call in the morning. They'll have no idea that rolling out the pink carpet is really just for special school occasions."

Rapunzel looked at the girls surrounding her. They were the greatest friends anyone could ever want. But their concern was making her feel better *and* worse. Snow's eyes were wide. Ella looked nervous. And Rose had just offered to help in the morning even though it would mean getting up early — something she hated to do. They all seemed genuinely worried.

Rapunzel swallowed hard. Maybe the situation was more dire than she thought.

Chapter Eight

Writing on the Wall

Rapunzel walked slowly down the path toward the tower. Val had a last-minute jousting practice, so she was walking home by herself, but Rapunzel didn't mind. She had a lot to think about — the weird stuff going on in Cordial Correspondence, her troubles with Madame Gothel, getting ready for exams, her jealousy about Rose and Val, and the worried looks on her friends' faces as they talked together in the stables.

It's no big deal, she told herself. *They're just looking out for me. That's what friends do.* But needing help was not a familiar feeling. And Rose was coming to help her tomorrow. That was okay, except that Rose was coming with Val. And if they couldn't get Rapunzel out they'd be walking to school together, alone!

Val would probably love that, Rapunzel thought miserably.

Taking a deep breath, Rapunzel untied her cape

and swung it off her shoulders. The strange weather had cleared. In fact, it had turned into a glorious afternoon. The sky was a deep cerulean blue with a few puffy white clouds. A light breeze was blowing, making the leaves whisper happily on the forest trees.

"Rose probably just wants to see Val," Rapunzel said aloud as she gazed up at the sky. The cloud above her was shaped like a flower. As she watched it pass, a lump grew in her stomach. Rose and Val. She hated the way she felt about their relationship. It wasn't like her to be jealous. They were both her good friends. She was glad they got along. So why did their friendship bother her so much?

Ahead of her the path widened and the tower came into view. Rapunzel stared up at it for a minute. It looked different — straighter, rounder — more welcoming somehow. Seeing it made Rapunzel feel oddly better.

Stop being such a sad jester, Rapunzel scolded herself. *Things are never as bad as they seem.*

Whistling a tune she'd learned from Snow, Rapunzel skipped forward and began to climb. A minute later she swung her leg over the edge of her windowsill.

Rapunzel peered around her familiar room. Madame Gothel was nowhere to be seen, but she had left a soufflé of wilted greens and a glass of milk on the small table next to her bed. Rapunzel looked at the food in surprise. Though they appeared to be the same bitter greens Madame Gothel always served, the old witch had never made anything as fancy as a soufflé before — and she'd never brought Rapunzel an afternoon snack.

She'd left Rapunzel something else, too. A letter.

Rapunzel eyed the note warily. It was probably filled with threats and accusations. Madame Gothel must have been furious when she'd brought the soufflé and found that Rapunzel was gone.

Maybe I can just ignore it, Rapunzel thought. She felt okay for the first time all day and didn't want to break the spell. But she knew she had to read it. And the longer she waited, the worse it would be.

Bracing herself, Rapunzel picked up the letter. It was written on thick, earthen-colored paper, which was folded and sealed with pea-green wax and stamped in the shape of a cast-iron cauldron.

Sitting down on her bed, Rapunzel broke the seal, unfolded the letter, and began to read.

Rapunzel,

Perfect potions. You have been like a daughter to me these last ten years — filling my cauldron with just the right things. Do not worry your head over changes, young Rapunzel. I will make sure things remain the same forever. Forget about Princess School. You have me. You do not need friends. They will only abandon you in the end — something I will never do.

Madame Gothel (Mother)

Rapunzel stared down at the paper in her hand. There had to be a mistake. She looked at the outside again to make sure it really was for her. The letters of her name were clearly written in Madame Gothel's sharp scrawl.

Why would the old witch write such a letter? Rapunzel read it again, and her mouth dropped open even farther than it had before. This time she read each word carefully . . . including the signature. The last word hit her like a slap in the face. It said *Mother.*

Somehow Madame Gothel had received the letter Rapunzel had written to her mother! Even worse, she thought Rapunzel wrote the letter to *her*!

Filled with fury, Rapunzel leaped to her feet and began to pace the floor. How could Madame Gothel *ever* believe that she thought of her as a mother? What mother kept her daughter locked up in a tower for years on end? And what did Madame Gothel know about friends?

"My friends *are* real!" Rapunzel cried to the empty room. "They would never abandon me!"

Rapunzel glanced at the letter again. She ripped it to shreds and threw the pieces out the window where they scattered in the breeze. But she still felt furious. She had to think of something else to do — something that would make Madame Gothel understand her mistake.

Rapunzel looked over at the small hearth. Since the weather was warm, there was no fire burning. But the blackened stick she used to stoke the fire caught her eye. She could use it like a quill to write a response. Since she'd torn up the only paper in the room she would have to write the response right on the wall.

Rapunzel quickly picked up the stick and began to write.

MG,

That letter was not for you.
You are not my mother, and never will be.
I am not a bird in a cage.
You cannot keep me trapped forever.
And you do not know my friends.
Unlike you, they would never betray me.

R.

She had to blacken the end of the stick in the flame of her candle a few times to complete the message, but the effort was worth it. The note said just what she wanted it to.

Satisfied and exhausted, Rapunzel ate a few bites of her soufflé and fell into a dreamless sleep.

Morning came quickly. Still curled up on her lumpy mattress, Rapunzel was suddenly aware of a blinding light. It burned right through her eyelids, giving her a headache. Was she dreaming?

Very slowly Rapunzel opened one eye. She wasn't dreaming. Her tower room was filled with a light so intense it hurt just to be in its presence. Using her hand to shade her eyes, Rapunzel looked around. She spied a bowl of boiled greens and a mug of tea on the table next to her bed.

"So much for better food," Rapunzel said, closing one eye and reaching for the fork. The greens were overdone and especially bitter.

By the time she had swallowed the last bite, Rapunzel could almost squint around her tower room without shading her eyes. Through lowered lids she saw a response from Madame Gothel written on the wall:

Birds have wings. Bees have stings.
You, little bird, shall never fly.

You shall stay in this tower
Until the day you die.

Rapunzel felt the blood pound through her veins.

"I will not be trapped! I will come and go as I please!" she shouted to no one. She hurried to the window to flee for the day. But if the light inside her tower was painfully bright, the light outside was truly blinding. It seemed as if all the sun's blazing energy were pinpointed on the stone tower in the forest.

Shielding her face with her arm, Rapunzel tried to look down to the ground. It was impossible. She couldn't see anything. Her head ached even more than before. Closing her eyes, she retreated into her tower room.

How was she going to get out of there?

Rapunzel tapped her foot on the stone floor in frustration. The soft sound echoed in her ears. And then she heard another sound — voices.

Familiar, friendly voices.

"Rapunzel!" Val shouted. "Are you okay? Stay away from the window! It's too bright!"

Relief flooded through Rapunzel. Then she smirked. "No kidding," she called back, teasing. "I thought it was midnight out there."

The next thing Rapunzel heard was a scraping sound — the sound of someone climbing up the tower.

But Val was terrified of heights. He'd only ever climbed up the tower once, and it had taken an hour of coaxing.

Then, all of a sudden, the light dimmed.

"Come on out," a different voice called. It was Rose. But the figure swinging its leg over the windowsill in Rapunzel's tower and successfully blocking the blinding light looked more like a knight. A knight wearing a dress.

Rose quickly pulled off Val's jousting helmet and tossed it to Rapunzel. She looked around at the tower room. "Put this on," she said matter-of-factly. "And pull the visor down to protect your eyes."

"What about you?" Rapunzel asked, taking the helmet. She was grateful for it, but wanted to make sure Rose had a plan for herself, too. "How will you see?"

Rose wrapped a gauzy scarf around her face several times. "I can use this," she said. "My eyes have adjusted a little. This will dim the brightness just enough."

Rapunzel pulled down the visor of the helmet and followed Rose out the window.

Climbing down wasn't easy. The bright sunlight made the tower stones scorching hot. Rapunzel kept banging the top of the visor on the tower wall. And Rose had to stop twice to retie the scarf around her eyes.

Finally Rose and Rapunzel stepped safely onto the ground.

Even under the shade of the forest trees it was still bright and unusually warm. But at least Rapunzel could see without the helmet. She pulled it off so she could recoil her hair. She handed the helmet to Rose. "Thanks," she said. "I could never have gotten down without —"

"A fine rescue, m'lady," Val said, interrupting Rapunzel. He took the helmet from Rose, then bowed low and kissed her hand. "Truly daring."

Rose giggled, and Rapunzel felt her thanks catch in her throat. She'd wanted to tell her friends everything about the letter mix-up and Madame Gothel's horrible reply. But not now. Clearly Rose hadn't come to help her. She was just trying to impress Val!

Without another word Rapunzel turned and stomped toward school.

Chapter Nine
Heating Up

Ella wiped her brow with the tiny lace handkerchief she kept in her sleeve and hurried down the road toward Princess School. She was late, and though the sun had only been up a few hours it was already blazing hot. Ella wished she had left her cloak at home, but after yesterday's hailstorm she hadn't known what to expect.

The weather was the least of Ella's worries. If she was tardy one more time she was not sure what Madame Garabaldi would do — probably pop her corset! But there was no way of getting out of her stepmother Kastrid's chores. That morning, in addition to the long list of usual tasks, Kastrid needed a dress pressed for a tea party she was hosting that afternoon, and her stepsisters Hagatha and Prunilla requested poached eggs *and* waffles for breakfast. And there would be more chores later, too, Ella was sure.

What in the kingdom makes me think I can make it to

Rapunzel's tower next Monday to help Val? Ella wondered.

Ella almost laughed at the idea of having "extra" time. But the thought of Rapunzel being stuck in her tower, unable to get to school, wiped the smile off her face. It was just too terrible to consider. Princess School needed Rapunzel. Ella needed Rapunzel. She was so fun and outspoken and spunky and bold — all of the things Ella wished she could be.

In the distance Ella heard the first trumpets peal. She only had a few minutes to get to hearthroom.

"Blast," she murmured, hoisting her skirts and hurrying faster.

Ella had reached the turnoff for the lane into town when a noise made her stop and turn. It sounded like branches scraping on windows. Or worse — Hagatha's laugh!

"Hagatha, don't you try to get me in trouble!" Ella called. There was no response. Maybe it was her other awful stepsister.

"Prunilla, you'll only make yourself late, too." Ella backed down the lane, looking right and left for Kastrid's nasty daughters. Despite the heat of the day, a chill went up Ella's spine. The screechy cackling sound was now directly to her left.

Whirling, Ella clapped her hand over her own

mouth to stifle a shriek. What she saw was worse than her stepsisters. Two nasty-looking Grimm witches were crouched in a stand of trees, waving twisted wands and laughing cruelly. In front of them a small whirlwind spun madly, throwing up sticks and dust and small rocks.

It was an impressive little tornado. But that wasn't what was making the witches cackle. A tiny, very scared-looking field mouse was caught in the vortex, squeaking for all he was worth as he was whirled around and around.

"Miserable mousie!" one of the witches mock-whined between guffaws. She had pond-water-colored hair and an orange-and-green-spotted dress. Ella couldn't see her face because she was bent over, clutching her stomach.

"Rotten rodent," the other witch chortled. The second voice was awfully familiar. Leaning farther forward, Ella spied the witch's black-and-red-striped stockings and lethal-looking boots. It could only be Hortense Hegbottom — one of the grisliest girls at Grimm School! Then Ella saw something lying by one of Hortense's huge boots. It looked like —

Snap! Suddenly a twig broke beneath Ella's soft slipper. All at once the cackling stopped. The two witches looked at each other, then turned in her direction. Ella did not stay to see if they saw her. Gathering her skirts, she ran toward Princess School as fast as she could.

As she slid into her hearthroom seat, Ella could still feel her heart pounding in her chest. She tried to quiet her breathing before Madame Garabaldi could point out that "panting is for poodles, not princesses." She could not wait to tell her friends what she had seen. She motioned Rose, Rapunzel, and Snow toward her.

"I think I know who's been messing with the weather," she puffed. "And mucking up the mail, too."

"Who?" Rose whispered.

"The Grimm witches!" Ella breathed. "I think you *did* see one with a scroll yesterday, Rose. I saw a pair on my way to school making whirlwinds and tormenting a field mouse. And I think I saw a scroll under Hortense's boot!"

"Hortense Hegbottom?" Rapunzel asked. Her face was contorted as if she smelled something foul.

Ella nodded.

"A field mouse?" Snow gasped.

Ella nodded again.

"There's something else —" Rose started to say. She was interrupted.

At the front of the room Madame Garabaldi took her throne and impatiently tapped her ringed fingers on the ornate arm.

"I hope I don't have to ask for your attention," she said softly. "Monarchs do not beg." The room went completely silent. The Bloomers knew better than to make Madame Garabaldi ask twice.

Pleased with the silence, Madame Garabaldi began scroll call. She announced each name as if she were reading from a grand guest list. "Rapunzel Arugula!" Rapunzel stood to answer.

Ella looked at Rose, a question in her eyes. What was the other news? Was it bad? Good? Rose pointed at Rapunzel under her desk and shook her head discreetly back and forth. Ella sighed. It looked as though there was more bad news about Rapunzel.

When Ella's name was called she stood and curtsied to Madame Garabaldi. "Present," she replied. Then she sat as patiently as she could until scroll call was over and Madame Garabaldi began the day's proclamations.

"As you all know, exams are quickly approaching. If you wish to improve your performance, as I am sure you all do" — Madame Garabaldi looked smilingly at her students — "I suggest you take advantage of your time here in hearthroom to prepare. In fact I suggest that you take every opportunity both at school and at home to study. These exams require only one thing — that you spend the time to prepare for them properly."

It was all Ella could do to keep from dropping her

head on her desk. *What time?* She barely had time to get to school, let alone study before and after!

Maybe I should be the one locked in a tower, Ella thought. *At least then I'd have a moment to myself!*

When Madame Garabaldi stood and turned toward her desk the princesses in hearthroom opened their texts. In an instant, Snow, Rose, and Rapunzel were huddled around Ella's desk.

"The little witches aren't the only ones mucking around," Rose whispered to her friends. "Gothel was trying to cook Rapunzel this morning. Val and I barely got her out!"

Rose related the whole story to Snow and Ella. When she finished, Snow's eyes were as big as saucers, and Ella had changed her mind about wanting to live in a tower.

"That's not all," Rapunzel said glumly. "Now Madame Gothel is acting like she really *is* my mother."

Ella cringed. She didn't think she could stand it if Kastrid started pretending she was her mother. And Kastrid wasn't even a real witch.

Rapunzel explained the letter mishap, twisting and untwisting her hair all the while. "She is flaming mad. And when she sees I am out of my tower again she's going to be even more determined to keep me in — forever!"

Ella was trying to think of something comforting to say when a trumpet blasted in the doorway, announcing a visitor.

"A thousand pardons!" Sir Spondence burst into the room followed by a page carrying a basket of scrolls. Madame Garabaldi rose slowly from her desk to greet the unexpected guest.

"To what do we owe the honor of your visit, Sir Spondence?" she asked. She didn't sound particularly honored.

"Good lady, I beseech you. Grant me but a moment to direct the deliverance of these late letters and I will trouble you no longer." Sir Spondence bowed low and smiled sweetly at the hearthroom teacher.

Madame Garabaldi did not return the smile, but she didn't banish the visitor, either. "Do it and be done," she said, waving her hand.

"Ah, gracious lady. May the stars —"

"Quickly," Madame Garabaldi enunciated.

Sir Spondence was uncharacteristically quiet as he took the scrolls from the page's basket and passed them to the girls.

"There are but a precious few," Sir Spondence whispered to all of the princesses looking expectantly at the basket. "A preponderance were pounded to a pulp by the hateful hailstones!"

Snow hastily opened the orangish scroll Sir Spondence had held out to her. "It's from Hans Charming!" she cried out.

"Of course it is, silly," Ella said in a hushed tone. Madame Garabaldi did not look up, but Ella could swear she saw her raise her eyebrows. "Didn't you write to him?"

"Yes, but he wants to meet me by the wishing well!" Snow burbled. "Ooh, Rapunzel, who wrote to you?"

Rapunzel had an unopened scroll on her desk, and Ella thought she looked a little nervous as she turned it over to examine the seal. It was a tiny dragon. "It's from Val," she said. She sounded surprised. And glad.

"But isn't your correspondent Oliver Eggert?" Ella asked.

"You know Val," Rapunzel said, ripping the scroll open. "He probably . . ." She trailed off.

Ella read the beginning of the letter over Rapunzel's shoulder. *My blooming Rose,* it began.

"That's not your letter," Ella said. Rapunzel must have realized the mix-up at the same moment because she quickly rerolled the scroll and thrust it toward Rose. But not before Ella read the next line. *I must speak to you* alone.

What a prince! Ella thought. Of course Val would be worried about Rapunzel. Of course he would want to ask Rose how to help.

Ella smiled, remembering how this same group of friends had gotten her through a tough time. They would do the same for Rapunzel. Together they could do anything!

Rapunzel did not seem so sure. She sat in front of Ella, staring straight ahead. Even though Ella couldn't see her face she could tell her friend was frowning.

"I'll come by on Monday to make sure you can get out," Ella whispered. She placed a reassuring hand on Rapunzel's shoulder. "Don't worry."

With all of her homework, extra studying, and chores to do, Ella didn't exactly know how she was going to make it to Rapunzel's on Monday morning. But she would. Rapunzel needed her, and Ella would not let her friend down.

Chapter Ten
Unraveling

When the final trumpet sounded, Rapunzel stood up slowly and filed with the other Bloomers into the unusually warm hallway. She had been listening all afternoon for the signal that the school day was over but now, facing a corridor of Bloomers bent over their trunks, she was not sure what she'd been waiting for. She certainly wasn't anxious to go home, especially since the sun was still blaring. What if she couldn't get into her tower? And assuming she could, the weekend loomed ahead of her like a waiting dragon.

Rapunzel pulled her embroidery hoop from her trunk. Her Stitchery project was going to make a terrible purse, but at least it was useful as a fan. She glanced up and down the corridor, scanning the faces for one of her friends. She needed cheering up.

She spotted Rose, surrounded by admiring girls, two trunks down. Rapunzel started to raise her hand.

Then she remembered the note in Val's scroll and pulled her hand back down like she'd touched fire. How could she forget Val was walking Rose home today — alone?

Ducking down so Rose wouldn't see her, Rapunzel fumed. It just wasn't fair. Val had been walking to and from school with her since the day she started Princess School. Princes were supposed to be loyal! And he wasn't just any prince, he was her friend — her oldest friend. If she couldn't count on Val, whom could she count on?

Maybe Madame Gothel's right, Rapunzel thought grimly. She felt her life was unraveling like an untied braid. *You have other friends,* she reminded herself. Hadn't Ella volunteered to come and make sure she got out on Monday morning? Rapunzel blew her bangs off her moist forehead. Monday was a long way off. And Rapunzel wanted to talk to somebody now.

The halls cleared out quickly as princesses collected their schoolwork and made their way toward waiting coaches. Rapunzel walked slowly several paces behind Rose. She'd walked right past Rapunzel without even noticing.

When they got outside, Rapunzel stopped on the stairs and watched Val introduce himself to Rose's father and her guardian fairies. *He probably has to talk them into letting Rose walk home!* Rapunzel thought.

Her father is probably terrified that she'll trip and stub her toe. She almost laughed. Living under such watchful eyes would drive Rapunzel crazy. But was it really that different from being locked in a tower?

Though Rose's father looked worried, eventually Rose and Val were allowed to walk together down the path toward Rose's castle. Rapunzel did notice one of the fairies — a blue one — flying a short distance behind. She tried again to laugh. Rose's parents treated her like such a baby! But she couldn't even smile. Her stomach was tied in knots, and watching Rose and Val together was only making the knots tighter.

Ella dashed past Rapunzel with a swish of worn taffeta, her arms full of books. "I'd love to walk home with you, but I have to get the tea and crumpets ready for Kastrid's party," she apologized. "And then I have to study!" She waved over her shoulder as she ran. Rapunzel was tempted to run beside her and tell her how awful she was feeling. She jogged a few steps but then stopped herself. Ella was such a good listener. But the poor girl had her own problems.

Besides, there was another person Rapunzel could talk to. If she hadn't rushed off, too.

"Is he there? Can you see him?" Snow's singsong voice was music to Rapunzel's ears. Snow was just coming out of the castle and gazing across the moat toward the Charm School.

"Who? Val?" Rapunzel asked.

"Oh, no!" Snow twittered. "Hans! Hans Charming. Do you see him by the wishing well? Do I look presentable?" Snow did a little curtsy demonstration for Rapunzel. She looked great but Rapunzel felt her heart sink. It was on a collision course with the knots in her stomach.

"Perfect," Rapunzel said a little glumly. She wasn't about to ruin Snow's first meeting with her pen-prince. So she kept her mouth shut and waved Snow off. "You'd better get to the well. Your prince will be there soon."

Snow skipped away, giggling. Rapunzel stood on the hot castle steps watching her last friend go. There was nothing left to do but head home.

Rapunzel's feet felt leaden on the woodland path. The sun beat down, making her coiled hair feel heavy on her head. Though she'd taken off her cloak she was sweltering under her gown.

I don't think I have ever been this hot, she mused. *Or this lonely.* The last thought echoed in Rapunzel's brain.

Before she started Princess School, Rapunzel didn't even know what lonely was. She had been alone for so much of her life it just felt normal. She used to entertain herself in her tower with whatever the wind happened to blow in her window — leaves, feathers, dandelion seeds. . . . Back then, spiders were her best companions. Then, when she was seven, Val had appeared and coaxed her down to the ground. And this year she'd started attending Princess School. Now, after having a taste of friendship, everything had changed. And not necessarily for the better.

When she reached the clearing, Rapunzel squinted up at her tower. The sun was lower and not nearly as bright as it had been that morning. But when Rapunzel touched the rounded rocks on the tower wall they were still hot. With no place else to go, Rapunzel climbed up quickly so she would not scorch her hands.

After pulling herself in the window Rapunzel collapsed on her bed. She closed her eyes but they could not shut out the thoughts whirling in her mind. She wished she could just stop thinking for a little while. When she opened her eyes again she saw her dinner sitting on the table — two toadstools and a handful of unwashed greens. Beside the dirty roots was another scroll from Madame Gothel.

Rapunzel,

Toad's tears! Somehow you manage to get out of your tower in spite of me. Your ties of friendship must be very strong. Are they binding? You are right. I do not know much about friendship, but

*neither do you. I see all with my witch's sight. If
you continue to escape you will receive a terrible
slight.*

M. Gothel

Rapunzel cast the scroll across the room before she
even read the last word. *What does that old hag know
about my friends?* she fumed. Then she picked up the
letter and read it again. *Toad's tears,* indeed!

Rapunzel grabbed the blackened stick from the
hearth and wielded it over the back of the scroll like a
weapon. She was about to start her reply when she
heard a voice in her head. Not her own angry voice. A
different one, a flowery one — Sir Spondence!

'Tis true delight what courtly courtesy doth rend, the instructor said.

Slowly a smile spread across Rapunzel's face. Her
grasp around the stylus loosened, and she began to
write.

To the ever-thoughtful Madame Gothel,

*However can I thank you for your kind letter of
warning? Allow me to assure you that the salty
offerings of a sad amphibian have nothing to do
with my escaping the tower. As for my friends, I*

*think I do know them. I am confident they will
stand by me no matter what, for they are royally
loyal.*

*Yours truly,
Rapunzel*

Satisfied, Rapunzel smoothed the scroll on the table and read it over one last time. It was certainly courteous. Sir Spondence would be proud. But with a pang Rapunzel wondered if her words were true.

Of course my friends are royally loyal, she reassured herself. *Aren't they?*

In a flash Rapunzel saw each of her friends rushing away from the Princess School steps, and away from her. Only a few days before, Rapunzel had been certain of her friendships. She couldn't have imagined doubting them. But everything was so topsy-turvy right now that Rapunzel didn't feel sure of anything.

Chapter Eleven
Secret Valentine

"Wow, they really look out for you, huh?" Val raised his eyebrows and nodded toward the blue fairy darting around Rose's head.

Rose batted at the fairy like a fly. "That's putting it mildly," she said. "Actually, I'm surprised they let me walk in the woods without more bodyguards than just Petunia."

"M'lady, you are safe in the presence of a prince." Val pulled a handkerchief from his waistcoat pocket and twirled it twice before bowing. When he stood up he was grinning.

Petunia crossed her teeny pudgy arms and *humphed* softly. She was obviously not sure about this "prince."

But Rose was. She admired the way his green eyes twinkled and gratefully took the handkerchief he offered. Daintily she dabbed tiny beads of perspiration from her brow. She could not wait to hear what Val wanted to talk to her about. But he'd said they needed to talk alone. And they weren't alone just yet.

Rose noticed Petunia was sweating and flying slowly. The heat must be getting to her, too. And it gave Rose an idea. Gently Rose held the handkerchief in the air for the fairy, and Petunia gratefully flew toward it to wipe her face.

"Oh, thank you, dear," the fairy squeaked, burying her whole head in the hanky. As soon as Petunia's eyes were covered Rose looked at Val and put a finger to her lips. Then she made two of her fingers walk quickly and pointed toward a bush. Rose loved Petunia. She was actually one of her favorites of the fairy pack. But right now she wanted to ditch her.

Val nodded his understanding and Rose quickly draped the handkerchief over Petunia's whole body, covering her — antennae to toes.

"Ack! Rose dear, what's happened? Where are you?" The fairy's tiny voice was muffled under the starched linen and the weight of it was pushing her down toward the forest floor. Rose stifled a giggle as she dove for the bushes. Val was right behind her.

"Oh, dear, oh, dear, oh, dear!" Petunia cried when she'd freed herself from the hanky. "Rose has been kidnapped! I must warn the king!" Petunia disappeared as fast as her small wings could propel her round body.

As soon as she was gone, the bush beside the trail erupted in laughter.

"I didn't know you had that in you!" Val said. He sounded impressed.

"I didn't, either." Rose laughed. "Poor Petunia!" Holding their stomachs, Val and Rose stumbled back onto the path.

"So, we're alone now. What did you want to talk to me about?" Rose asked. "And talk fast — it won't take Petunia long to tell my father I've been abducted!"

Rose dusted off her skirt and looked at Val sideways. She felt a little funny. Usually she hated to be around boys. They always acted so dippy. But Val was different. Besides the eyes, he was —

"I'm worried about Rapunzel," Val said. The laughter from a few seconds before was totally gone from his voice. His worry was genuine. "You know, she just hasn't been herself lately. And with Madame Gothel on her case, well . . . it's just that she used to be so carefree. I never worried about her. If anyone can handle living with a witch, it's Rapunzel. I mean, she always beats *me* in a fight." Val blushed a little and looked away from Rose. "But that was before. She doesn't seem so sure of herself now."

Rose nodded. She knew just what Val meant, but she was impressed that he'd noticed and that he cared so much.

"When we first met she had been alone for so long she couldn't even remember seeing anyone except for Madame Gothel, and maybe a Grimm girl going to school, or a woodsman passing by. She thought she made me up — like I was a figment of her imagination. She used to make up lots of games to make the time go by."

Val jumped up onto a large rock on the side of the path and pulled down an oak leaf. "She showed me how to make a kite with a leaf and a strand of hair." Val pulled a dark curled hair from his head to demonstrate. But it was too short and curly to tie to the leaf. "Her hair, of course. And she made up riddles, too. She can make fun out of thin air."

Rose just nodded as Val went on and on. She'd never thought about how alone Rapunzel was before she had Val.

"Most kids have toys and playmates and gardens and stables — lots of things to do. Rapunzel just had herself. She never even had a birthday party! She doesn't even know when her birthday *is*! I don't think she was ever very sad about it. You can't miss what you don't have. But the more time we spent together, the happier she got."

Val looked at Rose a little shyly. "And even then she wasn't as happy as she was when she made friends at Princess School." Val paused for a brief moment. "I guess what I'm saying is, we need to keep her spirits up or she won't have a chance against that old witch. I want to do something. I just don't know what."

Val, who had been walking and talking with increasing speed since he started his speech, came to an abrupt halt and let his hands drop to his sides. Rose bumped right into him. Her feet stopped but her mind was racing ahead. She couldn't believe everything she was hearing!

No birthday party? she thought. *Ever?*

Rose suddenly felt awful. She had always thought that Rapunzel had it easy in so many ways. She practically got to live by herself. She made her own rules. And nobody was ever looking over her shoulder.

But just that morning when Rose saw the tower room for the first time she had been shocked by how small it was. And now hearing Val, Rose had a new view. As much as Rose hated being coddled by her overprotective parents and pestering fairies, she couldn't imagine what it would be like if nobody *ever* made a fuss over her. Maybe that was just what Rapunzel needed. A little fuss.

"I've got it!" Rose grabbed Val by both his shoulders and looked into his surprised green eyes. "A birthday party!" she said. "We can throw Rapunzel a surprise birthday party."

Val's mouth dropped open, but he didn't say a word. He didn't have to. Rose was on a roll.

"It's perfect!" She clapped her hands together and started walking faster than ever down the path. "Snow and Ella will love it! Ooh, and I just remembered — soon we have to compose invitations for Cordial Correspondence. We can invite the other princes — Allister, Hans, and Oliver! And you, of course." Rose smiled over her shoulder at Val.

"It's a great idea!" Val grinned. "But we have to do it soon."

"We'll do it Monday," Rose said. "I can talk to the girls over the weekend."

"And I can teach you some of the flash signals so we can stay in touch about plans during school," Val said, catching Rose's enthusiasm. "It's going to work like a charm!"

The plan was perfect . . . except for one thing.

"It'll be great," Rose said thoughtfully. "Just as long as we can get our invitations properly delivered."

Chapter Twelve
Rising Waters

Rapunzel woke up staring at a bowl of acorns and torn lettuce. She rubbed her eyes. All night she'd dreamed of salad. Now her nightmare was sitting in a bowl beside her bed.

"About time you got up," Madame Gothel croaked. She was standing right next to Rapunzel's small table. Her arms were crossed and the green smoke that always marked her appearance was settling around her feet. She must have just arrived.

Hazy morning sunlight shone through the window, casting a ray onto the parchment on the table.

"Is this for me?" Madame Gothel asked. She picked up the polite response Rapunzel had written the night before, and with her back to Rapunzel began to read.

Rapunzel opened her mouth to speak, then closed it again. She had nothing to say to the old witch. At least not anything nice. Besides, she was curious to see what her reaction would be.

At first it was difficult to tell what Madame Gothel was thinking. Especially with her back turned. Then Madame Gothel's sharp shoulders started to creep closer to her ears. Her neck poked forward and Rapunzel could feel the sneer on her face. The witch was not amused.

The room grew darker as a rain cloud covered the morning sun. Madame Gothel whirled to face Rapunzel. Outside, rain began to fall.

"Troll snot!" she cursed. "What do you know about loyalty? You certainly don't know how to show it!"

Rapunzel's stomach clenched. "What do *you* know about my friends?" she replied, keeping her voice steady.

"I may not know them personally, but I know you won't be seeing them again," Madame Gothel growled back. "Not if I can help it."

Rapunzel looked at the floor. She wanted to hold her tongue and let Madame Gothel stew in her own juices. But she couldn't keep silent. "What do *you* know about *anything*?" she mumbled.

"Well, I *used* to know you, little girl." One of Madame Gothel's eyes grew narrower when she was mad. It was practically closed now. "There was a time when you were glad to see me. We had fun, you and I. Don't you remember anything I taught you?"

Madame Gothel reached out with gnarled fingers toward Rapunzel's braid. She strung a long lock through the fingers of both hands, leaving a little opening for Rapunzel to insert her own hand. It was an invitation to play Cat's Cradle, one of their favorite games when Rapunzel was younger. But Rapunzel had no interest in playing now.

She pulled her hair away and began to deftly fashion it into an elaborate tiara twist. Rapunzel did not look at Madame Gothel, but she could hear her cursing and fuming.

"Gnats! To think I taught you some of my best potions! Now you are so full of princess ways with your fancy hair and flowery speech. I . . . I barely know you!" Madame Gothel spat.

"Maybe you never did," Rapunzel spat back.

Madame Gothel's eyes burned. She did not wait for Rapunzel to unravel her hairdo and lower her out into the rain. Instead she waved her arms and disappeared in an angry cloud.

"And stay out," Rapunzel muttered, flopping down on her hard straw mattress.

Unfortunately, making Madame Gothel feel worse did not make Rapunzel feel any better. She knew it was foolish to make the witch angrier. It would only make her more determined to keep Rapunzel locked in her tower.

All through the long afternoon and evening, Rapunzel tried to study for her exams.

After all of this work to stay in Princess School, I can't *flunk out,* she thought with a wry smile. But she couldn't concentrate. She had no room in her head for memorizing the names of ancient monarchs. Every bit of her brain was consumed with worry — worry that she might never again see her friends or Princess School.

Time and again Rapunzel went to the window and peered out into the rain. It was never ending. And when she looked down at the base of her tower she saw the puddles starting to flow together. Water was inching its way up the rocks.

When Madame Gothel returned with Rapunzel's dinner of sour sorrel soup, the greens and acorns she'd brought for breakfast sat limp and uneaten right where the witch had left them.

Hiding her books under the mattress, Rapunzel pretended to be asleep. She heard Madame Gothel sit down on her small stool and let out a raspy sigh.

Rapunzel must have fallen asleep for real, because the next thing she knew it was morning. Though she could hear the rain falling on the thatched roof she hurried to the window and looked out, hoping for a change. Rapunzel felt her shoulders droop and her head tip forward. Things had changed all right.

Below her the water swirled faster and higher up the sides of the tower. The forest around her home was officially flooded. The flowers had been washed away. Bushes were almost entirely submerged. And small trees were in danger of drowning.

I'll never get to school now, Rapunzel thought, looking at the roiling waters. Even if her friends were as loyal as she hoped they were, how could they possibly get near her in this?

Rapunzel stared at the falling rain for the rest of the weekend. She gave up trying to study. She gave up eating. And she gave up hiding from Madame Gothel. When the witch appeared to bring breakfast and dinner that day Rapunzel did not pretend to be asleep. She didn't do anything but stare glumly out at the falling rain.

On Monday morning Madame Gothel arrived in a gray-and-red witch's dingy and moored it to the side of the tower with one of Rapunzel's braids. "Give up?" she asked, cackling as she tossed more wilted salad along with a few nuts and berries into Rapunzel's bowl.

"Never," Rapunzel said. But she said it more strongly than she felt it. Truthfully, Rapunzel nearly *had* given up. Though she had planned to swim for school that morning, whether her friends came through or not, a second glance at the churning floodwaters had changed her mind.

When Madame Gothel had gone, Rapunzel laid her chin in her hand. *There's no way Snow, Ella, Rose, or Val can make it through this mess,* she thought. She hoped the thought would comfort her. But it didn't convince her that her friends would come if they possibly could. She still felt alone and abandoned.

Wind sent the rain over the edge of the sill. It soaked into Rapunzel's skirts and dripped down her face like tears. Rapunzel squinted into the wicked weather and gasped. Straight ahead she saw a warm glow.

Rapunzel's jaw dropped when a purplish boat came into view. It looked a bit like an eggplant, and in the hands of the funny-looking, shimmery woman steering it, was a large wheel . . . of cheese.

"Hang on, dearie," the woman called. She was jerking the wheel this way and that in an attempt to steer the boat around trees and floating logs. Rapunzel wasn't sure who she was talking to, but the woman could certainly use the advice herself. The eggplant boat was turning in all different directions and looked in danger of capsizing as it zigzagged toward the tower through the frigid water.

"Rapunzel!" a familiar voice called. Behind the

woman steering the cheese, Rapunzel could just make out Ella's and Val's smiling faces. Ella was waving madly.

Suddenly the boat hit a snag. "Lurlina, look out!" Ella pitched forward. The boat almost careened into the tower, but Val reached forward and pushed the boat away from the stone wall. When she got to her feet, Ella was still smiling. "Ahoy!" she called.

Rapunzel returned her friend's grin before grabbing her texts and cloak, descending a foot or two, and leaping aboard. It wasn't a traditional rescue, but it would do.

Chapter Thirteen

Woodland Worry

Skipping outside, Snow stretched her arms and looked at the sky. The air felt electrified and the clouds above the treetops were an ominous gray-green.

"Thank goodness it stopped raining!" Snow chirped. Nearby, two bluebirds busily pulled worms from the drenched grass outside the dwarves' cottage. "Hello!" Snow called merrily. The birds looked up briefly, then turned back to their work. It had rained all weekend long, and they weren't sure what would happen with the weather next. They didn't have time to sing with Snow this morning. They needed to get food and get home!

"Bye-bye now," Snow called as the birds flew off. The busy birds and the gloomy clouds weren't enough to bring Snow down. She'd had a wonderful weekend, starting with her visit with Hans Charming at the wishing well. He was even more adorable than the dwarves! Then on Saturday morning, Rose and a pair of fairies had slogged their way to the cottage with some very exciting news.

Just thinking about Rose's news made Snow beam. She was planning a surprise party for Rapunzel! And Snow simply *loved* surprises.

"Oh, please, can I make the food?" Snow had pleaded.

Rose had easily agreed. And as soon as she did, Snow jumped up to begin. The rest of Snow's weekend was spent peeling and stirring, boiling and baking. The dwarves wanted to help, but Snow refused. She wanted to do everything herself as a special gift for Rapunzel. Snow had so much fun cooking that she almost forgot to study! Luckily Dim and Gruff were willing to help her there. They took turns holding her texts for her so she could read while she was rolling out dough or beating eggs.

Between the rain and the cooking, Snow hadn't made it outside in two days! "I wonder how my woodland friends are doing?" she said aloud. As soon as she'd spoken the words her smile faded. She had forgotten all about the forest animals. The grim weather had been particularly hard on them lately and she'd meant to check on a few of her favorite creatures to make sure they were okay.

Hoisting her skirts a little higher, Snow padded

over the sodden ground. She picked up her pace. If she hurried she would have time to look in on a few of her furry and feathered friends on her way to school.

"Robin!" Snow cooed, stopping by a low nest. "How is your wing?" The little bird's wing was newly healed. She looked well, if a little nervous. Snow stroked her feathers and skipped on.

"Hello, Buck," she spoke softly to a thicket. "Are you in there?" The young deer stepped shyly out of the bushes. He looked timid and shivery, but unhurt.

"Are you cold?" Snow asked. She touched his soft fur. It was wet through.

"Ooh, somebody ought to stop those bad Grimm girls from messing with the weather!" Snow said after stopping at the rabbit burrow and finding the bunnies huddled together to keep warm.

Snow stomped her slippered foot. It came down in the mud with an embarrassing squelch. For a moment Snow wished *she* had a way to stop the Grimm girls. Then she giggled at herself. The thought was preposterous. She couldn't even pass the gate to the Grimm School, let alone stand up to all of those witches! And with everything that was going on — the party planning, invitations, and exams — she wouldn't have the time even if she did have the nerve.

Slipping and scurrying, Snow hurried the rest of the way to school. She wondered about poor Rapunzel, shut up with that awful witch all weekend, and hoped she was okay — and that she got out this morning! Lately it seemed there was so much to worry about. But Snow could never fret for very long. There was always something to look forward to — and today it was a party!

As the spires of Princess School came into view, Snow spied Ella and Rose talking to another girl on the school steps. Though the other girl's back was to Snow, the telltale coil of hair made Snow clap her hands together with glee. Rapunzel had made it to school.

"Goody! You made it!" Snow cried as she rushed up to her friends.

"You should have seen it." Rapunzel's eyes were bright with exhilaration. "The water was practically up to my window, and suddenly a giant, floating, purple vegetable appears out of nowhere to rescue me!"

"Lurlina has a way with plants," Ella said humbly. "You should see what she can do with a tomato."

"Ella's fairy godmother is back," Rose explained to Snow, catching her up on the conversation.

"And just in time," Ella added. "She made a boat and helped get Rapunzel out this morning."

"Thank goodness," Snow said, giving herself a little hug. "If you hadn't made it to school we'd have had to cancel the pa —"

Rose stepped in front of Snow, cutting her off. "Say,

Ella, how did you get a fairy godmother, anyway?" she asked loudly. She gave Snow a look over her shoulder.

"Oops, I . . . I have to change my shoes!" Snow clamped her hand over her mouth and rushed up the stairs. She had almost blown the surprise in the first moment she'd seen Rapunzel! It was just too exciting.

I've never been good at secrets, Snow thought. She was just going to have to keep her distance in order to keep the party a surprise.

But staying away from Rapunzel was harder than Snow thought it would be. In hearthroom, Snow bent over her studies and tried not to look at any of her friends. She managed to keep her mouth closed, but she could not keep the smile off her face.

"*Psst*. Snow." Rapunzel leaned close to her ebony-haired friend. "Is the duke fourth or fifth in line for the crown in a kingdom without an heir?" she whispered.

Snow gulped. She looked at Rapunzel. The questioning look in Rapunzel's eyes was too much to take. Snow clamped her teeth together to hold back the secret waiting to burst out of her mouth.

"Frog got your tongue?" Rapunzel asked, looking at Snow a little sideways.

Snow looked back at her desk. Luckily, the trumpet sounded at that very moment. Snow jumped to her feet and ran for her trunk. It was a close call.

Correspondence class was even harder. Not only did Snow have to keep the party a secret, she had to make her invitation for Hans Charming without Rapunzel seeing it! She leaned close to her desk, using her dark hair as a curtain. She wrote quickly, not in her best script, and with a quick glance to see if anyone noticed, she sealed the scroll and breathed a small sigh of relief.

Sir Spondence was strangely silent. Usually he strolled around the chamber exclaiming over a fine seal or a sweet turn of phrase. Today he just stood at the front, gazing out the window and tugging his goatee.

When the missives were ready for delivery, Sir Spondence led the girls down the spiral staircases to the grand foyer. Snow hung back. She did not want to walk beside Rapunzel.

The school doors whooshed open. Outside, the clouds felt lower and darker than they had that morning. But the thick air could not hold Snow's excitement down. She hopped over puddles like a bunny, and when Rapunzel paused to ask Sir Spondence a question, Snow sprang ahead to catch up with Ella and Rose.

"Do you think she knows?" Snow whispered.

Ella and Rose looked toward Rapunzel. They didn't

know what she had asked the instructor, but she was scowling at the answer.

"Not yet," Rose said. "But let's stick together until these invitations get out. We don't want to ruin the surprise."

At the willow, a flock of mourning doves was perched and cooing softly.

"Ooh, doves!" Snow giggled. She'd been looking forward to trying winged delivery.

With their shoulders pressed tightly together, Snow, Ella, and Rose tied their scrolls around the birds' legs.

"I wrote my invitation to Oliver," Rose explained. "Val already knows all about the party."

Ella nodded. Snow let another giggle escape. She glanced over her shoulder and saw Rapunzel's scowl deepen. "Rapunzel needs a party. I hope this works," Snow whispered.

Rose still looked serious. "Me, too," she said quietly, holding her dove up on one finger. "The princes have to get the invitations today!"

Rapunzel sidled closer and the other girls stopped talking. "Is it almost lunchtime?" Rapunzel asked grumpily. "I am starved. And it had better not be salad. What I wouldn't give for a slice of pie."

Ella, Rose, and Snow exchanged glances.

Snow lifted her dove into the air and watched it fly toward the dark clouds. She bit her bottom lip. It was all she could do to keep from telling Rapunzel about the delicious apple and berry pies waiting for her — and her party!

Chapter Fourteen
News Flash!

Rapunzel was in a mood. Her face looked as dark as the storm clouds hanging over Princess School. She had grumbled all through lunch in the banquet hall and now, in Looking Glass class, the look she was giving her reflection was almost enough to break the mirror.

Rose knew her friend was dealing with enough to make any princess cross. But Rapunzel's disposition was positively ferocious. Rose hoped the party would be *enough* to cheer her up — and that Rapunzel wouldn't do anything drastic before then!

Under the circumstances, Snow's tactic of steering clear of their friend until the surprise seemed like a good idea. Rose turned her cushioned stool so she couldn't see Rapunzel. Then she arranged a spiral curl down the nape of her neck.

A quick flash of light in her mirror made Rose close her eyes briefly. What was that? A second flash followed. Then two more in quick succession. It was a signal. Val!

Rose glanced around the chamber to see if Rapunzel had noticed. She and the other princesses were busy trying to perfect their curls. Snow's stick-straight hair was hopeless!

Sliding off her cushion, Rose made her way to the window ledge and the cut-glass jar filled with hair combs. Pretending to pick a new comb, Rose snuck a look out the window. It was Val all right. He was standing on the Charm School lawn tilting his shiny belt buckle this way and that in an effort to catch a ray of light. The sky was still cloudy, so he had to wait for small breaks in the building storm.

He must be desperate if he is trying to signal me now! Rose thought. She racked her brain trying to remember the parts of the code he'd tried to teach her on their brief walk.

Was it two flashes for "meet in the stables"? Or two quick, one long? Rose asked herself. She could not remember. And there was only one other person who would know.

Rapunzel had a single lock of her long hair wrapped around a heated iron. It circled the metal so many times it looked like a ball of yarn. She unwrapped it as Rose approached, and only an inch at the end had curled. The rest hung straight.

"Lovely," Rapunzel muttered sarcastically.

"I like your hair better braided anyway," Rose said, smiling widely.

Rapunzel rolled her eyes. "And how does Val like *your* hair?" she asked. Her voice was full of sarcasm.

This was going to be trickier than Rose thought. She had suspected Rapunzel was angry that Val had walked home with her the other day. But she'd hoped she would be over it by now. Besides, all they had talked about was her!

"Val doesn't talk about hair," Rose said lightly. "But he did tell me about the code you created. I think it's so clever that you two can talk while you're in two different schools! How did you come up with it?"

Rapunzel looked at Rose suspiciously. "I don't know. I just did, I guess."

"It's just *so* clever," Rose went on, using a tone she usually reserved for talking her parents into something. She knew flattery was a powerful tool, but she'd never tried it on Rapunzel. And her friend was looking royally annoyed! "Can't you tell me some of the things the code says?"

Rapunzel put her hairbrush down on the dressing table with a thud. "It's simple. Anybody could do it. One flash means 'yes.' Two means 'no.' It's very basic." Rapunzel sighed.

Light flashed again in the mirror behind Rapunzel —

two long, two short. Rose hoped Rapunzel hadn't seen it, too. She just had to figure out what Val was trying to tell her before Rapunzel caught on!

"So, what would two long and two short mean?" Rose blurted. She felt like her smile was plastered to her face.

Rapunzel narrowed her eyes. She suspected something. "It would mean 'trouble,'" she said. "Why?"

"Oh, no reason," Rose said, waving a hand in the air. She hoped Rapunzel couldn't see her face starting to flush.

"Who's in trouble?" Ella peeked around Rapunzel's looking glass. Her hair cascaded in yellow curls around her face.

"Nobody!" Rose said quickly. Ella's distraction came just in time! "Ella, your hair looks perfect. You just need a comb over your ear. I saw one with a butterfly over here."

Rose led Ella back toward the window. "Something's gone wrong," she whispered when they were far enough from Rapunzel. "Val is telling me there's trouble."

While Ella pretended to busy herself with the combs, Rose peered down at Val. When he saw her face in the window, he dropped his belt buckle completely and signaled frantically with his hands. He held up three fingers, then two. He held up three again and covered one with his hand. At last he pulled a scroll from his pocket and pointed to it, then gestured like a court magician making something disappear.

"It's the invitations," Rose whispered frantically. Her fears had been confirmed. "One of them is missing!"

Chapter Fifteen

A Change of Scenery

Rapunzel's mind raced like a stolen coach. Everything around her was so strange, starting with the weather and ending with her friends. Wasn't it enough that she had to contend with a witch at home? Why did everything have to spin out of control at once?

Making her way toward the Self-Defense classroom, Rapunzel felt grateful for her assigned princess duty. There would be no wolf evasion practice today. Today she would be there by herself. And all she had to do was switch the scenery. Maybe because she spent so much time alone growing up, Rapunzel felt she did her best thinking that way. And she had lots to think about.

"Rapunzel! Wait for me!" Arinda, the miller's daughter, ran down the hall. "I have scene-changing duty, too. I saw your name on the roster. Isn't it great to have a free period? I have been studying so much lately. Not that I'm worried about the exams. My father says I can do anything! So I'm sure to get a golden mark."

Rapunzel glanced at the girl chatting rapidly by her side. So much for a moment to think! Arinda was always talking. And most of the time she was bragging, too. *Someday her bragging is going to get her into trouble,* Rapunzel thought.

Pushing open the door to the large hall where the princesses learned to protect themselves, Rapunzel spotted the woodland props. Trees and bushes and rocks were placed around the room to imitate a forest path. They needed to be taken down and replaced with village scenery.

"Would you like to see my skip-trip?" Arinda asked, eyeing the forest. "It's practically a flip. My father says I could take down a whole pack of wolves with it and the woodsman, too."

Rapunzel wrestled the bush toward a large storage compartment. *If I don't reply she might stop talking,* Rapunzel thought. Her head was crowded enough without Arinda's crowing!

Rapunzel pushed the bush to the back of the compartment and pulled out a village stall, one of the props used to create a mock town lane.

"I heard we're taking on rats and pipers in Self-Defense next," Arinda kept on. "That should be no problem for me. I'm not afraid of rats. And Father says I'm very musical. Practically a lark, he says."

Arinda kept talking. But Rapunzel found if she held a prop between herself and the chatterbox, she could hear her own thoughts in spite of Arinda's constant din. But as soon as she heard the doubts about her friends and Madame Gothel flooding back, she wished they were drowned out again. Rapunzel was confused. And sad. And angry. She didn't want Madame Gothel to be right about her friends. But maybe she was. Maybe they would disappoint and leave her. Just like her parents.

Ella and Lurlina did *come to get me out*, she reminded herself. She was grateful for that. But Ella had seemed distant since then. And what was with Rose? It wasn't enough that Rose was walking home with Val and Rapunzel was walking alone. Now Rose wanted to know their secret code, too. The one Rapunzel had made up!

Then there was Snow. She always acted a little funny. Rapunzel thought it was because she lived with dwarves. But today? Every time she looked at Rapunzel she looked like she'd swallowed a toad. Rapunzel set a stile prop on her foot.

Ouch! She would have thought that Snow of all people would understand what it was like living with a witch.

But the thing that had felt the worst was when all three of her friends completely ignored her during Cordial Correspondence. They kept their backs to her and didn't ask her to tie scrolls with them. She might as well stay locked in a tower if this was how her friends were going to treat her!

All she'd wanted was to talk to them about the awful food and letters Madame Gothel had been leaving her. She'd tried again at lunch to tell them. She'd started by saying she hadn't gotten any studying done. "I'm going to have to spend at least two hours in the royal library after school today," she'd confided. Then she had actually seen the girls exchange smiles — like they were happy she wasn't going to do well! And nobody had said a thing. She felt like her friends didn't listen anymore — or worse, didn't care! It was enough to make Rapunzel stop talking.

Arinda, on the other hand, *never* stopped talking. "I think this is the best village setup ever. Except for that crooked stile over there. Did you put that up, Rapunzel? Don't worry, I can fix it. Father says I have an eye for arranging. I can spot a flaw no matter how slight."

As Rapunzel pushed the last tree into the storage compartment, Madame Gothel's words echoed in her head. *Continue to escape and you will receive a terrible slight.* Was her friends' aloofness the slight Madame

Gothel was talking about? She said her friends would betray and forget her. Was that what was happening?

"No," Rapunzel said aloud.

"Oh, yes." Arinda nodded vigorously. "And I can feel a grain of sand under twenty mattresses."

"I don't believe it," Rapunzel said to herself. She had to give her friends another chance. Dusting her hands on her skirt, Rapunzel headed for the door.

"It's true. Every word!" Arinda called after her.

But Rapunzel didn't hear her. All she needed was a moment alone with one of her friends. Just a few minutes to talk and she knew she would feel better.

The trumpet blasted as Rapunzel entered the corridor and the halls filled with swirling skirts and sweet voices. It didn't take long to spot Snow and Rose, but they were headed outside and Rapunzel was too far away to catch up to them through the crowd.

Rapunzel waited by Ella's trunk, watching as the last princesses filed outside. Still no Ella. A new and terrible thought stormed into Rapunzel's head. They all were avoiding her — on purpose!

Feeling wilted, Rapunzel pulled her scrolls and texts from her own trunk and let the lid slam with a bang. *Fine*, she thought. *I don't need those traitors. I don't need anybody!*

Rapunzel stomped toward the cupola that held

the royal library. She yanked the door open with a vengeance and was surprised to be greeted by a friendly face — Ella.

"There you are!" Ella grinned. "I was hoping to have someone to study with."

Rapunzel felt her anger start to thaw the moment she saw Ella. She desperately wanted to be wrong about her friends. She also desperately wanted to talk to someone about the maelstrom of feelings she had been having.

"I'm glad you're here," Rapunzel said as she followed Ella to a carved, round table. The huge multi-level chamber was quiet. Enormous pastel-colored banners hung down from second-level banisters. And shelves upon shelves of books spread out of the circle room like spokes.

"Me, too." Ella nodded. "I think this may be my only chance to study for exams. I have been so busy with chores I haven't even had a minute to myself! You're so lucky you live alone!"

Rapunzel snorted. Was she joking?

Ella sat down daintily in a high-back chair, opened her text, and began to read. The look on her face was pure concentration.

Sinking into her own chair, Rapunzel felt frustration fill her once more. With a sigh, she spread her own text on the table and began to read in silence.

Chapter Sixteen
Snow Storm

Snow nibbled on the corner of her thumbnail and glanced anxiously around for Val.

"He'll be here," Rose assured her, leaning on the rail of the Princess School drawbridge. Rose held up her arms like an arch and raised one slightly in imitation of Val's pantomime. "I'm almost certain he was saying 'bridge.'"

Snow nodded and tried to smile. All of her excitement about the party had turned to nervousness. It seemed as though everything was starting to go wrong. Ever since Rose told her that one of the invitations was missing, Snow had been trying not to panic.

It could be anywhere, Snow thought. *The doves could have given it to Rapunzel and ruined the surprise. Or worse.* Both of Snow's hands crept toward her ruby-red lips. *The invitation could be in the clutches of a Grimm girl!*

The clouds overhead that had been building since

the early morning seemed darker now. And in the distance, Snow thought she heard the rumble of thunder.

"Hey, are you trembling?" Rose put her hand on Snow's shoulder. "There's no need to panic, Snow. Val is on his way and Ella is with Rapunzel. We'll have plenty of time to get the food and get to the tower. Rapunzel doesn't suspect a thing."

Rose's reassuring words helped Snow relax a little. She took a deep breath and let her hands drop to her sides. She admired Rose's coolheadedness. And Rose was right, Snow knew. Ella was with Rapunzel in the library and under strict orders to keep her there for at least an hour. They had time.

"Sorry I'm late!" Val galloped up the path toward Rose and Snow, pausing to tip his crown and bow slightly when he drew near. "I just had to give the princes directions. They asked me to relate that they are most honored to be invited and will certainly be attending."

"Did you find the missing invitation?" Rose asked.

"No, Oliver never got one. But he's coming. You should have seen his face when I told him you would be there." Val grinned.

"Okay, let's go!" Rose said, rolling her eyes. She walked briskly toward the willow and the path to Snow's cottage, gracefully leaping and dodging puddles on the way. Val tried to walk ahead of her and when Rose paused at the edge of a big puddle, even offered to lay his cloak on top of it so that she and Snow could walk across it.

"No time for gallantry," Rose said, waving Val off with her hand. She gathered her skirts and leaped the puddle easily. Val jumped after her and came down on the edge, splashing his boots and making them both laugh.

Snow smiled, but she couldn't seem to catch her friends' playful mood. She accepted Val's hand and made it across the huge puddle herself. As she landed, something behind the trunk of the willow caught her eye.

Crouching, Snow peeked cautiously around the tree. Five small rabbits were huddled together, shivering and looking up at the sky as if it were about to fall on their fuzzy heads. They were frightened and muddy.

"Oh, you poor bunnies!" Snow scooped the rabbits into her skirts and dried them off with her hem. "Just look at them, Rose!"

Rose was already at the edge of the woods, but she came back and crouched beside Snow. She gently stroked one of the rabbits while Val leaned over her shoulder.

"What's wrong with them?" Val asked.

"They're frightened," Snow said, kissing the tops of their heads and making soft sounds in their long ears. "Has all this awful weather scared you?" She looked into the smallest rabbit's dewy eyes.

A mother deer and her fawn stepped timidly under the umbrella of the willow tree. They looked disheveled and upset as well.

"You, too?" Snow asked. Her voice was full of sympathy.

Suddenly the rabbits cowered further into Snow's skirts and the deer stood stock-still, clearly startled. There was a rustling overhead. "Ooh, that mean old thunder!" Snow frowned.

But the noise above them wasn't thunder. Three mourning doves flapped ungracefully down to roost in the willow.

"Aren't those the birds we sent to Charm School?" Rose asked. "Maybe they have the lost invitation!"

Finally, some hope! Snow thought. She tucked the rabbits into a dry knothole and held a hand up so the doves could fly closer. Two of them flew down to rest on Snow's outstretched arm. The third landed on her head. All of them wobbled woozily back and forth.

"Why, you're all worn out from the weather, too," Snow cooed.

"And if they did have that other invitation, they don't anymore," Rose pointed out. "I guess there's nothing left to do but go to the party and hope we don't have an uninvited guest."

Rose started toward the path with Val right behind

her, but Snow didn't move. She was trembling again. But this time she wasn't nervous. The gentle girl trembled with rage.

"It's those Grimm girls," Snow said in a tone her friends had never heard her use. "They're the ones. They are trying to mix up our mail with their bewitched weather, and they are frightening the animals. It's just not right."

Snow balled her delicate hands into tight fists. The animals that usually flocked to her looked shocked and kept their distance.

"Mischief is one thing," Snow said. She felt hot tears burning her eyes. "This is mistreatment, and I won't stand for it."

"They'll be okay, Snow," Rose said, trying to calm her. "Let's just get to the cottage and get the food for the party. You'll feel better then."

"No," Snow said more sternly than she'd meant to. Rose looked taken aback and Val stood with his mouth open. Snow knew she wasn't acting like her usual self — she was surprised, too. But she wasn't going to let her woodland friends be abused another moment.

"You go to the cottage," Snow said commandingly. "Pick up the food, then get to the tower and make sure everything's ready. I'm going to find Sir Spondence. Somebody has to put a stop to this. Now."

Chapter Seventeen
Ill Wind

When taking tea, a proper princess always extends her pinkie so that when the cup is tipped her smallest digit points directly at the ceiling.

Huh, Ella sighed. Though she would never tell an instructor, sometimes all of the princess protocol seemed to her like utter nonsense. Here she was trying to plan a party, stay out of trouble with her steps, and rescue her friend from the doldrums (and a witch). Was she really expected to memorize perfect pinkie positioning? It all seemed a little preposterous.

But even if what she was studying were more important, Ella knew she'd still have trouble concentrating. Rapunzel's miserable silence across the table was setting off alarms in Ella's head. She knew Rapunzel wanted to talk, wanted to ask a million questions. And she had every right to.

Ella hoped that Rapunzel would understand why she was being so coy when she saw what she and the others had been up to. They were trying to be good friends. But right now, from under Rapunzel's heavy hair, Ella knew it looked bad.

Gnawing on her quill, Rapunzel glared at her text. She stood quickly, knocking over her chair and getting a few looks of shock and displeasure from the ladies-in-waiting at the Table of Information.

"Where are you going?" Ella asked abruptly. They had only been in the library a short while and she was supposed to keep Rapunzel occupied for at least an hour!

"The little princesses' room," Rapunzel whispered loudly. Ella thought she saw her roll her eyes. She could follow her, but it might seem suspicious. And she didn't want Rapunzel to start asking questions now, with the party so close. She would just have to let her go.

Trying again to focus on her princess protocol text, Ella was surprised to see familiar slippers appear on the floor beside her.

"Come with me!" Snow whispered hoarsely. She grabbed Ella's arm and started to drag her out of the library.

"Snow! What is it? What's happened?" Ella ran behind Snow to avoid being pulled across the room. The pale girl was surprisingly strong!

"The animals!" Snow said as if Ella should already

know. "We have to talk to Sir Spondence about what the Grimms are doing to the animals."

"The animals?" Ella asked, unwrapping Snow's hand from her puffy sleeve.

"They are completely shaken from this unpredictable weather! You should see them, Ella. They're shivering and terrified." Snow stopped and looked into Ella's face. "We have to do something."

Ella had only seen sweet, cheery Snow this distraught once before, when she had been hiding under the bleachers at the Maiden Games. She'd been afraid to move, afraid to face the evil Malodora. She didn't seem fearful now.

"You saw them do it. You saw those girls make that terrible twister to mix up our mail. That's why you should be the one to tell Sir Spondence." Snow shoved Ella into the Cordial Correspondence classroom ahead of her. Sir Spondence was leaning back in his chair, asleep.

"What about the party?" Ella whispered.

"There will be time for that later." Snow picked up a stick of sealing wax and dropped it on the floor with a clatter.

"Heavens! Gracious!" Sir Spondence was startled awake and blinked at his two students. "Good afternoon! What have we here? I was just in a reverie. I dozed and dreamed that all of the epistles . . ." He shook his head mournfully. "Would that I knew what had happened to our wayward words."

Ella felt Snow nudge her firmly in the back. "I saw two Grimm girls casting weather spells in the woods!" Ella said abruptly.

Sir Spondence rubbed his eyes and tugged on his goatee harder than ever.

"Sir Spondence, sir," Snow pleaded. "One of our scrolls was there. The lost letters and horrible weather might be the Grimms' fault, and it's harming the innocent animals!" She stepped closer to the instructor, grasped the hem of his elbow-length cape, and looked at him with her round ebony eyes. "We have to do something."

The teacher shook his head as if waking a second time, got to his feet, and strode out of the room. "Quite right," he said crisply. "Right. Quite!"

Ella and Snow were close on his heels. "Where are you going?" Snow called, running after him. She still held the corner of his short cape.

"Perchance to see what foul players prey upon our fowl," Sir Spondence grumbled. "Could it be that the School of Grimm should conduct their course in Malicious Mischief at the same moment I conduct mine in Cordial Correspondence? Rest assured that if it *is* their ill wind that blows our letters astray I will put a stop to it!"

As they walked quickly away from Princess School, Ella heard a clock tower strike the hour. It was getting late. The party would be starting soon and Ella hoped Rapunzel wasn't going to be the one surprising Rose and Val!

Ella struggled to keep up with Snow and Sir Spondence. The closer they got to the Grimm School's grimy castle, the darker the woods got. The clouds looked caught in the tops of the gnarled trees and more and more roots twisted their way into the path to trip passersby.

Snow did not slow her pace as they made their way through the woods. But when Sir Spondence reached the frosted gingerbread gate that marked the boundary of the Grimm School yard, Snow stopped so suddenly Ella ran right into her.

"Oof." Ella stumbled back. "Snow, what is it?"

"Nothing," Snow said softly. Ella heard her draw in her breath. She knew what it was. Snow was scared. No amount of gingerbread or candy would make her set foot on Grimm School grounds. Her stepmother, the evil Malodora, was headmistress there. Snow had stood up to Malodora at the Maiden Games, but that was completely different from setting foot in her stepmother's territory.

Sir Spondence was halfway to the castle doors, and Ella wanted to catch up with him. She wasn't exactly feeling brave about hanging out in the witches' woods without her teacher. She opened her mouth to remind Snow they were there for her animal friends. But she didn't need to.

Snow let her breath out slowly, squared her shoulders, and stepped through the frosted gates.

A moment later they were at the entrance. The doors to the Grimm School were enormous — even bigger than the grand Princess School doors. The leering door knocker was almost too high for even Sir Spondence to reach. He stood on his tiptoes and grabbed the tarnished ring that hung from the mouth of a grimacing gargoyle. The gargoyle appeared to recoil slightly at being touched by a white-gloved hand.

Sir Spondence let the ring fall. The clang of metal on metal echoed inside. Ella wanted to run, but her feet wouldn't move. Even Sir Spondence was starting to look a little nervous.

At last the doors opened and Ella, Snow, and Sir Spondence were enveloped in a cloud of warm, stagnant air. Ella felt like the school had just belched in their faces. And the smell!

"What a stench!" Sir Spondence whispered. Princesses, cover your noses. Let not the reek of sorceresses enter your dainty nostrils." He produced several lace handkerchiefs and handed one to Ella and one to Snow. Ella gratefully covered her face before stepping inside the empty hall. Her handkerchief smelled like vanilla but could not cover the rank odor of sulfur and mildew mingling in the Grimm hallway.

Ella and Snow had to hurry to keep up with Sir Spondence. Face covered, he marched smartly down the hall, looking left and right into rooms filled with dusty texts and bottles of fetid potions. Snow slipped along on the slimy floor and Ella linked arms with her.

"Thank you," Snow murmured under her hanky. Ella nodded back but didn't say anything. She was hanging on to Snow as much for herself as for her friend. The empty hallways were giving her the creeps.

Suddenly something limped toward them. A bent witch with a crumpled hat and a twisted walking stick looked at them through one eye. The other was sealed shut. "What do you want?" she snarled.

"I seek an audience with someone in a position of power," Sir Spondence said formally. He started to bow, but seemed to think better of lowering his balding head before a witch holding a stick.

"Ha!" the old witch laughed, revealing yellowed and broken teeth. Her laugh caught in her throat, choking her. She started to hack, bending farther, but as she coughed she pointed with her stick toward a door leaning on its hinges. The splintery sign on it read JEZEBEL JEWELWEED.

Sir Spondence turned and gestured for Ella and Snow to stay close. Behind them the short witch's hacking echoed in the dank hall.

Using one of his handkerchiefs, Sir Spondence grasped the door handle and pushed his way inside the office. A silver-haired hag sat at an enormous desk. Though Sir Spondence cleared his throat, she did not look up when they entered. Instead she stared intently into a glowing crystal ball. Her long, silvery fingers moved near the shining surface, never touching the glass.

If Ella was frightened before, she was petrified now. She squeezed Snow's arm tighter. Snow wasn't even shivering.

Sir Spondence puffed out his chest and prepared to speak. "If you will excuse the intrusion, Madame Jewelweed, I —" He was cut off by a snort.

"Silence," the witch commanded, looking up from her ball. She surveyed the three royals before her with distaste. "Your saccharine speech will only give me a toothache. Besides, I know why you're here. And you're mostly wrong."

Ella looked at Snow, who did not look as surprised as Ella felt. But then Snow's stepmother was a powerful witch who used a mirror to know all. This witch must use a crystal ball the same way.

Jezebel Jewelweed stood and walked closer to Sir Spondence. She pulled his hand down from his face, uncovering his protected nose and mouth.

"Of course we would be proud if our little brats could cast such strong weather spells," she hissed. "As it is, they have simply been interfering a tiny bit with your foolish postal play — something we choose to allow. Every good witch stirs up trouble, after all."

Sir Spondence began to stammer. Jezebel put a gnarled knuckle on his lips. "Dear sir," she mocked him. "The spells you seek are beyond the capability of any Grimm student."

The hag chuckled and turned her attention from Sir Spondence to Snow and Ella, who stood almost hugging behind him. "The spells you speak of could only be created by an unusually powerful witch — a witch in danger of losing something she holds dear," she said softly. Ella felt Jezebel's gaze bore into her and shuddered. The witch's eerie smile grew. "A witch about to do something drastic," she added.

Ella wasn't sure if Snow pulled her or she pulled Snow, but the next thing she knew, both of them were bolting down the slimy halls, past the gingerbread gates, and down the path toward Rapunzel's tower.

Chapter Eighteen
Surprise!

By the time she reached the tower, Rose was completely out of breath. She stopped in the small clearing and put her hands on her knees. Panting wasn't very princessy, but neither was pushing a wooden cart of pies and cookies down a woodland trail!

Val bumped to a stop beside her. "Can I eat one now?" he asked, eyeing one of the cookies in the wheelbarrow.

"Not yet," Rose breathed. She pushed the cart behind a small bush in case Rapunzel showed up early. "We have to get them into the tower first." She gestured toward Rapunzel's open window thirty feet above them and let her eyes follow. The last time she was here the tower had been bathed in such bright light she could barely look at it. This time it was dark. Thick clouds swirled menacingly above the pointed roof, blocking all light save the greenish-gray glow of the sky before a storm.

Though she was still warm and flushed from hurrying down the trail, Rose shivered. The tower looked pretty spooky. But something else was bothering her, too. She couldn't shake the odd feeling in the pit of her stomach. And she couldn't name it, either.

"We have to get all this up there?" Val pointed straight up in the air. He didn't look like he felt very well. "Can't we just have the party down here?"

"Don't worry. I'll help you up." Rose walked closer to the tower and found her first toehold. "Then we can make some sort of pulley system for the rest."

Val started to shake his head but a crash in the bushes made them both jump. Rose looked for someplace to hide but it was too late. A pair of twig-covered figures stumbled out of the woods. Snow and Ella! Their cheeks were rosy and they were breathing as hard as Rose had been a minute before.

"Is she with you?" Ella gasped.

"Rapunzel?" Val asked.

"I thought she was with you!" Rose said. The odd feeling in her stomach felt like panic now.

Suddenly an auburn braid sailed out of the tower window and swung to a stop by Rose's side.

"Are you going to just stand down there all day?" Rapunzel's voice sounded like music to Rose's ears.

"I guess she got here before us," Val said, scratching his head. He looked a little disappointed.

"Climb on up!" The braid jiggled. "The others are already here. Let's get the party started!"

"So much for the surprise." Ella shrugged and started to climb.

"At least we're all together," Snow said, looking on the bright side. She stepped forward and hoisted herself onto the ropy braid.

When Snow was about ten feet up, Rose pushed Val to go next.

"I'll be right behind you." Rose tried to sound reassuring, but she wasn't feeling very sure herself. She knew she could climb up without a problem. But the uneasy feeling in her stomach was still there.

Rose helped Val position his feet, wrapping the braid around his waist so he'd be safe if he fell. "I still don't understand why we couldn't have this party on the ground!" he said in a shaky voice.

"Because it's not your party," Rose said. "Now keep climbing!" She tried to concentrate on the next handhold but a voice was clamoring in her head and getting louder all the time.

How'd she get here before we did? If she knew about the party at school, why didn't she just tell us? Rose didn't think it was like Rapunzel to be secretive.

Above them, Snow and Ella had reached the windowsill and climbed over. Rose thought she heard a gasp. Suddenly Val started to slip. His foot came down on Rose's head.

"Use the braid," Rose said through clenched teeth. For a charming prince, Val was a terrible climber. Taking Val's suede boot in her hand, Rose pushed up hard and foisted him in through the open window. She swung easily in beside him and gasped herself.

A stern-looking woman with a sharp nose and a witch's cloak stood beside the window glowering at the royal students assembled in the tiny tower room. She leaned on the end of a hard bed where the auburn rope Rose had just climbed was knotted. Behind her, three frightened princes sat bound together. It was a trap. The woman could only be Madame Gothel!

The witch's glower snaked itself into a sinister smile. "Well, if it isn't my *friends*!" she said in a perfect imitation of Rapunzel's voice. Throwing her head back, she cackled madly. And at the same moment a booming thunderclap echoed in the darkened sky.

Chapter Nineteen
Party

Rapunzel kicked the dirt, scuffling her way home. She had been hoping that when she went to the little princesses' room Ella would follow her so they could finally talk. Instead, when she got back to the library Ella was gone. Rapunzel had been deserted . . . again.

It didn't seem like Ella's style to just leave. All of her texts and scrolls were still on the desk. But there was only one explanation for the way her friends had been acting. They weren't really her friends after all.

It hurt Rapunzel to think that Madame Gothel had been right all along. She hoped the old witch wouldn't rub it in too much. Because all she wanted right now was to be in her familiar room, under her rough sheet on her lumpy straw bed. She just wanted this awful day to come to an end.

Hand over hand, Rapunzel climbed up to her tower room. The dark clouds swirling overhead and rumbling thunder matched her mood. "Go ahead and flood," she said, scowling up at the sky. "I don't care if I ever make it back to Princess School."

Rapunzel's cheek was wet. She wiped the water drop away with her shoulder. It wasn't a tear. "I would never sob for that pack of pampered princesses," she mumbled. But as soon as she said it she felt closer to crying.

With a final heave Rapunzel lifted herself onto her windowsill and stopped dead.

"Surprise?" Snow said softly, her eyes wide. Behind her, Ella and Rose managed small apologetic smiles. Val looked scared enough to vomit.

"Surprise indeed!" Madame Gothel echoed. She spun around to face Rapunzel. Her mouth contorted into a sneer and her hands were on her hips.

Rapunzel had seen Madame Gothel angry before. That was no big shock. But what were all of her friends doing here — and who were those three princes tied up on the bed? Then, slowly, it began to dawn on her.

"You were throwing me a party?" she asked.

"A birthday party." Rose nodded.

"To make up for all the ones you missed," Val added.

"We wanted it to be a surprise, that's why —" Ella's voice dropped and disappeared as Madame Gothel raised her hands and turned to glare at her.

"Rats and bats!" the witch spat. "The final surprise is mine."

Madame Gothel's voice cracked. Her hands trembled and thunder shook the tower. Rapunzel pressed her back against the stone wall. Though she'd seen Madame Gothel mad before, she'd never seen her *this* mad.

"Your time with your friends has come to an end," Madame Gothel shrieked. She said the word *friends* like it burned her tongue. "In a few short moments they will be blind as bats, and your window will be permanently sealed!" The witch raised her arms to cast a spell.

The three princes on the bed struggled with their bindings. Rapunzel recognized them from the Coronation Ball. Oliver Eggert wore a look of determination. Allister Arlington looked mad. And poor handsome Hans Charming was there, too, hiding his face in his knees.

Dumbfounded, Rapunzel did nothing to stop Gothel's spell. She was too shocked to fight back.

"No!" Snow gasped.

"You can't!" Ella cried.

Rose locked arms with Val and moved with the other girls to block the tower's only opening. The princes struggled with their ties. Seeing her friends' courage, Rapunzel managed to take one step forward, then another.

"You can't keep me in forever," Rapunzel said quietly.

"You can't leave me," Madame Gothel choked out. Her hands were still held before her, but instead of looking like she was about to start casting she looked like she wanted to get them around Rapunzel's throat. "You can't leave me," she said again.

"I have been leaving you for years," Rapunzel retorted.

Madame Gothel's eyes flared, but Rapunzel thought she recognized something in them — something sad, like the way she had felt on the way home today. "But I always come back," she added more softly.

The room was suddenly silent except for the rain falling outside. Madame Gothel slowly let her hands fall to her sides. Rapunzel could hear her friends' cautious breathing. Nobody knew what was going to happen next.

"You always come back," Madame Gothel repeated. She looked from Rapunzel to the floor and back again.

"Lizard lips!" Madame Gothel cursed, stamping her narrow black boot on the floor and making the students jump. "I guess you do."

Rapunzel raised her eyebrows and cautiously tried

a half smile. The old witch actually seemed a little disappointed that she didn't have anything to be mad about.

"Of course I do." Rapunzel gestured around her tiny crowded room. "How could I give up all of this?"

Madame Gothel was caving. Rapunzel looked at her friends and winked. They were going to be okay! Snow was biting her ruby lips but managed to return her smile. Ella, Val, and Rose still looked a little nervous. And although Oliver and Allister had stopped struggling with their bindings, Hans still had his face hidden and was whimpering softly.

Madame Gothel seemed to be going over what Rapunzel had said again and again. Her leathery face had lost its cruel expression. Her shoulders drooped. She looked plain stumped.

Rapunzel felt her familiar confidence returning. She thumped Madame Gothel gently on the arm. "You know I don't have anyplace else to go," Rapunzel reminded her. "And besides," she admitted, "I kind of like it here."

Chapter Twenty
A Break in the Storm

Madame Gothel stood in a sort of stupor. For a few long moments she didn't move or say anything. Outside, the rain stopped. Everyone listened silently to the water dripping off the trees. They watched as the clouds blew quickly away to reveal an evening sky of deepest blue. On the horizon a band of dark orange was all that was left of the setting sun.

"I thought this was a party!" Rapunzel said, breaking the spell. She moved quickly to untie the three captive princes. Hans wiped his face and looked up sheepishly, obviously unaccustomed to being saved by a damsel.

"Oh, the food!" Snow leaned out the window. The cart of pies and cookies was just where Rose and Val had left it. "I hope it wasn't ruined by the rain!"

"Should we all go *down* now?" Val asked hopefully.

"I mean, it will be awfully hard to get all that food up here."

"I'll take care of it," Madame Gothel grumped, rousing from her stupor. Hans Charming retreated again to the bed as Madame Gothel advanced toward the window. She dropped the braided rope out the window and, after a quick wave of her wrist, the rope wrapped like a tentacle around the cart and lifted it to the level of Rapunzel's room.

"It's so soggy!" Snow said. With her hands on her cheeks, she surveyed her baked goods.

Madame Gothel mumbled something that sounded like "damp salamanders," waved her hands, and suddenly the cookies looked crisp and the pies' flaky crusts were restored.

"Oh, thank you!" Snow threw her arms around Madame Gothel. The witch cringed but Rapunzel noticed she didn't pull away.

When the cart was unloaded, everyone gathered around. Ella produced a candle stub from her pocket, poked it into the top of the biggest pie, and placed it in front of Rapunzel.

The candle mysteriously burst into flame and everyone, except Madame Gothel, who was blowing on her index finger, sang.

"Make a wish." Rose smiled.

Rapunzel closed her eyes and blew the candle out. When she opened them she looked around at her friends and her wicked foster mother. She couldn't remember the last time she'd felt so happy.

"What did you wish for?" Snow asked.

"Not telling." Rapunzel grinned.

As the food was served, the party guests relaxed more and more. Everything was delicious. Madame Gothel even tried the apple pie.

"Apple is my favorite," Snow said sweetly.

"Humph," Madame Gothel snorted with her mouth full. "I prefer bat wing stew," she announced as she shoveled in another bite of fruit and pastry.

The princes flocked around Rose. Hans fetched her a plate. Allister knelt beside her to hold her water glass and Oliver stared, starry-eyed, into her face. Rapunzel watched as Rose tried to brush them off like gnats. She was completely surrounded.

"So you were planning this all along?" Rapunzel asked Val. Val held a cookie in each hand.

"Mmm-hmm," he said with his mouth full.

Suddenly Rapunzel felt a bit foolish. Why would Rose try and steal her friend? She already had too many princes paying too close attention to her!

Ella sat beside Rapunzel on the bed and discreetly gestured toward Madame Gothel, who was lingering over her apple pie. "I still can't believe you made her mad enough to cause all of those storms!" she whispered.

"What?" Rapunzel asked.

"What?!" Madame Gothel roared, turning toward the girls.

"I didn't think you could hear. . . . I mean, it's just that Jezebel Jewelweed said . . . Well, I was only repeating —" Ella stammered.

"Spit it out," Madame Gothel said sternly, standing over poor Ella.

"She said the horrible weather could only be created by a powerful witch in danger of losing something she holds dear," Ella said quickly.

"Jezebel Jewelweed said that, did she?" Madame Gothel's mouth turned up into something like a smile. "Well, warts and warthogs. She used to be a pretty powerful witch herself until she took that desk job." Madame Gothel stood a little taller and smoothed the white streak in her hair.

"You did that?" Rapunzel asked. "I mean, all that weather was because of me?"

"You should be ashamed," Snow scolded, suddenly remembering that it was Madame Gothel who was responsible for most of the mess of the last week. "You mixed up all of our messages and the poor animals. They could have been really hurt!"

Madame Gothel turned to look at Snow. Snow took a step back and her voice got a little meeker. "I mean, it wasn't very nice," she finished.

"I mixed up the mail? And frightened the animals?" Madame Gothel laughed. It was practically a giggle. "I'm sorry," she said to Snow. But Rapunzel didn't think she seemed a bit remorseful. In fact she seemed a little proud. "I suppose I was angrier than I knew."

And it was all over me, Rapunzel marveled. She looked at Madame Gothel again and felt her own tug of pride. The old witch had quite a few surprises up her long sleeves.

The party lasted until the moon rose.

"I'd better go home," Ella said reluctantly as she stood to go. "It must be nearly midnight!"

Snow and Val left soon after Ella. "Many happy returns!" Val called when he reached the ground safely.

"Happily ever after!" Snow called before scampering into the woods.

Rose fought her way out of the circle of princes to give Rapunzel a quick hug. "We'll do it again next year." She smiled. "See you at school?" It was a question.

Rapunzel looked at Madame Gothel to see if she had heard. The witch was cleaning up the party mess, and at the mention of Princess School she began to bang things around a little harder.

"I hope so," Rapunzel said softly. Things had gone so well, but Madame Gothel's moods could change like, well, the weather.

Rose nodded her understanding and moved toward the window.

"Allow me!"

"No, me."

"Climb upon my back and I will carry you down." The princes began to vie for position to help Rose out the window and down the side of the tower.

Rose winked at Rapunzel. "Back off, boys. I can do this myself." She slipped gracefully out and disappeared over the window ledge with a last wave.

"May I escort you home, Beauty?"

"Please, allow me?" The princes followed, still clamoring for Rose's attention.

Rapunzel watched them go, grinning. Poor Rose! She hoped she could lose them in the woods. If she couldn't they would probably spend the rest of the night serenading under her window!

Rapunzel grabbed the last empty plates and stacked them with the ones Madame Gothel had already cleared. Neither of them spoke, but the silence wasn't awkward, like it had been before. It felt comfortable.

"Mmm." Rapunzel licked a little berry pie filling off her thumb.

"You like that?" Madame Gothel asked. Her wild eyebrows almost met in the middle. "It's too sweet for me. But I might be able to make a pie for you once in a while."

"Thanks," Rapunzel answered. She was grateful. It would be nice to eat more than toadstools, eggs, and bitter greens. But another question hung in the air unanswered.

"So, uh, about Princess School," she started to ask.

"Oh, toads' tears," Madame Gothel cursed, sounding a little defeated and balling her hands into fists. "Just don't let them make you too royal!" she pouted.

Rapunzel laughed out loud. "Not a chance," she replied, looking straight at Madame Gothel. "Haven't you heard? My foster mother is a powerful witch." Rapunzel looked at Madame Gothel and smiled. Her birthday wish had just come true.

This summer uncover
Little Secrets

By Emily Blake

Book 1

PLAYING WITH FIRE

One family. Two sides.
A whole town caught in between.

In this new series, when a rivalry between two families turns nasty, cousins Alison and Kelly go from best friends to bitter enemies. Kelly steals Alison's boyfriend, destroys her reputation, and pits her against her insanely wealthy—and manipulative—grandmother. But Alison isn't going down without a fight...

Available May 2006

■ SCHOLASTIC

www.scholastic.com

More Series You'll Fall In Love With

by Lauren Brooke

Dylan, Malory, Lani, and Honey discover that academics, horsemanship, and rivalries are par for the course at this exclusive all-girls school in Virginia.

www.scholastic.com/chestnuthill

Jesse Sharpe is an orphan, a genius, and a secret agent. She trails suspects and cracks codes in a world where she can trust no one but herself.

UNDERCOVER GIRL

by **Christine Harris**

JIM BENTON'S Tales from Mackerel Middle School

DEAR DUMB DIARY,

BY JiM BENTON

In Jamie Kelly's hilarious, candid (and sometimes not-so-nice) diaries, she promises everything she writes is true ... or at least as true as it needs to be.

www.scholastic.com/deardumbdiary

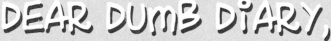

FILLGIRL5